A HANDFUL OF DUST

A HANDFUL OF DUST

By

Charlotte Gardner

An Imprint of
B. Jain Publishers (P) Ltd.
An ISO 9001 : 2000 Certified Company
USA – Europe – India

A HANDFUL OF DUST

First Edition: 2008

All rights reserved. No part of this book may be reproduced in any form or by electronic or mechanical means without permission from the publisher. This book is a work of fiction. Names, characters, places and incidents either are products of the author's imagination or are used fictiously. Any resemblance to persons living or dead is purely coincidental.

© with the author

Published by Kuldeep Jain for

Pegasus

An imprint of
B. JAIN PUBLISHERS (P) LTD.
An ISO 9001 : 2000 Certified Company
1921/10, Chuna Mandi, Paharganj, New Delhi 110 055 (INDIA)
Tel.: 91-11-2358 0800, 2358 1100, 2358 1300, 2358 3100
Fax: 91-11-2358 0471 • *Email:* info@bjain.com
Website: **www.bjainbooks.com**

Printed in India by
J.J. Offset Printers

ISBN: 978-81-319-0332-2

Dedications

*For Rockwell and Adelaide in memory of the Manota
that once flourished.*

Publisher's Note

We have been successful in serving our adult readers with high quality books on Homeopathy, Health, Spirituality, Fitness, Business and Fashion. At the beginning of 2008 we launched our new imprint Pegasus. In Pegasus we are publishing high quality fiction and non-fiction books for our young and adult readers and aim to set a high quality standard in this genre. We have roped in various experts from their respective fields in our expert panel to write different books as per the requirement of the young readers.

We launched hundred preschool books under Pegasus in February 2008 for which we got a tremendous response and now we are starting with the adult fiction. This novel is one of the two novels written by Charlotte Gardner. The novel "*A Handful of Dust*" is a story about old Anglo-Indian families of India .The story is written in the times of 1970's. The story revolves around four characters, the way they grow up, their emotions, relationships, ties, impulsive behaviors and twists and the turns their lives take.

The writing style of author is so lively that it gives you a feeling as if all the events are just happening in front of your eyes. Read this saga of a sea of emotions and impulsive reactions which changes lives. The events take shape in a manner which keeps you engaged till the end.

Kuldeep Jain
CEO, B.Jain Publishers

Acknowledgement

Special thanks to Mrs. Puri a wonderful mother and friend and to Yogesh and Sonia Puri whose encouragement and warm friendship made a huge difference in my chaotic life. Their perseverance in leading me to excellent publishers through Anuradha Varma, to whom I owe much, is highly appreciated. Many thanks to Nitin Jain, Dr. Geeta, Dr. Harpreet and the others at B. Jain including other Editors and all involved in the process of getting the novel published and marketed. Many thanks to Mr. Rajan and Mr. John who peppered their encouragement during the writing of the novel and its research with humourous interjections! Most of all I owe thanks to my mother Adelaide Mary Gardner who said, "don't ever give up, I will always pray for you and all my children and that's half the battle won." My father, Rockwell Gardner, who told me, "you should always have the courage of your convictions." My children, Alannah and Nihar whose love supported me through the difficult times when trying to juggle home, career and writing. My brothers and sisters who believed I was meant to be a writer especially my sister Annie who called me, 'Drama Queen' believing I was transferring imaginative creation of scenes to real life ones. Thank you all!

About the Author

Charlotte Gardner is an Anglo-Indian who spent several years in Darjeeling first at a Methodist Mission School then as a wife and mother. At Kanpur one of the venues at which she worked her first novel was created, 'A Handful of Dust', based on her family home 'Manota', followed by 'The Curse of Garibagh' culled from Kanpur experiences. However, writing was put on hold for a while as the demands of her job as CEO of a Tea Company at Nepal occupied most of her time. She is currently writing full time at Dehradun where she presently resides.

One

The train rumbled into the overcrowded station in the early morning, its wheels rhythmically churning as it came to a halt with a screeching and burping as the brakes took hold. Disembarking passengers pushed and pulled to remove their luggage and the noise escalated a few decibels almost deafening. Along the length of the train the disembarking passengers squeezed past the embarking passengers not helped by the vendors who persisted in adding to the bustle. Perspiration, unwashed smells, sticky hair oil smells, *pan masala* and cigarette smells, *puri-sabzi* smells, odours enticing, suffocating and stifling. Thankfully a bottom berth had ensured my privacy. I could talk or not depending on my mood. Opposite, a family of nutmeg, brown and shiny were discussing, the little earthen pots of '*mishti doi*' clutched in their hands. The curly haired infant whose antics of bending over and looking between her fat, dimpled thighs, gurgling through her four teeth while spittle drooled, attracting more mirth than was deserved. The mother squashed flat on the berth like a balloon from which much of the air has dispersed. Wilted and shrivelled, her well oiled hair scrunched into an angry bun at the top of her head. I wondered how difficult her life could be, that she had such an air of suffering. She sat inelegantly, her legs spread wide in a parrot green *salwar*. She noticed my attention gingerly hoisted to beneath her knees to expose rounded calves on which ugly burn marks, bloated and raw weeped angrily amongst long, black hair unshaved, unwaxed. I looked away quickly before her eager eyes could collide with mine and collided with her husband who was watching me with a furtive look while his hands did the scritch scritch of scratching his private parts absently. The bouncy older child who grabbed at his mother's '*mishti doi*' asking her if he could finish the sweet curd in a piping, musical voice. I glanced at her again, then up at the fan, she was still watching me. Small, round and dusty, black and whirring loudly then out the window at the fleeting landscape through a dirty windowpane. Fleeing green and brown fields with waving mud coloured bunches, lonely, tilted poles supplying electricity, trees and more trees.

Boarding the train at Delhi had required nerves of steel with passengers pushing and squeezing, somehow managing to shrink into the compartments of the train. Another feat was to successfully cocoon myself against the inquisitive stares of other passengers who waited for an opportunity to begin conversing. It was the nature of Indians to offer food along with desultory conversations and various questions during train journeys. Antecedents were examined carefully, tracing them minutely through remembered recollections of vocations and dwellings, the number of children one had, siblings, parents and ancestors strewn over India and other countries. Frequent stops teeming with humanity who clambered on and off the trains, clogging the stations like jettisoned flotsam, buffeted by the wind scattering in all directions, some aimless, some challenged, some bewildered, some desperately seeking. Sleep eluded, bug-eyed, dark-ringed found no solace, disturbed constantly by sounds and noise, which often rose to a crescendo.

Another stop and more passengers this time one addition to the family of four, a bearded *kurta* clad man who glanced in alarm at the woman's weeping wounds, concern written all over his face (Is it contagious? Will I get it? What has she touched?) I could almost hear him think!

"The kettle of boiling water overturned" she said, now that she had an audience. Her voice was low, almost husky. His relief was palpable, it lifted into the air stunning the lone fly which had attempted to compete with the fan and fell squished to the ground to be pounced on by a gleeful baby who attempted to stuff the morsel into her spittle filled mouth.

"*Nai, nai*", yelled the mother, hurriedly snatching the now further squashed fly and throwing it under her berth. Danger averted, she proceeded with her explanation while the kurta clad man listened eagerly (now that he was in no danger of being contaminated). "We were in a hurry, my *dupatta* tassle got caught in the spout, it tilted, *uri maa*, the pain was awful.."

while she showed him the tablets and ointment she regaled him with the doctor's visit, the drive to the station, boarding the train (with much difficulty because of the pain). His expression now polite but glazed, he was obviously thinking his own thoughts and she droned like the dull buzzing of a bee in the distant hum of voices rising and falling, rising and falling...

Pretending they didn't exist and managing to avoid eye contact, I spent the entire journey looking inwards at my thoughts. It was 1995; The Rao government was attempting stability. The last time I had made this journey Ivan had travelled with me. It was not my nature to be so reserved and antisocial. In normal circumstances I would be peeping into bits and pieces of passenger's lives, sampling snacks, pickles and sweetmeats, which were an inevitable offering to break the monotony of train journeys. Manota evoked exactly what the name depicted, 'boiling feelings'. Perhaps in some distant past a lonely ancestor overwhelmed by turbulent feelings smiled with wry humour and christened his domain 'Manota', feelings that boil. A tryst with destiny, that's where I was headed, a place which touched the heart and erupted emotions, a simmering cauldron which bubbled until the fires were doused. Everyone has a special place they grew up in, a place they call home, mine was Manota, deep in the interiors of Kasgunj. Like myriad grains of sand we scattered across India spilling over into other countries. Those left behind met infrequently, the camaraderie of the past had vanished with the mists of time. For me this was the final episode of Kasgunj, the last leg of the journey to commune with ghosts and lay them to rest.

A few days back I had been spring-cleaning. The time when along with cobwebs the old and useless were discarded and given away. The gray jacket with corduroy cuffs had been a favourite and worn often, now faded and musty smelling. I began folding it prior to placing it in the cardboard carton marked 'Sisters of Charity'. The noise of paper crinkling in its pockets had me reaching to pull out two leaves of a letter stained yellow probably having lain in the pocket a long time. The handwriting was familiar, well remembered, but not thought of for a while. The date was 12th June, 1990. Beneath the date was written Kasgunj. I sat abruptly onto the lid of a box. Gem...her mother had called her Gem because she had said that's what she was, a precious stone. But precious stones can be flawed too and Gem was flawed. But flawed or not like her namesakes she had her own special beauty. I settled myself more comfortably among the opened lids of the tin trunks and the mildewed smelling cardboard cartons and began to read. The bright light from the open window threw into relief the closely written lines, a little faded here and there, she had always tried to pack as much writing into each page squeezing the words together in an effort to use the maximum space. For a moment the sounds of birds chirping intruded and I could smell the scent of roses and jasmine which wafted in from the garden below. A slight breeze swayed the white muslin of the curtains and I felt her presence, a gentle touch as I began to read. The letter had no beginning and no end.

'I'm going to Delhi finally. Anil has employed me as a nanny for his kids. I'm so excited I'll be together with him. I can see the frown between your eyes. There's no need to be prudish, he's gorgeous and rich. He's promised to take care of me. I don't know if you've ever experienced this great enveloping feeling which burns the body making one feel divine. You've always had it easy, I don't think you've ever craved anything the way I have. It's a consuming emotion, which ignites the mind and makes one aflame. I'm aflamed and my desires can now be fulfilled. I've dreamed of this moment all my life, of leaving Kasgunj and finding love. Imagine the things I shall see, the places I shall visit. I'm a little nervous having to take the journey alone, but I know I can manage. Mum can see well enough now to take care of herself. Aunty Sarah is managing and Chris, he will never know why I am going. He thinks it's just a job. I always wondered if it was possible to love two men at the same time, now I know. Chris is kind and gentle but he waits for me to take the initiative. Anil is exciting! He not only takes the initiative, he commands and demands and is able to draw from me more than what I thought was within. When a woman joins with a man each time it is different, even if it is the same man and it makes for many experiences. Have you ever wondered what it would be like with different men? Imagine the wealth of experience that would enrich life. Could it be possible to love each man individually? You frown some more, you've been brought up to believe love is for only one man, the rest are prohibited. Why should we believe that? Who made it a rule? If I'm scandalizing you, I feel it right to do so. I *want you too to be fulfilled but in order to do so you have to be intrepid and uninhibited. Who is it that ever bothered what life I lived? Is it your straitlaced Aunt who could improve my circumstances? It is Chris who is trapped, but in saving myself I save him also. When he realizes I have flown the coop and discarded the old life perhaps he will make the effort to leave. The world is big and wide and I've yet to taste its nectar. You once said I was a radical and a free thinker and that religion would mould me. I have no religion. If God did exist then there would have been a touch of divinity in me. My mother lacked it and I inherited from her a realism which sees us without the rose that tints others visions. We evolved with something missing, the spark of belief that makes you believe there's good in everyone. Who defined good anyway? If being good is suppressing enjoyment then how can it be good? Should guilt be a degree by which we measure our actions? Is conscience the rule by which we assess the degree to which we have fallen? I don't feel any guilt, perhaps I don't have a conscience. Marriage was invented by women who wanted sole access to a single man. People are born free, so why should they then be bound in chains? I disagree with what you wrote about laws being made to suppress crime by instilling fear of consequences. People should be a law unto themselves. Who better than the person concerned, to judge their own actions. How can someone other than you judge your own conduct? Who decides what is right and what is wrong? Who can read the mind of a person and give fair judgement? A person's actions are not taken without a motive in the mind and circumstances surrounding that action. So how can a person, other than the one taking that action, know why it was initiated, for what purpose?*

You won't agree with me, however, so I beg to differ. I have tasted heaven and it was not through following the rules. If in breaking the rules of morality I'm deemed wicked, so be it. I go now not to be a nanny but a mistress, to lead a deceitful life, a slave to pleasure. I know that despite my non-conformity you will continue to be my dearest friend for the obvious truth which makes me smile. We are two sides of a coin. One day perhaps, victory will be yours and like a lamb to slaughter I shall be docilely led into sweet conformity. As yet I don't feel the arrows of condemnation but should it engulf you, spare me the barbs...

The unfinished letter ended there. If only she had known to what degree I had failed. Had I heeded her warning and dispensed with conformity and embraced freedom I might have escaped being trapped like a moth in a glass cage beating futilely with tired wings, despairing of ever getting free.

I had both loved and hated her and like a Gem she had continued to lure me with her mystifying qualities. Perhaps she had attracted me because she was different. Despite her claim to wickedness, she had her own code by which she had lived, she was honest and frank. She could be trusted to live openly according to how she felt and she fiercely protected those whom she loved. She didn't see any merit in pretence. Her emotions were the force, which controlled her actions. Anil Sharma, the philandering doctor with his aquiline features and his knowledge of sex had corrupted Gem. But perhaps I was being unfair to him. Perhaps Gem was incorruptible, maybe she was born corrupted. But her corruption was not the type that kills, it was the heady experience of 'being born old', of forbidden pleasure laid out in the open with no barriers, bared naturally like something joyful not dark and secret to be hidden away. She made illicit pleasure seem as a matter of course not something extraordinary or dirty. Natural desires were not to be suppressed but base nature was indulged and she revelled in being liberated. I hated her for her liberations. She only highlighted my confinement, the chains that bound me grew more heavy with social restrictions and imposing bans on behaviour. Laws and rules handed down by tradition, religion and family values that had been inbred. While I suffered the pangs of repression, she roamed free and seemed none the worse for that freedom. I couldn't break the mould; she had never been moulded.

Darkness had crept in without my noticing, so deep in thought had I been. The sounds from the garden had changed. The singing of the crickets and cicadas were more pronounced. A bat swooped past the window and I heard the hoot of an owl. I stood slowly, easing the cramps from my legs. Faint light from the window was sufficient to grope my way to the door where the switch was. As light flooded the room it took with it the shadows of the past. But a resolve had been born, a resolve to go back. Leaving the box room behind I entered the living room, switching on the lights as I went, dispelling the darkness. As I entered the kitchen, which looked out onto the garden, I admired the silver light of the moon which bathed the garden with its luminosity. There were no shadows, all was pure clarity. The moon's light was cold, it changed the character of the garden, which during the day was warm and inviting, kissed by the glow of the sun. Shaking off the eeriness of a moonlit garden, I flooded the room with bright electric light.

I couldn't sleep that night, thoughts screamed through my mind. Unanswered questions pounded my brain. Where were they, would I ever meet them again?

Finally with no answers forthcoming and sleep eluding I climbed out of bed and took the stairs to the terrace. Cool breeze soothed my skin. Ivan and Chris, Gem and I, were we really so different? Hadn't we all wanted the same things?

Perhaps it was time to close the chapter, to come full circle. Did I have the same values or were they so frayed with time that I had ceased to feel them. Fragments of the old remained, slivers which stuck doggedly like bits of food lodged irritatingly between the teeth refusing to be dislodged by a worrying tongue. The new had to be painstakingly fitted into the slots left by the old, little pieces of puzzle fitted together to form a complete picture but the cracks showed.

And I wondered just how visible they were. Gem had lived honestly, her kind of truth had freed her to live joyfully. My life had been fraught with pain. Shackles bound in childhood could never entirely be broken. I knew now I would go, there had to be an ending or perhaps... a new beginning...

We arrived at Kasgunj.

No longer clean, the station was like any other station not its old pristine self. Crumpled bits of paper, dirty unpolished floors, and betel stained pillars from which the smell of stale urine made one gag. Garbage bins filled to overflowing with paper cups, butts of cigarettes, biscuit wrappers and spat out *paan* which coloured everything. A black bull foraged among the filth discovering a discarded plastic filled with something edible and began to chew the packet with complacent movements of its jaw. "Not good for you" I muttered while gazing round the station. No one I knew, no one to meet me, a mixture of relief and something indecipherable...could it be disappointment? I left the platform and strode into the sunshine not feeling as confident. It was a relief to leave the station with its closed in smells behind. It didn't take me long to find a vehicle to carry me the distance to Manota.

Kasgunj had evolved from a sleepy town to a bustling, humming city constantly moving, the colours and odours changing from minute to minute. Restlessness pervaded the air, or was it only me? As the hired jeep sped through the city out onto the canal road I breathed a sigh of relief. Wide-open spaces, dust which rose in a cloud behind us, and green rice fields which stretched for miles. The driver glanced at me inquisitively from time to time.

"It's very interior," he commented, "you live here?" I looked at the curly haired, mustachioed driver whose oil stained vest and shorts added to his grimy appearance.

"Used to, there were only dirt roads before. Mostly we crossed over by boat."

He nodded his head uninterestedly and we lapsed into silence, each with his own thoughts, unbroken for miles. Almost dreaming thoughts with hot air blowing into the face along with sand and grit. A dark room in a tomb...I could almost feel the coolness, the musty odours and the clammy feeling...rudely awakened with a bump into a ditch and a rattle of the jeep suspension like the groaning and winching of tired springs in an ancient sofa. When would they make a proper road? The British had thought a grand acquaduct was good for Kasgunj. Didn't the Indian government think it deserved attention too... dust, heat and dust... creeping sleep thoughts, jumbled and disjointed... I dozed again dulled by the drone of the engine and the heat which made one almost comatose.

A bend in the road, and suddenly the fort came into view. Wide awake now I gazed at it with mixed emotions, what would I find there? No longer our family home, it had changed hands, been sold to people I didn't know. What foolishness had brought me traipsing the many miles on a whim? Impulse often ruled my actions and now as we drew near to my destination I was filled with a sense of anticipation and dread. I couldn't change my nature, but jumped headfirst into any and every situation. What would I find? I didn't know and I couldn't wait to find out. As we stopped beneath the high walls I heaved a sigh of relief as the dusty jeep came to a screeching stop, its brakes squeaking in protest at the sudden pressure.

It looked deserted. Not so brave after all, I thought. Gingerly stepping out of the jeep I stretched languidly easing the kinks out of my back. The driver stared at the walls in mute amazement, a natural reaction when the walls stretched upwards unendingly. A dog barked in the distance. I was struck by the silence and the stillness. Time seemed to be in suspension holding its breath waiting like I was, not a breath of air...not a whisper of sound...it was almost eerie. I turned in slow motion to look at the cemetery, which sprawled a little distance away to the left. It looked neat and clean, well cared for. The new owners were in residence then, or else they had a caretaker... A hail from above and I jumped letting my breath out in a whoosh, which I hadn't realized I had been holding. The driver grinned in amusement as I glanced upwards at a man whose head was swathed in a turban. Something about the figure was familiar but I could not place him.

"Come up," he said gruffly, then disappeared from view.

Asking the driver to wait for me I negotiated the stable area where lethargic buffaloes flicked their tails at flies and the smell of animal urine was strong. The cobbled path, which sloped upwards beside which the old castor tree grew, loaded with the spiked globes, and onwards into the compound still filled with white river sand.

"Chris!" my astonishment was tinged with excitement. "How wonderful to see you!" hugging him, "Where's Gem?" He was older, laughter lines had made deep indents on the side of his mouth but his features had not changed much.

"I knew you would come. Everyday I've scanned the roads for you..." his eyes mirrored the excitement I was feeling. Somewhere along the way he had lost his atrocious accent and had acquired a gruff, clipped speech, which somehow suited him, as did the tan that made his eyes look even greener though they were not as bright as before.

"You knew?"

"Of course, what kept you?"

"I didn't know what I'd find. I wondered if the house

would even be standing. When I last left here it was in a sad state of neglect."

"It's eaten a big hole in my savings but I think it was well worth it?"

"What are you doing here? Where's Gem"

"I've bought the house, fighting to reclaim the land..." I gaped at him.

"What?"

He laughed mockingly, his moss green eyes defiant, "Never thought old Chris the nowhere person would come back to buy your family home did you? Well I did and what's more, I own it all." I took a deep breath, what did I feel?

"Well?"

"There wasn't anything left Chris. Uncle Cyril came to stay after Grandma and Grandpa passed away, he broke up the 21 acres of farm and fruit gardens and sold them to people for a pittance. Uncle Sunny got ill and just withered away and died. Uncle Wilfred was starved to death by Mercy and Cyril and they put Buddi into an asylum somewhere. Even the very bricks of the house were sold to someone. You coming here, rebuilding, fighting to regain the land. Its like a dream. None of us would have done it, so I'm glad," I said simply, "I'd rather it was you and Gem than anyone else. Most of all I'm just glad to see something still standing."

"You mean that?" his voice was hesitant and I nodded my head. I did, I was relieved there were no strangers but Chris and Gem. He looked pleased. Why did it matter to him how I felt? I wondered, did he need my acceptance?

"Come," he said quietly "you can rest in the living room, I'll get Bhim to bring your luggage and give the driver refreshments. This is Bhim," as a stocky figure came out of the newly built *chappard* and said "*namaste*". I folded my hands in return, wondering where Gem was. He had changed, evolved; this was a new Chris, a Chris I didn't know. Gone were his prickly sensitivity, his discomfort, and his awkwardness or had he always been like this and I had not noticed? I wondered about that, had Ivan occupied so much of my thoughts and emotions, I had not observed Chris growing up? I followed him through, lost in thought.

The living room was reminiscent of Chris' wanderings. Bits and pieces of Rajasthan tapestries, Khurja pottery, bright blue of Jaipur ceramics, mirror work cushions from Gujarat and inlay-work boxes from Kashmir. It had the odour of wax polish freshly applied...and the coolness of thick walls and high ceilings. It had the smell of nostalgia and the familiar whisper of voices trapped in the sands of time almost heard if one stood still and listened. A silver framed picture of Gem caught my attention and I knelt near the low peg table to take a better look.

It had been taken at Agra, the Taj Mahal in the background rising in all its splendour, awe inspiring as always. "She was so thrilled to see the Taj," Chris said behind me and I turned towards him.

"Chris?"

"I know, I'll tell you about her, come sit." He patted the couch and I seated myself beside him as Bhim returned with tumblers of fresh squeezed lime juice.

"Gem died while giving birth to a child."

"Oh Chris," I stared at him wide eyed, shocked into speechlessness.

"We didn't know the baby had died and Gem's system got poisoned," he continued, his eyes bright with unshed tears, "I couldn't save her. By the time I got her to a doctor it was too late". I reached out to squeeze his hand in sympathy, remembering the love they had shared, which had begun turbulently and ended so sadly.

"I'm so sorry," I whispered, inadequate words for the sorrow I felt at having lost one of my dear friends. We had shared so much; our lives had been intertwined over the years until the time she and Chris had disappeared.

"Your Mum?" I asked him.

"She died a little after Gem, quietly and in her sleep. Steve disappeared around the time we left here. I've tried locating him but no information has been forthcoming." I looked at his tired face. Although he had matured and his red hair was not bright any longer but interspersed with gray, his features still retained some of its boyishness.

"Ivan met Steve," I told him.

"Where?" He sat up straighter.

"On the train when he was returning from Delhi, he didn't tell him where he was going but he was happy. I'm sorry there isn't much to tell." I couldn't tell him further details he was already so grieved.

"And Ivan?"

"He married an Irish lass and is settled in Ireland. He writes when he remembers."

"But I thought that you and.."

"So did I, but Ivan never looked at me as a woman... well.." I shrugged my shoulders and Chris laughed.

"Do you think if I wrote to Ivan he might remember something on Steve?"

"You could... but I think he didn't know where Steve was headed, you could ask him though."

"Where would you like to sleep? The big room?" he asked and I nodded my head.

The big room...a roomful of memories, memories of a time long ago. Suddenly it all came rushing back and the years fell away and I wanted to remember then.

Then was being thirteen, that special age when those adolescent changes and hormonal disruptions occur. I could feel the changes occurring, but I didn't understand them. Strange stirrings, deep yearnings, for one thing I had developed beasts and it wasn't only I who noticed them, they seemed to have become the focus for eyes. Most people who spoke to me seemed to let their eyes wander to my chest and linger there making me want to look down to see if they were in position or doing something they shouldn't. Wearing bras didn't seem to solve the problem but aggravate it. I suddenly had shape, much more than I wanted. I was so aware of my body. Sometimes after bathing I caught myself standing in front of the mirror just looking at it. Boys began to hold some sort of fascination especially their hands, which seemed to catch my attention. The shape of the nails, the length of the fingers, attractive hands gave me the urge to caress them. I had a fetish for hands. I would look at the face. The lean hungry look sort of got my pulse racing, latently I realized I was attracted to the 'predatory male' which didn't make for much happiness but lots of excitement.

Ivan had had that lean hungry look which had me behaving so out of character. Confusion reigned supreme. One moment I was on a high, the next plunged into inner turmoil which I least understood or knew how to handle. I wanted to ask Roxanna if these feelings were normal or was I the only one boiling turbulently.

Something even worse was taking place. My olfactory sense had gone haywire, instead of wrinkling my nose at the male musky odour of sweat; I seemed to want to inhale it.

Then was Chris and Gem and worst of all then was embarrassing myself in the cemetery, the day Ivan came to say goodbye...

Two

It all began with being a Gardner. Someone threw a Gardner into Kasgunj and the ripple effect was created. Ever thrown a stone into a pond and seen the ripples created in ever widening circles? That's exactly what happened they spread everywhere, when Kasgunj became too full of them, acute indigestion prevailed until it belched! Before that happened, however, cough and one fell out of a tree, clap your hands and they'd be popping up out of the bushes, trip and you could be absolutely sure it would be a Gardner you were tripping over. They had a peculiarity distinct touch to the family, Gardners from one village married Gardners of another village, so they all got related and interrelated that is, until the ripple effect created sometime after the First World War, threw them into other corners of the country and the world. One might ask, where in the world is Kasgunj?

Fifty kilometre from Agra in Uttar Pradesh, a State in India, is Kasgunj, a sleepy town in the district of Etah, with nothing to distinguish it except nearby the village of Chhaoni exists, which was once the cantonment of Colonel William Linneaus Gardner, originally from Coleraine in Ireland, who distinguished himself with 'Gardner's Horse' a cavalry regiment formed during his service with the British army, when they were in occupation, later becoming 2nd Lancers. His palace, which had housed his Muslim *begum*, now stood in ruins but their tomb and family vaults were still intact as well as the Turkish baths, which were still standing. Two other villages as well were still peopled by succeeding generations. Manota, which was styled on an English fort, and Fatehpur, another village. Remnants of Mughal architecture dotted the landscape in and around the villages. Red brick domes, arched walls, circular edifices, with determined grass growing in the crevasses and birds nesting in apertures. Beautiful birds in vibrant colours like precious jewels, purple amethyst, yellow topaz, blue sapphire, emerald and black agate flew among the bushes, perched on the branches of trees or pecked at insects frantically burrowing into the earth.

The villages were like other villages in Uttar Pradesh. Brown sandy soil, clumps of yellowing sword grass, rough to the touch with sharp edges difficult to dislodge, as the roots grew deep, pockets of broom grass with their fluffy heads. The grass if unattended, which it mostly was, grew to almost four to five feet high, forming screens along the well trodden paths providing shade to the tiny creatures which scuttled among the bushes or to humans who ventured out in the fierce heat of the sun. Dust flew along with the hot winds, which parched an already parched earth and stung the eyes and exposed skins, filling the nostrils with the smell of the earth. Fields of bright green and gold, mustard or wheat, lentils and pulses, refreshed the eyes. Fallow earth which lay waiting to be planted, its brown muddiness exposed to the scorching heat of the sun. But the sun set the vivid azure of the sky flaming a bright orange with fingers of gold and purple, gently fading to deep dark night and stars popping into the big black void making it sparkle while the air cooled and soothed, bringing relief after the heat.

Evenings saw the deep green of the fruit trees, the orange *gulmohurs*, the red squirrel tails, the yellow rain trees, the *banyan* trees with their twisted vines flushed with the nesting birds, lime green parrots squawking and screeching, cawing grey and black crows, red breasted robins, striped-hooded woodpeckers, beige and brown wood pigeons, gray and white doves, dust coloured magpies who fought raucously, blue jays, black birds, handsome mango birds with their distinctive calls, the faithful sarus cranes and the common sparrows. The soaring large winged eagles, alighted on the tallest trees together with kites and hawks. White egrets, and the tiny jewel coloured bush birds darted in and out among the creepers, co-existing, and noisily settling in at night.

Manota still retained twenty-one acres of rich farmland with guava and mango gardens although most of the land had been given back to the Government with the abolition of the *zamindari* system, which had given landlords land grants from which part of the revenue generated was paid to the

Government. Stewart William Gardner, grandson to Lord Gardner had married Colonel Gardner's granddaughter Hurmuzi and been given Manota and its fort as a land grant. The family had shrunk sizably with most emigrating off to foreign shores but those left made it a point to gather for winter vacations as the weather was conducive to comfort. Kasgunj, like most of Uttar Pradesh had extreme climates summers that scorched and winters that froze. We preferred to freeze than fry as most of the family worked in hill stations where due to cold winters, schools gave a three month break, making it the ideal time to migrate to warmer climes or visit the family.

Dacoits were a menace during Great Grandpa and Grandma's time, the old iron ball cannon stood sentinel in a corner near the wall in an attempt to psychologically demolish the dacoits before they began an attack. Iron balls were already a scarce commodity to come by so when the cannon had served its purpose it was retired to a museum.

It was customary for our family to congregate at the farm. Aunts, uncles, cousins, nieces, nephews and a plethora of fun, games, gossip and food. We ranged from old to young, from fat to thin and the in between, tall to short and medium dark skinned to fair skinned, red hair, brown hair, black hair, curling hair, straight, short and long hair. Mine, yours and ours collected together, sharing and discoursing. The discussions ranged from hair care, to bread making, jams and pickles to sewing, hunting to religion. Imagine if the walls could talk the imposing battlements could tell the tales of mother-in-laws chutney and other culinary delights, the births of babies (sometimes buffaloes). The dancing of the village belles who slyly peeped at the men enticing when the wives were not looking, or the old men who sat around a glass of whiskey, their companion and garnished the tales of their younger days, reliving them all, well embellished and spiced like the duck which had been marinated, liberally sprinkled with Indian spice and roasted in the oven.

"We had this lovely brick club house over which creeper roses had spread all over the roof, deep maroon, light pink and pale lemon intertwined. Showers of petals floated down if there was a slight breeze." Stewart, who had retired from the railways was relating one of his tales while we sat in the compound gazing at the stars, bright sparks of light in a navy sky, listening to tales of his younger days. The air was heavy with the intoxicating scent of *'raat ki rani'*, which grew in profusion in the cemetery and wafted on the breeze, surrounding us with its heady perfume.

"It must have smelt divine," said Mum

"Oh yes and the gardens had these well manicured lawns with creamy jasmine, mauve jacaranda, 'flame of the forest', and magenta, yellow and pink bougainvillea intermingled round the perimeter and in the night the firefly lanterns which hung in the branches of the trees while the railway band played soft instrumental music," he said. "The dances and gala evenings were really splendid, the women came all decked up like birds of paradise, perfumed and powdered and the men in tails and bow ties looking like penguins and just as stiff with formality. I hated the stiff white collars we had to wear." He grinned at his captivated audience, "Can you see me with a bow tie and looking so handsome?" We looked at each other skeptically, it didn't seem possible, Uncle Sunny who shuffled the halls in brown *keds*, vests and striped *pajamas* only adding a *khaki sweater* to his outfit during winters, and a sola *topee* during shikar, in a bow tie and that too looking handsome? I shook my head. He was right I couldn't visualize it.

"Do people change so much when they grow old?" I wondered aloud.

"Of course they do," said Roxanna.

"I won't," said Anne, "I'll be Miss World and I'll always be beautiful."

"You'll have to make sure your pugees don't fall down first," said Neville ducking to avoid the handful of sand flung by her. She glared at him, annoyed that he had reminded everyone her knickers had a tendency to circle her ankles from time to time. She was sure they had a life of their own; it really puzzled her how they kept creeping down again and again.

Most of the stories had railway colony backgrounds and exotic tales of army dances and alluring ladies who were unforgettable. Glamorous tales which were wonderful on long balmy nights with a sky full of stars and a gentle breeze blowing and the family sitting around in comradely affability.

Pride in previous generations who had excelled themselves in the armed forces or made names for themselves among Indians and British alike with their intrepid adventures and dare devil exploits. Grandpa's story of how he rescued the Raja of Kasgunj's heir from a sticky situation during the war of independence and conducted his safe passage on the railway to deposit him safely with his father was one such. There were other tales of Anglo-Indians they knew who had aided Hindus, Muslims and Sikhs to escape death during the time of communal unrest. The older generation was fond of discussing that time and trying to depict just how dangerous and exciting it had been. We egged Grandpa on as much as possible and he never disappointed us.

"Jimmy actually had Sukhbir hiding in the closet," he said one time. Jimmy Smith was a friend of his who worked in the map survey department for the Government, "and he began to shout and create a terrible din" he continued, "the damn-fool fellow has run off with my money! The blackguard! The lily-livered cur, wait till I get my hands on him, I'll beat the living daylights out of him!" Then he turned to the British soldiers and started berating them, "you ... what are you still standing here for, go chase the nincompoop, can't you catch the thief, damn...."

"Enough cursing Leo, we get the point," Gran interrupted him. Leopold's stories were normally high drama and he waved his hands around to express himself better. He was good at upsetting his daughters-in-law by encouraging his grandchildren to be less than obedient while his large store of cuss words besides spicing his stories introduced us to a wide range of colourful vocabulary.

It was Leo who explained how the British had segregated the Indians from them. They had overpaid their own countrymen and underpaid the Indians who worked for them. "They introduced corruption to India," he said. "The Indians who worked in government service were so poorly paid that they took bribes and gifts to enable them to live better. The British were clever, they got loyalty because the Indians who worked for them were afraid of losing their jobs only because of the extras they got."

"Weren't they aware of what was going on?" I asked.

"Of course they were," he told us, "but they pretended ignorance, they paid them poorly on purpose."

"What about the Anglo-Indians?"

"We became a sort of bridge between the two cultures. Anglo-Indians were put into all the responsible posts and because of them the government ran in a well oiled manner."

"But you told me that Gramps helped the Indians during the mutiny, didn't the British suspect?" I asked him.

"No child, the British trusted them but we were half Indian too and the Indians trusted us. We all had friends among the Muslims and Hindus, we couldn't abandon them, so we aided them and since most of us were in posting that allowed a certain leverage we made sure that many of our friends were moved to safety. We hid them in our homes, fed them, we did whatever we could."

I was silent pondering what he had said.

"Not all Anglo-Indians were half British," he continued, "there were many who belonged to other foreign countries as well, but to make it easier the term Anglo-Indian was used for almost everybody who had a foreign ancestor in his background."

Anglo-Indians understood India and Indians and they copied the British style of living. He went on to tell us that it was only after the Constitution was made, when India gained independence, that Anglo-Indians were defined as those who had either British or European descent from the paternal side. It was rare to catch Grandpa in an expansive mood but since Grandpa had not yet brought him his tea he seemed content to chat awhile as he waited.

I knew Grandpa sometimes thought I was too serious, "little book worm", he called me. Often he found me hidden in some dusty corner in the shade of the compound pouring over one of the books from his store. I wasn't like the other girls. I didn't play with dolls or runaround in some fantasy game and I knew they thought I was too quiet, always lost in some other world. All this changed, as I grew older. Trying to make up for lost time I indulged in repartee which made siblings, friends, cousins and all in range bide their time waiting to practice lobotomy on the part of my brain related to speech.

"Tea Leo," Grandma handed him his mug. He refused to drink in anything except his white enameled mug. She looked at him fondly. The years had been good to them, he worked so hard and they had plenty but sometimes I wondered if Gran ever wanted electricity and running water and to go shopping in a fancy shop and to have a house where sand didn't get into everything. She sighed as she looked out over the wall. I wondered what she thought.

"What are you thinking?" Grandpa had been watching her noticing her sad expression.

"Why don't you make a visit to Sarah, go shopping in Kasgunj."

"Next week maybe."

"Granny, may I have some ghee and *chapathi*," Anne tugged at her skirt, interrupting them.

"Hungry again, are you?" she smiled at my sister who didn't have a stomach but some monster thing which gobbled food and still remained hungry, "who can resist this curly haired angel," Gran said. I wondered how she was able to call the curly haired thing an angel. Perhaps Gran had different ideas to what angels looked like, all a matter of perception I supposed.

"Come on, let's see if there's any *chapathis* left." Gran seemed to have forgotten she had a rotten temper and loved to grind her teeth and lie screaming on the floor when thwarted. I didn't think angels did that but one never knew. Maybe that's how they got God to take notice of them.

Grandpa was a farmer and he was good at it, guavas thrived in his garden, fields of mustard, wheat and rice flourished and waved thickly, grandly announcing to the passers by the richness of the soil, well watered while the bullocks turned the water wheel, to which old kerosene tins had been nailed emptying the water into the troughs that ran into the fields. Grandma suited him just fine, she was pretty and gentle with gossamer skin which gave her an appearance of delicateness (didn't answer him back much) and when required would nurse all the villagers and the servants without complaining, while making sure the house ran well and meals were on time. He didn't believe in being soft and took his responsibilities to the village folk seriously. In his early years he had worked in the Kanpur Cotton Mills and had lived in

Manchester for sometime too. He had also been in the British army during the First World War and had been decorated repeatedly but it was difficult to get him to talk about his experiences, as he was awfully busy with the farm, either it was planting time or harvesting time and he had no time to indulge in idle talk. He must have done something to make Gran love him so much because after he died she could not bear being without him and followed him to the grave soon.

Food was plentiful at the farm but hard cash sort of eluded Grandpa's grasp after the crash where he lost most of his money in the Jawala bank and in what he thought was the perfect solution to this ailment, he kicked his two elder sons into the Airforce and the Navy. Rockwell stayed the course and the Airforce became his vocation for a period of eighteen years but Nelson sobbed into his mother's ears and much to the relief of the Navy, who preferred robust recruits, to waif-like ones, secretly funded his education from her own resources until he was able to stride into the teaching profession.

Rockwell, Leo's eldest, in rapid succession or perhaps because he had learned the skill of keeping his wife occupied from the old male buffalo, or maybe he wished to help the Government by giving them the added incentive to introduce family planning, increased the population by two boys and three girls. Neville, his eldest had a special quality. He could never be found. He seemed to think studying airplanes taking off or landing would stand him in better stead in later years than sitting in a classroom and attending lessons where arithmetic seemed to be the conspiracy of aliens and grammar a new language the teacher had just invented.

He was suitably surprised at being discovered in a circle with his current compatriots in imitation of the colony sweepers, smoking the butts of their discarded *beedies* and protested quite volubly when Adelaide cured him of this sudden addiction with the aid of well smeared chillie powder on his puckered lips and a few hard smacks on the rear of his rump.

Roxanna was just as spirited with calf brown eyes, which were often deluged by tears, they couldn't help themselves but of their own accord gushed from the tear glands, which seemed to think they had license to flood the earth at every opportunity. Unlike Noah, we rarely had warning to initiate some damage control but were at continuous risk of a flood. However, weak tear glands were never a deterrent to escapades, which were attributed to anyone else in the vicinity except the one who had perpetuated them. Wide hazel eyes which looked out at the world in perplexity and long shiny hair which framed a face no one would have dared to call mischievous was a perfect cover for committing crimes ordinary mortals would have balked at. In contrast having stretched a few inches more to her five foot nothing frame and loaded with somewhat heavier apparatus, I was frequently called upon to dispatch salivating beaus, who refused to believe she didn't return their nauseating ardour and desperately groped to embrace her hastily retreating figure while she yelled for assistance. Having no choice but to assist, I soon learned the art of repelling *'persona non gratis'*.

"You'll earn the reputation of being a bouncer," was Mum's warning comment. At that time it seemed an interesting proposition and I took to reading western novels despite Roxanna's entreaties to sample her tame diet of Mills and Boons. The 'Sudden' series by Oliver Strange provided sufficient material to encourage progress with that vocation while making Adelaide despair she would ever turn her robust daughter into a demure lady. Rockwell consoled her with the thought that female wrestling was fast becoming quite a sport and might earn their daughter laurels someday.

While I munched on western novels and adventures, Anne made a study in the art of evasion. She deliberately avoided Adelaide's watchful eyes at parties and tried her best to satisfy the ravenous monster, which egged her on from dish to dish. Much to Mum's chagrin we never left a party without the host or hostess congratulating her on the healthy appetite of her curly haired daughter. I attributed it to the fact she had curls which required more nutrition. Her nickname of 'pugee Ann' followed her until the time we no longer visited the farm. By then she had learned the art of keeping gravity in abeyance or else she might have dispensed with the offending articles altogether, I never did remember to ask her.

Andrew, our youngest, despite growing teeth, refused to be weaned at two and a half and became adept at exposing Mum's mammary glands until in desperation she resorted to the use of powdered quinine on her teats to make him believe that the milk tasted awful. He never touched it again much to our relief and we were saved having to think up explanations for the startling exposes.

I always felt inconspicuous like brown mud. Nothing distinguishable. I didn't have Ann's flamboyant good looks or Roxanna's beauty. I was this brown person who could blend into the background unnoticed. Quietness was my trademark and after a time people forgot I was there. When I was a baby I would disappear under the dining table to sleep. Sleep was my panacea for all ills. I could curl up anywhere and gently slumber. I didn't try to be pretty. If I did get noticed it offended me and I would retaliate by behaving obnoxiously. I preferred the fantasy world to the real world. I didn't share my feelings, thoughts, and aspirations with others but used banter to parry questions. People don't concentrate for more than a few minutes at any time, so it was easy to introduce a new topic and I would be forgotten, until the time I turned thirteen.

What we liked best were the tales of dances and nights at the clubs in the railway colonies or in the cantonments where white coated waiters served five course meals and ladies in gowns paraded on the arms of well dressed gentlemen. Narratives of the big bungalows with huge verandahs and large gardens where lanterns were hung and parties held in Victorian style, of ladies in hats and parasols, of horse riding and polo and food which was described with mouthwatering elaborateness. We girls expressed our penchant for those stories; Sunny was the one who answered us.

"If Gurly was alive," he said, "you would have been told such interesting tales of the fun we had at the clubs. One time she dressed herself as a Sardarji and went around planting kisses on all the ladie's cheeks. She caused quite a stir I can tell you."

"Didn't they recognize her?" asked Roxanne

"She stuck on this huge beard and she wore glasses with thick lens, of course nobody recognized her."

"But how did she disguise her chest?" Neville asked wickedly while we laughed.

"Bandaged her chest," he replied grinning.

"Then what happened?"

"Marjorie Williams was our Chief's wife and Gurly waltzed upto her and said;

"*Namasteji*, I, Sardarji would like to dance with you," in a gruff voice. "How did you get in?" she asked in annoyance wrinkling her nose for all the world as if he smelled bad. 'Bearer'! she shouted and Gurly bowed to her and said, "No need to scream Madam, I dance better than him," and twirled her moustache while the poor bearer kept asking the Sardarji to leave and then Mr. Williams came up and said, "Marj there's no need to create a scene," and Gurly grinned at him and took off the spectacles and said "Gurly at your service, Sir," and bowed to him with a flourish. Everyone laughed so hard, I tell you. I think they were relieved it wasn't a real Sardarji who was contaminating their hallowed club. There was a lot of discrimination; sometimes I didn't feel like associating with the bosses. We didn't have a choice ofcourse, if we were given an invitation to be present at a function, we had to be there."

That was the nice part of our family, scratch the surface and the cracks showed.

Brian, Aunty Noreen's son tried to toughen Neville by often kicking him down the stairs. Mum scolded him for being so boisterous and was resentful that his mother refused to discipline him. Lynette bit me at the village fair for having the audacity to take the horse she wanted and got bitten in return by Roxanna who felt she just had to retaliate since I didn't. Dorothea, Nelson's wife and Lynette's mother slapped Roxanna and Mother came to the aid of her brood sounding nastily on her. A brawl was averted by the hasty separation of antagonized females. We noticed Gran was a little in awe of her two younger daughters-in -law. Ruth the dignified, at all times polite, refusing to be anything other than lady like, married to Jefferson, a teacher born not made, and Thea married to Nelson, whose sharp tongue held nothing sacred but demolished all her opponents with knife-cutting sarcasm. Mum was different, Gran related better to her only because she felt more comfortable with her. Mum didn't have to be asked, she happily took over the cooking, organized all the children and did whatever had to be done but secretly, I think, she wanted a little praise for her efforts but sadly everyone took her for granted. Beneath the calm surface ruffled feathers tickled but superficial politeness prevailed among the adults. Children, however, have short memories; nothing remained the same minute to minute. We fought, we played, we laughed and we forgot what we were angry about. Life just went on!

Three

1984 has a hallmark in the Indian history. Indira Gandhi had been assassinated by her own Sikh bodyguards who felt she had desecrated their shrine at Amritsar by killing Bindranwala, the Sikh rebel. It had been a hot topic of discussion all along the journey and continued deep into the night as the family were disturbed that with Indira Gandhi gone, Anglo-Indians would be relegated to the ranks of the forgotten unless some action was taken by prominent members such as Frank Anthony. He shouldn't be a voice crying in the wilderness but a voice that has been given a body by our community's united support. How this was to be done was being debated heatedly.

I looked around as the family gathered round a bonfire. What an assortment we were. Grandpa was with his short white hair close cropped in the army style he was used to.

His bearing was still that of the Army but his face was a mass of wrinkles and his skin burnt a deep gold by the sun. Gran sat beside him, her fine white hair knotted in a bun at the back of her head, her features serene in repose as she sat gazing into the fire lost in thought. Rockwell, resembled his father but not to the height, he hadn't quite been able to reach that far but that was Gran's fault she had the short genes being diminutive herself. He had literally tripped over Adelaide in a basketball game in Bangalore where he had been stationed during his Airforce days and she had dug her well manicured claws into the little of his retreating back and hauled him back so firmly he had never been able to extricate himself. She gave him five very good reasons to stay, there would have been six but one got buried among the flowerbeds in a soap dish in Poona. Guess he suddenly wised up and decided to practice self restraint but the damage had been done and he buckled down to ing his duty. But he couldn't prevent his roving eye, which seemed to have a life of its own and refused to be subjugated to verbal chastisement and sometimes it was necessary for Adelaide to dispel her mortification by driving home point with the aid of a missile.

Built like a fort to withstand the siege of many battles, Manota had withstood the siege of generations who had clambered its walls, run screaming in the compound, banged doors, laughed, cried and sang. The walls still held the secrets of new loves and old, of dark mysteries, beautiful moments, all captured within the bricks of time. The wide staircase leading to the verandah reminded one of the entrances to an open theatre and, infact, the compound had been the venue for many a family drama enacted daily, the actors and actresses changing according to time and circumstances. The stairs had seated a generation of spectators and lead the frequent visitors to the long verandah with the round Roman pillars, which formed the imposing entrance to the dining hall, a long room with antique furniture. Further back, the living room had more antique furniture and several antique curios. A three-piece glass vase hung on the wall, its globes a delicate pink and opposite a similar one patterned in white. Sleeping beauty, the fairy tale, in a series of depictions graced the walls, the pictures still retaining their beauty despite their age. The store housed a number of old books in ancient bindings and rustic broad swords, pointed spears, fencing swords, bows and arrows and other paraphernalia pertaining to the war like leather saddles, harnesses, tapestry and an assortment of bric a brac. It was a paradise for the adventure seeker who could lose himself in flights of fancy among vivid imaginings.

The other side of the compound housed the kitchen with its old fashioned *chulas* which still used the old method of fuel, the local '*kandas*' or cowdung pats and next to it the pucca '*dillan*' or strong room which in the old days was the armoury but which now Grandma used as a kitchen store. Rice, wheat, *ghee*, *dals* and spices, the odours of aromatic herbs mingled with the stronger smells of spirits and tinctures with which Grandma used to treat the ailments of the villagers.

Behind the house, leading down to the stables was a little pathway and this was a favourite haunt for us children to sit and stare at the livestock. Their odours permeated the air, which coupled with the heat, and dust made one uncomfortable until one could almost imagine that we smelled the same. It was the most interesting vantage point, as anyone who entered the house or left it had to pass below discomfort notwithstanding; it was still a favourite haunt.

Opposite was a huge door where the hand operated machine was plied to cut fodder for the cattle. Beyond the door was the pathway leading to the village and beside it were two platforms called '*chabuthras*' where village plays were held during visits by nomadic actors and actresses. Themes from the Ramayana, Mahabharata and other mythological stories made up most of the repertoire. Their plays were dance dramas and hilarious portrayals of village and family life. It was the only form of entertainment back then, there being no television sets, or electricity.

Brown predominated. Shades of brown beginning with a light tan to a deep dark chocolate. Lord Krishna, Arjuna, Shiva, myriad Sitas, hilarious Hanumans and mustachioed Ravanas. Wide girth Parvati who being the Goddess of beauty probably squirmed at her mountain like reproduction who stormed the stage in enthusiastic swirls of diaphanous drapes. Wincing at the startled gaze of a captivated audience her flesh developed a life of it's own and the jelly like mound of her torso quivered and wiggled in a stupefying dance refusing to be quelled.

Reproductions of the Mahabharata and the Ramayana were favourites especially since enthusiastic warriors inevitably fell off the stage in the frenzy of fighting adding to the already comic spectacle. Relationships, the mainstay of all interactions were frequently woven into all the plays with village folk tales. Desire and conflict in a relationship, contradictions in the masculine and feminine visions of life, through it all one idea persisted, the clashing of personalities being the main reason for discord and disharmony in a marriage. I supposed even if a partner is given what he or she wants the result is still dissatisfaction because people are beings with opposing desires. Life and love always intertwined with battles.

"Wish we could put these people up on our stage at school," Neville remarked, "I can just see the reactions of some of our teachers."

"You kids should take some tips," said Dad and I wondered if he meant the acting or the bits of wisdom. But plays were not always available for entertainment, the nomadic troupes moved on and we were left to our own devices.

We acquired a new skill that winter, the art of making '*kandas*'. Elbows deep in cowdung, which we kneaded well with straw, mud and water, then fashioned into flat, round cakes and left to dry. This was not our normal occupation but the work of Kamla, the sweepress. Zestfully she applied herself to the task squatting on her haunches. She didn't deem it necessary to cover her face with the '*ghunghat*' and her sharp features were clearly displayed with an enormous silver ring nestled on her nose. Mum had exhorted us to do something constructive. What more constructive work could we do than this, which would provide fuel for the kitchen '*chulas*'? In emulation of Kamla we undertook the task with absorbed enthusiasm not realising we had an audience until shrill screeches assaulted our ears and talons dug into the flesh of our arms and we were unceremoniously hauled away in cacophonic confusion. Mother had found us.

The beating we got was not as bad as the scrubbing which made our hands raw for almost a week. What took longer to get over, however, was the teasing we had to endure from the elder cousins, not to mention the beaming smiles from Uncle Sunny, Grandpa's elder brother, who dazzled us with a brilliant imitation of a glowing sun as he thought it a great lark. We had finally got the treatment we deserved. Well revenge has its rewards too and tomato red toenails somehow clashed with striped pajamas, but we didn't get as much satisfaction as we expected because no one commented on it preferring not to embarrass him or perhaps nothing he did surprised them and he calmly went around oblivious to the whole thing. I frowned in annoyance and his brown scalp shone mockingly. I wondered if he polished it?

"Do you ever take a bath, Uncle?" I asked inquisitively as this had been haunting us for a long time. His stomach wobbled as he chuckled. Far from being annoyed, he was amused at the question.

'You keep track of baths huh? I only have oil baths," he informed me, "water makes you sick." He chuckled fatly and we grinned back at him quite forgetting our annoyance.

I thought of Adelaide and her fetish for cleanliness, I didn't think she would be pleased. She wasn't, especially when, Andrew, took it as a license for him not to bathe with soap and water either. He thought sand baths were to be recommended over any other bath and everyday a tussle would ensue as he tried to escape on his chubby legs and wallow in the sand again. Only when Gran threatened to feed him worm medicine if he didn't behave did he decide to admit defeat. Mother in ballistic form, rounded on Uncle Sunny for filling our heads with silly ideas. But we were quite sure he had not been fibbing.

Christmas entered glitteringly. The Christmas tree with coloured fairy lights twinkled and winked, the silver tinsel shone shining brightly and the different hued balls and bells glowed against the deep green of the tree. The angel at the top looked down benevolently, smiled a blessing. The aroma of roasted duck wafted in each time the door to the dining hall was opened. Brown onions in ghee and the garlic sizzled to a light gold in melted butter. Sips of ginger ale, which tickled the throat and the reek of whiskey and fumes from the brandy in hot water added to the already pervading aromas.

"Why do we eat such a lot during festivals?" I asked nobody in particular.

"You don't have to eat. I hope Gran made *biriyani*," said Neville.

"You're just a stomach."

"So don't get J, you could lose some weight if you didn't sleep all day".

"I don't.."

"Okay you two, can we hear some music instead?" asked Roxanna "Where's the guitar?"

"Neville, where are you sneaking off to." I asked him.

"I was just going to check on my goat."

"Maybe that's what they cooked for dinner."

"Yeah, I heard Mum say we were getting roast leg of mutton," said Anne

"And duck and fried fish."

"What's for pudding?" I asked

"Something they're planning on lighting...hey think anyone's looking, want some wine?" Neville had returned and was sniffing some of the bottles on the small cupboard reserved only for liquor.

'They're coming..' I teased him.

"Idiot, you made me nervous.." some of the wine slopped onto the floor and he mopped at it with a paper napkin.

"I thought I heard footsteps."

"Okay, keep a watch, which one you want?"

"I only want the ginger."

"Hey you guys, come and sit near the bonfire, bring the guitar...what are you up to?" said the cousins from Dad's siblings.

"Nothing, want a sip?"

"Come on, you'll become a drunkard and I'll tell Mummy." Roxanna said.

"I'll tell her I saw you kissing that red haired guy near the stables.."

"Liar...which red haired guy?"

"Come on..." we followed them out to the compound which was covered in sand deliberately placed there from the river by Grandpa who thought it delightful to have kids wallow in it and build strange, imaginative buildings which we thought were castles but tended more to look like insect accommodation.

The bonfire glowed brightly; sending sparks shooting in a spiral each time more wood was added.

"We should have a piglet roasting over it." Bobby, Sunny's grandson said.

"Che, the piggies are so cute, Edene will scream if she hears you. Muslims don't touch pork." I replied.

"Who wants ginger ale?"

"I do," holding out my glass and Mum carefully measured in a little.

"When will Santa come?" That was the fifth time Ann had asked the question.

"Later," Mum replied and she subsided onto the carpet again to watch the antics of the older people. Alcohol played an important role at parties it seemed, that slightly heady feeling of intoxication where eyes blurred, feet seemed to move in opposite directions and body parts didn't belong together, not to mention the curdling in the brain where speech impediments resulted and the tongue swelled up to confuse words that were rushing to escape but sadly tumbling out with h's in everything. Liquor brought out the dormant personality of a person. Liquor did to people what was supposedly impossible. A quiet, smiling man becomes garrulous, a calm, gentle-spoken person becomes one's worst nightmare with prowling hands and a happy go lucky individual becomes crazy picking fights with all and sundry. Rockwell waxed eloquent with Rudyard Kipling in keeping with the high spirits and high on spirits, he was an excellent example of garrulousness.

"If you can keep your head about you when all around are losing theirs and blaming it on you..." that did seem rather apt, I grinned and looked down at the shoes, his were black and polished to a shine, his right foot pointed a little to the left, next to his shoes a brown pair, turned slightly outwards, then a ladies pair of low heeled pumps, the right foot tapping a little in time to some inner music, I surmised. Further on a pair of while sandals...back to Dad, it didn't take much encouragement to get him singing, he had come to the end of that poem and had swung into his old airforce song, "The chicken in the army, they say, is mighty fine. One fell off the table and broke a leg of mine..." everyone joined in and were laughing by the time he switched to his Hinglish "*Nanhi se meri jaan, hua qurban, I love you all my darling, de dungha meri jaan, cheeks tumhari beautiful ...*" while pinching Mum's cheeks and she smiled in amusement but couldn't help feeling awkward as all eyes were on her. She had quite forgotten the argument they had only that afternoon over some petty matter like *Sundari* the washerwoman who slyly allowed her *ghunghat* to slip every time she went near him and his eyes had been riveted.

The *verandah* became the venue for dancing. Neville and Brian belted out tunes with the guitar. Heaving, wiggling flesh were perfumed by talc, scents, aftershaves and deodorants. Energetic *chachachas*, dreamy waltzes and graceful tangos interrupted sometimes by uncoordinated jiving, hip grinding, chest jiggling and arm-flinging gyrations of nieces and nephews who were intent on oozing perspiration and ensuring that the maximum amount of dust rose from the floor in clouds with their enthusiastic stomping.

"Dinner's on the table." Grandma disturbed our wide-eyed concentration of people whom we had known as serious, calm and cool but had somehow converted to contortionists. They laughed a lot to cover the embarrassment they were feeling, behaving so out of character. Once in the dining room, my stomach juices calmed after being in revolt of frenzied perspiration, which had mingled with cigarettes, perfumes, deodorants, brandies, and the smell of something delicious wafting through the dining room door.

'Nourishments on the table." Uncle Sunny prodded us to move quickly while I stared at the entrance. Was this our dining hall, maybe I took a wrong turn somewhere. The table sparkled with coloured candles in silver holders and poinsettias in a sparkling rose bowl. Two ducks in a brown glaze surrounded by a mound of peas and mushrooms. Roasted potatoes, white sauce cauliflower, *biryani* sprinkled with cashewnuts and raisins, thick gravy mutton, which we hoped had not been sourced from Neville's goat, and big creamy *rotis* spread with *ghee* piled on a platter. Round dishes of *chutneys*, pickles and salads. Plum pudding which Leo couldn't light with brandy and a match, fizzling out like a damp squib tasting bitter and which Grandma drowned with custard and cream to make palatable. By the time I had scooped the last spoon of cream from the bowl I knew what the duck had felt like when they had stuffed it and no wonder it had lain on it's back with its belly up and legs protruding.

Santa Claus made an entrance at midnight laughing his merry 'ho, ho hos'. Despite the disguise, Dad was recognizable as he entered the room well-stuffed with pillows and dressed in Santa's clothes with a white cotton beard and a *dhobi* bag slung across his shoulder filled with gifts for distribution. One of the babies who didn't seem to think much of Santa bit him in fright instead of kissing him. We pretended not to recognize him in keeping with the spirit of fun, winking shyly.

I went to sleep with Christmas carols ringing in my ears and the sound of the reindeer bells tinkling softly.

Christmas was over and life returned to normal. Lazy days were spent in weaving childish fantasies or poking through Leo's store of books, roaming in the guava gardens or playing in the sand which filled the compound and where castles could be built to our heart's content. Having clean river sand to play in everyday was an aid to using our imaginations. The day after Christmas we scooped up bucketfuls of sand and spent hours building a model of Manota, but when it was completed, a sudden winter shower poured from the skies and we scurried to the verandah laughing with glee. Rain was fun, the earth smelled so good!

When a watery sun showed its face we scrambled down the stairs to take a look at our model. It was gone! Dispersed into tiny grains of sand under the onslaught of water as if it had never been there. The dismay on our faces was comical I expect, because they found it something to laugh over. Only Wilfred commiserated with us; he understood it had been a labour of love.

Four

Bess, our gentle buffalo, was going to given birth again and we sat at our vantage point and watched the whole process. She seemed to be having a bit of a struggle but Grandpa was assisting. As she lay on her bed of straw her huge black body quivered with effort, heaving and straining she trembled and tried again and again but the baby didn't seem too keen to come out. Grandpa watched for a while, talking to her softly then nodding his head as if he had come to a decision he pushed his hands in up to the elbows while Ramsai and Shyamlall held her to prevent her struggling. Then he tugged and out came the head, Bessie heaved some more and the little calf just slid out in a mess of stuff. Grandma was stroking Bessie's head and talking to her but she seemed more interested in investigating her baby. In a little while they had her standing and the calf got shakily to it's feet aided by

Grandpa. It stood trembling for a while looking so strange with it's big head that we all laughed. Bessie was busy cleaning it and the calf wobbled a few steps blinking its huge black eyes. After that experience, Bess might have thought to be a little more circumspect. Instead she continued to attract the old male buffalo who was jealous of his stud status and feared being replaced by a younger generation one. She always seemed to be in some stage of pregnancy. We wondered what secret enticement Bess used, to make her more attractive than the younger female buffaloes. He had been bought to increase Grandpa's buffalo population but he seemed to have married Bess and forgotten there were other prettier females he could add to his harem. In fact, he didn't have a harem.

"Our men could learn something from him," Mum had said to Gran, "he doesn't roam." Gran clicked her tongue reprovingly but her eyes were laughing.

Bessie's calf Jennie from an earlier marriage was determined never to get married. She rebuffed all the males that Grandpa introduced to her. One young bull in frustration began chasing the old she cow who had been put out to pasture, too old to do anything except eat and sleep. He didn't seem to know the difference between buffalo and cow. In fury she lowed angrily at him and lashed out with her sharp horns. He looked so forlorn with a deep gash on his neck dripping blood, that Grandpa took pity on him and bought a pretty gentle she buffalo just for him.

During mating season all the animals and insects ran riot. The mosquitoes flew around dizzily clinging to each other while the birds jumped on their mates, flattening them, pecking lovingly at their heads to let them know that they were loved. The rooster crowed happily. He was well satisfied with his current brood, he had had a go with all of them and it prqmised to be a good crop. Puffed up with his own consequence he perched on the hencoop roof and did what all cocks do so well. He crowed loudly informing the world of his prowess oblivious to the chuckling and gossiping of the hens who exchanged notes on his aptitude and giggled at his cocksure manner while busily pecking at the grain. Even the cobras got hit by the love bug and a pair slithered into the barn and copulated for hours much to the dismay of Grandpa who locked the door to keep everyone out of danger. The men were quite envying their stamina, at that time 'viagra' had not yet made an appearance and they had to depend entirely on what they possessed, which when we thought about it, never amounted to much anyway.

"What is it uncle?" I asked Wilfred the question. He was standing near, watching Shyamlall rub Bessie down with straw.

"It's a female," he replied, after inspecting Bessie's calf, "you'll get something special as a treat tonight."

"What? What?" I tugged at his shawl.

"Piyushi, the thickened milk that comes after the birth, you'll enjoy that." The calf distracted me from what he was saying; it fluttered its lashes as it blinked seemingly surprised to find itself on the outside. Then it jumped a little and bounced up and down as if testing the strength of its legs before collapsing near its mother who nudged it to help it stand again.

Wilfred was the only person in the family who dressed differently; he swathed his head in cloth turbans and wrapped shawls around him when it was cold. He did wear trousers and shirts under the shawl but all the same he managed to look like he belonged in the village, he could blend in a crowd at a village fair.

"It's my disguise," he told us when we asked him, "I'm a secret agent and I send messages by pigeon courier to my boss...sshhh, this is our secret." Ofcourse, it was our secret, if any of the adults heard him they might think he had to be removed to some special place where the white coated men and women would dose him with pills and talk endlessly trying to make him believe he was normal. We liked him as he was, infact he was more normal than the others were, and it was easy to understand him. He was different but he always seemed to be in hiding, I supposed he felt more comfortable with himself than with anyone else. He didn't tell us what he was investigating or who was after him but it was fun to enter into the spirit of his game and to keep his secrets. For a while after that we crept around trying to follow him and see where he went and we always informed him if there were visitors in case one of them was after him. He rewarded us with shells he had collected from the river and once he even gave us a snake's skin for luck.

Looking round his darkened room we wrinkled our noses at the disorder. Bird droppings dotted the floor, the smell of animal urine was strong as he often had a collection of wounded or ailing animals, which he healed with strange concoctions before releasing them again and the faded gray blanket, which served as a curtain was coated with a thin film of dust.

"Uncle, how do you stay in this place," Roxanna wrinkled her nose in disgust.

"If I clean it, Grandma will start poking around in here and then you'll have everyone trying to discover my secrets, this way no one wants to enter."

We nodded our heads in understanding our secrets were always in danger of being exposed. Mum seemed to think she had license to rummage whenever she felt like.

"But how do you sleep here?"

"I don't, I sleep in the granary in the hammock."

"Oh!" we said in unison and he smiled at us thinking how easy it was to fool us. We grinned back innocently but I was thinking, "who does he think he's fooling, no wonder Mum doesn't want us to come here, what filth!"

"Poor chap," Roxanna whispered, she actually looked like she was about to begin the deluge of her tear glands. I knew they were weak but this was ridiculous. "Maybe I'll come and clean it when he goes out," she said. Thankfully the brimming tears didn't fall and I was able to distract her by reminding her that Mum must be looking for us.

After the gloom of the room the sun struck our eyes with sufficient force and we blinked like round-eyed owls in the startling brightness.

"Where were you?" Neville asked emerging from the stables where he had been to untether his goat. "Look, it's getting fat."

"He looks the same, infact he's grown thin, poor thing, what have you been doing, eating his food?"

"Jealous cat,"

"J of a goat, you're a clown you know."

"Come on, Mum's looking for us." Roxanna pulled at my arm while Neville shook his head at us in mock annoyance. We cuddled the sleek goat before marching off up the path. No goat had ever had such tender loving care. It's coat was brushed until it gleamed; it got the best feed and got cuddled the most. I did wonder how Neville would be able to sell it to the butcher when the time came. It seemed likely his business was in danger of being a total failure.

The afternoons were always hot, unabated sunlight poured down on all and sundry and it was imperative to escape the heat. The grown ups took the chance to catch up on their sleep and invariably we youngsters would creep off to the guava gardens to climb trees or play in the cool shadows beneath if we had managed to escape the authoritarian hand which vainly tried to regulate our days with the inclusion of a couple of hours of the siesta. I say vainly because it was only they who strictly adhered to the routine of the afternoon nap which seemed imperative after a huge lunch while we used the time to indulge in whatever caught our fancy.

The farm was mostly guava gardens with some of the land being tilled with rice, wheat, various lentils, mustard and sugarcane. There were some groves of custard apple and mango as well but since we only visited in winter, we never got to taste the fruit of the mango groves. Dad would regale us with stories of his boyhood and how when he and his brothers returned for their summer holidays they would indulge in mango eating competitions. Huge '*dekchis*' of mangoes would be soaked in water and they would sit around it peeling and eating the succulent fruit in quick succession until they could eat no more, the winner being the one who had managed to down the most mangoes in the given time.

"Didn't you get your stomachs out?" Mum asked him.

"Not often," he replied, "my mother made us drink a glass of cold milk each time or we would drink glasses of water afterwards, that's supposed to prevent the runs."

"Yuk, imagine sitting several times a day on the chamber pots," I had a horror of going to the toilet. We were not allowed to use the toilet, which had a door being reserved only for adults. We were expected to use the chamber pots, which lined in military precision, biggest to smallest, were kept in the shade of the compound and the venue for desultory conversations. Those who used this ancient method of relieving themselves had to have a good idea of the size of one's gluteus maximus to make the correct selection. Ears came in handy if one was enthroned and someone approached, the best remedy was to remove oneself from the immediate vicinity chamber pot and all, and set it down in a more convenient place. The chamber pots were carted away by the sweepers who couldn't be used for any other jobs except to clean the toilets or the yard and make cowdung pats. The sweepers came from the village and were a caste that was only employed for the menial tasks. The cooking and other jobs were given to high caste workers and Muslims.

Grandpa did the actual farming and he never seemed to have enough money to modernize. The old ways were still in evidence but the grandeur had long since disappeared. There were still servants to do the work but not as many. Most were employed in the fields and apart from a cook, a sweepress and a man to take care of the livestock and one to fill water from the well, we never really got to know who the others were. There were hardly any new developments except for the introduction of a few tube-wells to irrigate some of the farmers' fields, and a special well which grandpa had made for the untouchables as it was pathetic to see them waiting to be given water when everyone else had plenty. They were not allowed to draw from the village well for fear of contaminating it, and the building of a new acquaduct across the '*Kala nadi*', nothing else was done and the land remained much the same as it had been for hundreds of years. Stories of bygone days were passed down to us through the word of mouth. What was fact and what was fiction, got intertwined and as is common with word of mouth, what was embellished what true, was difficult to decipher.

Our family had their own brand of snobbery. Descended on the British side from Lords, The first Lord to claim the title of the Baron of Uttoxeter in Staffordshire was Colonel William Linneaus's uncle and his grandfather from his mother's side was Colonel Livingston of the Livingston's of America. The third Lord was an Admiral and on the Indian side '*begums*' and princess who could trace their ancestry from Bahadur Shah to Genghis Khan. It was no wonder that they felt themselves in awe of their heritage. In later years, the story, which made headlines in the pages of "Tatler," a British magazine, gave us something else to be proud of. The baronetcy of Uttoxeter was lying vacant as the fourth Lord had not come forward and someone from the British archives had researched and discovered that Uncle Julian, Dad's cousin was the rightful heir. Unfortunately he couldn't claim his inheritance, as he couldn't produce the marriage certificate of his grandparents and to find the records would require a tremendous amount of time and money. In the days when his grandparents got married, the churches were makeshift tents and the visiting Reverend conducted marriages, christenings and such which had been pending his arrival. The records could be anywhere. When all this happened I was already a young woman but still it caught and fired my imagination to see all our names in print in the annals of Debrett's peerage.

Stewart William was the grandson of the first Baron and he married the grandaughter of Colonel William Linneaus Gardner who had built a fort and a palace fifty miles from Agra at Kasgunj. We were the descendants of Tandy who was the third son of Stewart William from Grandpa's side and we were related to William Linneaus as Grandma was descended from his line too. Grandma was distantly related to Grandpa and Grandpa's parents, George and Mabel, had arranged their marriage. Great Grandma Mabel had blue eyes and never called her husband anything but Georgie Sahib. She had come from Fatehpur and Grandma came from Chhaoni, which still held the magnificent tomb of William Linneaus and his *begum* alongside the family vaults. William Linneaus and his *begum's* story was a romantic one and related to me by Aunty Sarah who lived in the remnants of the palace in the rooms, which were part of the Turkish baths.

Aunty Sarah was Grandma's cousin and they had been brought up together as Grandma was an orphan who had descended from the last Emperor's brother's family but since her parents were not around she had been placed in a mission school from where she was later married to Grandpa. Grandma and Aunty Sarah were very close and whenever the opportunity presented itself, Grandma would pack us into the bullock cart along with baskets of fruit and off we would go for a visit to Chhaoni. There were not many Anglo-Indian families left in Kasgunj and most were related as it is, but Aunty Sarah stood out among them. She was diminutive in stature and could not be considered pretty, her features being too prominent, but she definitely made an impression.

She was never without her hats and her suits, not to mention her stockings and pumps. She was always well turned out no matter the weather. Aunty Sarah was a teacher in a mission school in Meerut and her Principal was a Britisher with whom she got along tolerably well. She was well-read and owned a number of well bound English books including a poetry book by Robert Burns with his signature, which she presented to me in later years along with her hat boxes and hats. The hat boxes had the N.F. Railway labels all over them, which made them even more interesting. Today excitement had us hopping; Grandma was taking us on a visit to Chhaoni.

Rocky and Nelson, two of the bullocks who were used for ploughing as well, had been harnessed to the cart, they had been named after Dad and his younger brother, and were rather stately in appearance. One was white and the other gray, and both stood tall with pointed horns looking disdainfully down their noses at us from their lofty height. Grandpa invariably named his livestock after his children and grandchildren except for Bess, the buffalo, on which we all took turns riding, as she was most complacent, not minding anyone who went near her, unlike the bullocks or her calf Jennie who menaced with their hooves and their horns. Only Ramsai, Grandpa and Uncle Wilfred could handle them safely. Uncle Wilfred helped around the house and farm. Unfortunately at an early age he almost got drowned in a tub of limewash, '*chuna*' and it seems the fumes affected his brain so he couldn't study very far but he was a whiz at making chapathis and he could do magic. The limewash hadn't affected his hormones though and he had grown to over six feet tall but seemed taller as he sported a longish crew cut, which stuck straight out, from his head adding to his height. He was reed thin too no matter how much he ate. We asked him to come along for the ride but he just shook his head. We hadn't really expected him to come along as he normally shied away from grown up company but he got along just fine with us kids.

"Don't stay too late," called Grandpa, as we started moving.

Several aunts and uncles waved from the top and Mum called down to us, "Be good!"

Feet dangling over the edge I looked out over the landscape. We passed the graveyard, parts of the guava gardens and the tiny village, which nestled among some mud hills. The grass grew in tall clumps and was rough and unpleasant to touch. It was easy to cut a hand on it, as the edges were very sharp.

"Don't touch the grass," admonished Grandma as she caught my sister trailing her hand over the grass, "there could be snakes hiding there." That was the most effective way to keep our hands out of it. The deadly King Cobra was definitely to be avoided. It was rare for a King Cobra to be the first to leave, more likely the human who came in contact would be speedily dispatched or take to his heels with the utmost dexterity. There were cases where the horrendous exterminator actually gave chase. If a Cobra was killed by a villager, they poured milk over the dead reptile and then burned it so its mate couldn't seek them out and take revenge.

The cart gently swayed from side to side as the bullocks moved in easy rhythm. Neville was the first to take the lead in singing and we sang a few tunes sometimes not so tunefully and we giggled over the rendering of 'Hang down your head Tom Dooley,' which Neville entertained us with while adding a few lines of his own, which would have probably made the song writer slap a defamation suit on him and which Gran reproved as 'ungentlemanly'.

There was only a dirt road and we didn't relish plodding along in the ankle deep sand. It was much easier to sit and gaze at the landscape. The most common sight were the mustard fields, which soothed the eyes and were pretty to behold. Bright green with a carpet of yellow or the green of the paddy fields, with the tubewells dousing them in water or the tall sugarcane or sometimes just miles and miles of sand and stones with clumps of dry looking grass.

"Perhaps, we'll see some wolves," said Neville as we swayed and bumped over the dusty road.

"They won't come near," said Grandma "even if we do see any, but you just might see peacocks. It's the mating season and sometimes we can catch them dancing."

Grandma looked very pretty in a light blue dress and sandals with a straw hat on her head tied under her chin with a blue ribbon. She seemed so used to the life in the village and never minded not having much. She told us Indian folk tales and stories of the 'Lu' a hot wind that carried disease and death whenever it came and which made an appearance in summer. Sometimes it blew so strong, moving with gale force winds that people were lifted into the air and carried off far away. Since none returned people assumed they must have died but some of the villagers said the wind came from hell and it came to claim the lives of the wicked people.

Grandma cautioned us not to trust everyone we met, she said a crook doesn't change his character but he can change his appearance and she related the story of the partridge, the hare and the cat. By using folk tales she thought we would remember her advice better. I remembered the stories but I didn't always remember her advice until it was too late. Her voice was soft and melodious as we sat silently listening to her speak.

"The partridge one day discovered a field which gave it plenty of food so it left the tree under which it used to live and began to feed. Meantime a hare came along and took possession of the partridge's home. When Madam partridge returned she wanted Mr. Hare to leave but he refused and an argument took place," Grandma wiped the perspiration from her nose, "they took their argument to Pundit cat. The cat was only pretending to be a Pundit but was in fact a hypocrite. He told them both to come closer so he could hear them better and then he pounced on them and had himself a hare-partridge meal. "See," she said, " isn't it better to stay away from people like the cat?" We nodded our heads in agreement.

"How will we recognize them," asked Roxanna.

"Listen to your instinct, the inner voice that everyone has," she said. I never did until the time I landed myself in trouble and remembered her words. Once I got used to listening to the inner voice I rarely went wrong. It was a nice way of giving us her advice. She followed up that one by the story of the heron, the mongoose and the serpent.

"It's not good to listen to everybody's advice," she cautioned us, "there are some people who you know you should stay away from. Sometimes they cause mischief instead of doing good. They may only be pretending to be your friends because of some benefit to themselves". I already knew a lot of people like that. I could have given her examples but I wanted to hear her story so I kept quiet. We had begun our journey early morning to escape the mid-day heat which was always fierce and we expected to reach Chhaoni well in time for lunch.

"What's that Grandma?" A yell from Neville interrupted

her.' He was almost standing with excitement upsetting our equilibrium in the cart.

"Sit Neville," Grandma said sharply and he immediately subsided but remained on his knees, "that's the aquaduct. It was built by the Britishers long ago. We're almost at Nadrai."

"Wow, it's so grand."

I had to agree; it was imposing, running the width of the river, all in red brick with rows of arches.

"We'll come over it on our way back, so you all can look at it properly and you can see the bell too."

The bell was huge and made of iron. It had been carried out from Burma on the back of 'William Linneaus' own elephant, which was also buried near his tomb. There was a big mound to mark the spot including one to mark the spot for his horse, but I sometimes wondered how come the graves stayed under mounds, shouldn't graves sink when the bodies decomposed? I didn't think William Linneaus was partial to mummifying things but then I could be mistaken. Or there could be a simple explanation like a pile of rocks over the skeletons.

"Can't we go closer now, Gran?" Neville was impatient to get a proper look.

"What does the aquaduct do, why isn't it just called a bridge?" I couldn't help asking.

"It's a sort of a bridge which has gates which control the flow of water from the river for irrigation," said Gran. "Put your hats on now, it's getting hot, but first wash your hands." We had been digging into the basket of fruit.

"Somebody is waving at us," said Roxanna and she began waving back enthusiastically but I stared at the figure in puzzlement. We had reached Chhaoni but the figure signaling us was not familiar.

"Whose that?" asked Neville.

"That must be Ivan," said Gran.

"We don't know any Ivan, is he a cousin."

"Ofcourse he's your cousin and I want you all to treat him nicely. His parents have died and he's going to stay with Aunty Sarah"

"How did they die?" I asked.

"Car accident," said Grandma briefly and from her tone of voice I knew she didn't want to talk about it.

Must be her relations, I thought and she was probably sad about their deaths. We had reached the lone figure and I could see he was tall and lanky with a shock of unruly hair and a whole lot of freckles. He was grinning at us and didn't seem in the least bit sad, so I discarded the idea of saying I was sorry about his parents. He looked cheeky but I was a little disappointed.

"You don't have green eyes," I said indignantly. By rights he should have had green eyes but his eyes were brown.

"Why should I have green eyes?" he was looking at me in astonishment as I climbed out of the cart with everyone else following. Only my younger brother Andrew was missing, as Mum had not allowed him to come.

"Don't you know green eyes go with red hair?" His hair was not really red, more a deep mahogany which looked reddish in the sun.

It was a common sight to see bare feet children with red hair and green eyes playing among the village children and who could not speak a word of English. There was controversy about their ancestry and many of the grown ups claimed they were descendants from the concubines line. Subsequent male generations had raging hormones, which necessitated them keeping a special village for their extra-marital dalliances. William Linneaus himself had lived like a *nawab* and had owned a number of villages under the Zamindari system. He had been a favourite among the English ladies, with his dashing good looks and his wit. Wit was common among our family, all the many shades of it, witty wit, sarcastic wit, dim wit, you name it and we had it.

Most of the land had been mortgaged to a moneylender in Farrukhabad and was lost during his grandson's time. The Colonel's son had his father's taste for adventure and had eloped with the last Mughal emperor's daughter. So there was a lot of Muslim blood mixed too with the Anglo blood.

"I'm going ahead," said Gran. We were glad to walk and stretch our legs. Besides we were curious about Ivan and could question him without Gran's watchful eyes.

"So where do you study?" asked Neville of Ivan. He was only trying to be polite but I could see he wasn't much interested in Ivan; he was too young for him.

Ivan was fourteen then and the same age as my elder sister. Neville was three years older but he thought he was full grown. He liked to do the adolescent thing like being very opinionated and a little rebellious. He had begun his first business venture. He had bought a goat with painstakingly saved pocket money and was trying to fatten it so he could sell it for a good price.

"Boys high school," he replied proudly, sticking his hands into the pockets of his trousers.

"That's where my Dad studied too," Roxanna chirped in, I could see she liked Ivan. I had not formed an opinion of him as yet.

"Do you read westerns?" they were my favourites and most boys liked reading them too.

"Yeah," he replied, "I like Sudden." The Sudden series were my favourite so I smiled at him cheerfully. I definitely liked him now. Anyone who read Sudden had to be likeable.

Aunty Sarah and various aunts and uncles were waiting to greet us. We did the dutiful hugging and kissing which was expected and then trooped into the living room. One thing our family never suffered from was a scarcity of relatives. Grayheads mingled with black and brown, T-shirts with jeans, trousers and skirts, blouses and dresses and ofcourse, with Aunty Sarah in her usual coat and skirt with her gray hair neatly pinned behind her ears.

"We'll have lunch first," she said, "then we can sit and have a long natter."

I knew she was eager to have a chat with Gran. Lunch consisted of *dal* and rice, chicken curry and vegetables fresh from Aunty Sarah's own garden. Gran and Aunty Sarah still referred to the dal as 'doll' and Kanpur as 'Cawnpore' as did most of the older generation Anglo-Indians and although we did try to correct them they soon reverted to the old way of speaking.

"Can we go to the tomb later?" Ivan asked her between mouthfuls, and she nodded assent.

The tomb had a dome, which was the favourite nesting place for parrots that screamed in frenzy at each other competing for the trophy of the loudest screech and abused each other with vociferous intensity just for the heck of it, enjoying the noise. Pigeons too found the accommodation to their liking and sometimes if you were not careful you could be christened with their droppings. It was better not to stand still in one place. We had two tame parrots in Manota to whom Gran talked a lot and we stuffed them with chillies and guavas but try as we did we couldn't get them to say anything except make parrot conversation which we couldn't imitate.

Ivan and I were the only two who eventually went to explore the tomb. Annie and Roxanna were busy talking with the other girls, Neville was in conversation with Uncle Oswald, and Gran and Aunty Sarah were deep in discussion. They didn't notice us leaving the room. Ivan didn't seem to have a problem with me being a girl. He took along his air gun and said he would have pot shots at the parrots.

"But you won't hurt any," I told him firmly, "you can't eat parrots and it would be a waste to shoot them." The mud was hot even with shoes on and we scrunched along the edges of the fields where it was a little firmer.

"I only shoot to kill," said Ivan glancing back at me.

"Then you won't shoot," I told him, "you might as well have left your gun behind."

"So typical of a girl," he grumbled, "as if I don't know

what to do, don't tell me okay.... walk faster or I'll leave you behind."

I stuck my tongue out at his retreating back, "bully!"

It wasn't far to the tomb but as we came in sight of it we were in for a pleasant surprise. Peacocks strutting like dandies, puffing their chests displaying their fine feathers, showing off their glistening blue-green plumage, dancing a mincing waltz to entice the sand coloured peahens who pretend they hadn't noticed the display being showcased for their benefit but pecked at the ground in studied indifference, gossiping together like rumour-mongering old women exchanging confidences, while secretly checking out the males, selecting the one they were going to procreate with.

"Why are the peahens so ordinary?" I exclaimed in surprise, "they should be the one's with the coloured feathers." To my way of thinking, females should be prettier, males didn't deserve such nice plumage.

"It's the males who have to attract the females," said Ivan, "See there's only three females and they have to choose from the males, I counted, there's seven of them."

The peacocks had stopped dancing and were walking around, dropping their heads to feed. Suddenly they were running and jumping as they scuttled in all directions. The peahens were faster than the males, perhaps since they had less baggage to carry.

"Wonder what frightened them off," said Ivan and quickly grabbed at my shoulder to prevent me from passing by him. "Wait somebody is coming."

"Nobody comes here," I stated positively, then stared in astonishment at the boy who was approaching the tomb.

"Do you have a brother here?" I asked Ivan.

"No," he said. Absently his gaze firmly fixed on the boy who was standing still staring at us. We were clearly visible as there was nothing in the fields as yet.

"Lets go meet him,"

"He's got red hair,"

"I can see that," Ivan had reached up to smoothen his hair. He had a habit of pulling at his ducktails, which stuck out behind his head. The boy looked poised for flight.

"He's not wearing shoes," I whispered as we came near him.

"I don't wear shoes half the time either," Ivan whispered back, I didn't either but I didn't want to tell him that.

"Hi," Ivan called out to him.

"Hi," the boy muttered. He did look a little like Ivan but maybe it was the red hair which gave him the similarity, and compared with his, Ivan's hair was more brown than red but he did have green eyes. Not an emerald green but like moss agate speckled with brown.

I was trying to figure out which branch of the family he came from, Ivan knew what I was at and openly ridiculed me.

"You're thinking of the red hair and the freckles, so which side have you put him on?" He had already been through the grilling of discovering his ancestry and was not going to have me begin all over again. "Give your brain a rest," he said irritably while I just glared at him indignantly.

The boy was looking at us with perplexity and he touched his hair in embarrassment. I think he thought we were making fun. His red hair had long been the bane of his existence and a target for many jokes by the village urchins.

"Our family has throwbacks to that colour of hair," I explained to him. "Are you also related?" he just shook his head.

"I don't know where my hair came from," he said, "I could ask my mother though".

"Do," I said, but the topic never did come up and I never did learn if he was related.

"Where did you come from?" Ivan asked him and he pointed backwards at the village.

He was staring at Ivan and as we stood and stared back at him, I noticed they were both of a height and he was equally thin. He didn't seem to like us for some reason but Ivan was determined to be friendly.

"We're going to explore the family vaults, want to come?" the boy just looked at us sullenly.

There was something in his eyes I just couldn't place. Later when I thought about it, I thought it might have been a surprise. I don't think he expected Ivan to want to be his friend. He was an enigma to us and I wasn't sure we should let him into the tomb, but I didn't say anything then.

"Chris," he said briefly when Ivan asked his name. We told him ours.

The tomb was typical of Mughal architecture. Aunty Sarah had said an Iranian had been the architect. The moment we entered the parrots started screeching and rustling. I was already having misgivings, "Ivan," I called softly, it was gloomy inside, "we shouldn't disturb the dead."

"Getting scared now huh?" Ivan demanded his voice sounding too loud and the parrots squawked some more in protest.

"We need a torch," said Chris, his voice gruff. It was cool inside but a little light filtered in from the dome, which had several openings around it.

"Where are the graves?" I asked in surprise.

"Down," said Chris; "there's a door on the side and stairs but its dark" obviously he had been here before.

"Is Chris the short name for Christopher?" I asked him, he had lost a little of his sullenness and looked more cheerful.

"No, Chris is just Chris."

"Oh, but normally ..."

"It's not," he said rudely.

There wasn't much we could do right now, so we went out into the sunshine and sat near the entrance to the family vault, which housed the graves of other ancestors. I was glad there was to be no more exploration right now. I didn't fancy facing the spectre of ancient ancestors coming out to greet me. Chris and Ivan were talking softly together, discussing his air rifle. Chris was fascinated with it and kept fingering it longingly. He refused our invitation to come along for tea and ran off waving madly when we decided to return.

"Aunty Sarah," I called out when we were back at the house.

"Yes dear."

"How many graves are in the tomb and how many are in the vaults?"

"Only two in the tomb, I don't know about the vaults," she replied her eyes twinkling, "so that's where you had gone to. Go wash your hands then come for tea."

"Have you ever been down the vaults?" I asked biting into a biscuit.

"Oh no," she exclaimed, "what ever would I want to go there for." She was pouring the tea. "Did you all go down?"

"It's dark, we need a torch," said Ivan.

"Tell us about him?" I asked her.

"Who, the Colonel?"

"Yes."

"What do you want to know?" Aunty Sarah told us a story she had heard once from the old Raja of Kasgunj. Somewhere there was a network of tunnels, which led to different areas in Kasgunj. These had been constructed underground and were used by the Colonel to keep his movements secret. In the old days, the Mughals especially liked to have secret passages and escape routes. It was common to find underground tunnels, which ran over miles of countryside normally coming out near a waterway as an escape route. The couriers used these secret passages to carry messages to their masters. I suppose the Colonel got influenced living among the Mughals. He was a military adventurer and in later years would hire himself out to various Rajas and help them defeat princes of other regions. One time to get news to Manota was imperative and it seems he would meet with members of his family secretly by using the tunnel, which led there. There was a surprise attack planned and he had to get word to the Raja he had hired himself out to, but he was being watched. Well, he did get word by making his way out through some tunnel. According to the old Raja of Kasgunj, one of the networks lead right to his palace, but he himself was never able to discover exactly where."So where are the tunnels?" asked Ivan, his eyes huge in his lean face. "As a kid, I searched for the openings all over," said Aunty Sarah, "but was never able to discover anything. It might have got blocked up when the palace started crumbling but my guess is it's located somewhere here. Easy for him to slip away from the *zenana*, while his wife covered for him. Coming from the house of Cambay she must have been used to intrigue." Cambay was on the coast of Gujarat. "If a tunnel led to Manota then we might be able to locate it from that end," said Neville excitedly, "we'll search when we return."

"Well time to head back," said Gran, "I think you have had enough excitement for one day. Besides we should return before dark or everyone will worry."

Five

When we returned to Manota, we were bustled off to the well to have our bath. Having a bath near the well was plenty of fun. Sometimes the village women would join us and draw water, other times. Dad would draw the water for us. We bathed with T-shirts and shorts on and more of the water got thrown at each other in games of splash than in cleaning ourselves and the village women would look and giggle at us. We three sisters were close in age and our games were lively. The well was a little distance from the house and next to it were the guava gardens. We would take turns holding the huge towel for each other while we dressed, this too amongst much giggling. Afterwards one or other of the village women would pull branches of the beyr tree down and we would pluck the fruit and fill the pockets in our T-shirts full to carry them back to the house. While we were plucking the fruit, Bhola, the water carrier came to fill his buckets. As usual we couldn't resist asking him to demonstrate his special trick. As a baby he had been lifted by the throat by a wolf and as it was making off with him, his mother heard his cries and came rushing towards the wolf banging on a utensil and screaming herself hoarse, the wolf dropped him in fright but he was left with a hole in his neck and with the aid of the muscles there he was able to expel the water he had drunk in a thin stream from the opening. All children were fascinated by this trick of his and several times a day he was eager to demonstrate his skill.

The way the women balanced the jars of water on their heads and their hips gracefully trudged their way home induced us to try the same thing but although it looked easy, it wasn't and we collapsed in a heap of giggles again and relinquished their vessels.

Some of the younger girls shyly asked us to visit their homes and we agreed on one condition that they feed us *makai* and *bajra rotis*, which were made from maize and buckwheat and they laughingly agreed.

When we returned to the house, everyone was in an uproar. Neville and Bobby were missing. Mum normally never supervised Neville's bath, so he had been left to his own devices. Cousin Bobby, Uncle Sunny's grandson from his daughter, Florence, was a fast friend of Neville's. He had been given an air rifle for Christmas and the two of them would often disappear to look for game. We were a little envious that they had so much freedom and were taken on the '*shikar*' but the men thought we were too little yet and would not be able to manage the long treks. In later years we were allowed to try our hand at duck shooting and it was fun to shoot at the mullet in the river and have Ceasar, our bull terrier, dash into the water to retrieve the game. Partridges were the most difficult of all birds as they only flew upwards from the bush for just a moment and it required some skill with a rifle to pot them immediately. Some areas along the river were inundated with quicksand, so we were constantly being warned about them, the snakes, the wolves and other wild animals. It was only natural that the whole family should be bothered that Neville and Bobby were missing.

"But why would they go hunting in the dark," I asked Mum, who looked like she was about to cry, "Neville's not so stupid, they must be somewhere around". "They didn't go hunting," she said looking anxious, "they went to the guava garden nearby and were doing target practice. One of the village boys wanted to see what they were doing and he got in-between the target and the rifle. Bobby told him to move but he was stubborn and I don't know how Bobby could do such a thing, but he shot the fellow in the mouth."

"Did he die?"

"No, but his mouth was all bleeding, It made a hole in his lip."

"How horrible!" I exclaimed.

"Auntie Flo gave Bobby's clothes off to the boy in a fit of temper and Grandpa said he was going to beat them."

"Is the boy going to the hospital?" Roxanna was very soft hearted and looked concerned.

"Grandma dressed the wound, he'll be alright, and he was very thrilled with the clothes. Where could these boys have gotten to?"

"Don't worry Mum, they must be somewhere around," I said. We were looking at each other and when nobody took notice of us, we sneaked off to do our own investigating.

They were hiding on the stable roof and they begged us not to tell on them. That night Gran must have thought the outing had invigorated our appetites, we pretended to be consuming more than our normal share of dinner. In actual fact we hid a few *rotis* and *subzi*, which we quietly passed to Neville and Bobby who had to deal with hunger pangs along with their fear of being found out.

"Couldn't you get some more?" Neville complained.

"Sure we could but we didn't think you would want more, after all remorse takes away hunger," I replied.

"Go get some more, I'm still hungry."

"Gran's put it away."

"So steal some," Neville said.

"Oh no," I retorted piously, "God is watching. Why don't you just give up and take your punishment like men."

"We're not men yet, this isn't how you're supposed to help us. If we die out here then you'll be sorry."

"I'll miss Bobby" I grinned waving an airy goodbye.

When the grown-ups anger had been genuinely replaced by concern, they quietly crept off the roof and came in to sleep.

The next day Roxanna and myself had a visual lesson,

which made us remember it in graphic detail for quite sometime afterwards. We climbed the neighbour's wall, which was coated with mud. Her name was Daisy and she was a Gardner too as were all the neighbours. She had an inordinate amount of children who were a range of colouring from absolute fair to varying darker hues. We had seen the family on their way to some unknown destination so we thought we would undertake some neighbourly explorations. A thatch was attached to their boundary wall neighbouring our house. Old and brown, the thatch had rotted in various places and from our perch on the wall we could see through. Something strange was happening inside. A round whitish globe was rising and falling in a mystifying dance. On further inspection two legs were discovered attached to the round appendage and beneath a pair of dark brown legs were spread-eagled. The legs were thrashing and writhing while the white buttocks bounced in unseemly ignominy. The toe rings and *payals*, which glinted on the second pair of upturned feet, could only belong to a village woman, as they were fond of such ornaments. Faint grunts and moans were audible and we were hardpressed to stem our giggles. Although we couldn't see the upper part of the body, it was enough to watch the antics of the lower half, which gave us an uninspiring view of the ridiculous. Seems not only the animals were on heat, I wondered if Daisy knew what went on in her home while she was away.

"What are you doing, there? Get down at once," scolded Grandma who had caught us astride the high wall and hastily we clambered down amidst a flurry of giggles and dust.

We laughed till the tears rolled down our cheeks but refused to disclose the source of our mirth. We had been privy to the copulation of animals on several occasions but it surprised us that humans became such caricatures in an action, which was considered natural but looked so absurd. We made a pact then and there we wouldn't be caught dead in the process of reproduction if it involved participating in something so ludicrous.

The next afternoon I wandered too close to the river and caught sight of Mira being done by the village *baniya*. Hiding myself in the grass I waited till the dumpy man left her. She waded into the river, her buttocks spread obscenely as she squatted to wash herself before adjusting her sari. Twice in the week Mira would promptly appear at two in the afternoon to massage us. While she slathered us with oil she gave us all the gossip from the village. We knew Mira suffered having been married to Ramu Pyarelall, the village idiot. Mira had been betrothed to him at the age of three and at the age of ten married to him. By then he was already showing signs of retardation but her parents had seven daughters and were eager to lessen their burden by marrying them off early and sending them to their in-laws. Ramu had adored Mira. She had told us how at first they had played together until she had turned thirteen. Then her mother-in-law died. She was required to help plant the fields they owned, as Ramu could do very little work and when he did, his father would beat him. He hated Ramu, she had told us. All his frustrations he took out on him. He taunted him mercilessly calling him 'good for nothing'. Ramu being his only child was a disappointment to him. One day, Swami, her father-in-law caught her working in the fields alone. He raped her, pushing her face into the soil, which she told us, smelt of damp rotting earth. "Ever afterwards, I associated that smell with him," she had told us. "Rotting earth and sour vomit. He made me sick!" When she had gone home dishevelled and crying she had screamed at Ramu, "if I had a proper husband he would avenge me but instead I have an idiot who can do nothing, nothing! Your father is a pig, a miserable cur. I will boil him in oil, I will roast him over hot coals till his skin swells from the melting lard and bursts from the heat and his flesh exposed to the coals becomes a deep golden brown and he begs for mercy. But I will have no mercy, I will feed him to the vultures and crows piece by piece, I will gouge his eyes.." We shivered at the hatred in her voice; she had a deep-rooted hatred for her father in law even though he had died. She told us how she had collapsed by the cot in a heap of anguish crying in despair not noticing Ramu leaving, the sickle clenched in his big fist. When she woke from the deep sleep she had fallen into she found Ramu seated beside her on the floor, a glazed look in his eyes, his mouth hanging slackly as spittle drooled from the corners. Horrified she stared at him in bewildered puzzlement. His vest was splashed with blood, as was the sickle, which lay beside him. Pulling herself together Mira had washed off the sickle and burned Ramu's clothes in the kitchen *chula*. Leaving him sleeping on the cot she had gone to the river to bathe where Laxmi, her sister, and a few other women were washing clothes. They had told her Swami had been found in one of their fields gruesomely murdered. The *panchayat* had called a meeting to discuss the tragedy and the police had been informed. Part of his face had been eaten away by pigs, Laxmi informed Mira. Trying not to show her jubilation Mira had returned home to prepare the evening meal. A few days later they were plunged into desperation again as Swami's brothers had claimed the fields and she and Ramu had not been able to stop them. Having no source of income, she took odd jobs to feed them but they were few and hard to come by. Neetu, her daughter had been a result of her rape and their lives became even more difficult. The rationshop owner, Motilal Hariali gave her credit, then demanded she pay him immediately. She told him she had no money and he had suggested she pay him with another commodity, sex. Having no option Mira gave him what he wanted and in return he gave her a steady supply of rations, which allowed them to eat decently. There were others she paid in the same manner, deeming it a matter of necessity, but the *buniya* remained her favourite. He had a termagant for a wife who harangued him daily for being a lazy, fat slob though he wasn't nearly as mountainous as her. Normally she wove her enormous body around their compound berating the clerk who wrote the books, his glasses perched on his sharp nose as he tried to drown the sound of her voice with loud calculations and additions and subtractions which he wrote in the ledgers perched atop a high wooden stool beside a rickety old table, worm infested, which looked in danger of collapsing any moment. Mira thought Motilal's wife had a secret desire for the clerk and so found every opportunity to yell at him just to make her presence known. We laughed at the pictures she conjured with her words. Kishan, her son was born a year later and she didn't know who the father was nor did she care. She kept telling us how lucky we were to be educated and at our age she had perforce to become a woman. Motilal despite what he did to her was a kind man who showered her with gifts; she felt he had fatherly feeling towards her. I could only shake my head at her simplicity. In some ways she herself was still childlike, in others she was as old as the mountains.

"Mira!" I called to her as she waded out of the water.

"You should not be here," she scolded, "you have wandered far."

"I saw you," I told her laughing and she looked at me sharply, unembarrassed at having been caught.

"Come let's sit under that old tree, there is some shade."

"Tell me how Kishan died?" I asked her sitting crossed legged, and her face immediately took on a sad expression. She had promised to tell us the story but never got round to it. I supposed it still bothered her.

"I loved that child, he laughed such a lot and Neetu really adored him. She hasn't gotten over losing both him and Ramu." She looked into the distance her eyes taking on a faraway look as she remembered.

Dusk saw the three of them, Mira and her two children hurriedly carrying home bundles of sticks balanced easily on their heads. Seven year old Neetu was a bubbly child who laughed a lot, a miniature replica of her mother who loved her three year old brother, Kishan, teasing him to make him chuckle. He looked nothing like his mother with his broad nose, thick lips and dark skin. Neetu danced ahead chatting and singing. Kishan's shorter legs tried their best to keep up but unable to catch her up, he lagged behind pulling a long stick behind him to create a pattern in the sand. They were unaware of the lone creature stalking them just on the other side of the grass, salivating as it watched the children. Calling to the children to wait a while, she stepped behind a clump of bushes to urinate. She could hear Neetu teasing Kishan as he complained his legs were tired. Mira had smiled to herself as she heard them. Sighing, she stood up adjusting her saree. "Come let's carry on, it's getting late." She had told them. Lifting the bundle of wood she placed it on her head.

Snarling and snapping its powerful jaws in a wicked grimace the creature had sprung out of the brush, hurling itself at the boy, knocking him to the ground, its fangs had sunk deep into the throat of the child. Blood had gushed in a steady stream, the screams and cries of Neetu and Mira piercing in the quiet. Growling deep in its throat it had turned to face the woman, the child-hanging limp from its jaws. For a moment in time, red baleful eyes had glared into horrified brown ones, then the paralysis of fear leaving her she had rushed at the creature screaming with all her might, but in a flash it had gone, taking the child with it. In bewildered agony she had run to and fro, beating the grass with her hands, parting the bushes, frantically searching. Neetu had sat in the sand stunned by what she had just witnessed. Then giving a howl, like a wounded animal she had cowered, tears rolling down her face. Fear had gripped her like a cold, wet blanket, which had pressed bands of steel round her chest. She had felt a searing pain as she fought for breath. She hadn't understood what she had just seen, terror contorting her features she had curled into a tight ball, whimpering into the soil. She had been afraid to look. Her mother had disappeared into the bushes, lost and alone she had cried, waiting her turn to be taken by the creature. "After that experience," said Mira, "she's become a nervous child, afraid of the dark, of being left alone, she still has nightmares." She continued with her story telling me how she had been unable to scream, her voice had become hoarse with anguish, her arms and hands had been torn and bleeding from the rough grass. Tripping over a stone, she had sprawled her length on the ground unmindful of the sting of the sand on her face or the stones grazing her cheek. Born of the desolation she had felt, a high pitched keening sound had erupted from her throat which would have sent chills down the spines of those who heard her but nobody had. She wailed for her lost child, for her own lost childhood, for the horror she had lived. She had wailed because she felt guilty. Horror, fear and despair had warred in her bosom. Devi Ma had cast her from her long ago; her child had been sacrificed for her sins. Humans are so conditioned that when thrown into despair due to sudden loss they inevitably attribute it to divine retribution and a rejection of the force they believe in. Blame has to be apportioned to someone, why not the self, especially so when the deeds we commit are sinful? But does not circumstance circumvent sin? Is it not that due to circumstances and in order to survive certain actions are undertaken. Guilt results due to the ingrained teaching and conditioning of society and archaic laws which we inherit. Guilt possessed

Mira, she had felt abandoned, rejected by the deity she worshipped. She blamed herself.

Returning from the fields, Ganshyam Behari had almost tripped over Neetu still curled on the sand, sound asleep. Lifting her into his arms he had woken her and questioned her. Whimpering with relief, she had told him about the demon that had attacked them and taken her brother. She didn't know where her mother had gone; she had run off chasing the creature. Carrying the child he had hurried to the village, to Nandaram Rawat's house.

Nandaram was the village headman. Nandaram's house was better than the other villagers huts only because it was made of bricks and had two rooms and a substantial compound where his wife grew vegetables. His compound was fenced by bramble thickets to keep intruders out though it was rare to have any thieves. He had only one son and three daughters. His wife a thin, tall woman ventured out only to go to the temple. She had taken Neetu into the house and given her a glass of warm milk as they listened to her story. Later the men had taken Neetu to Mira's house and had tried to explain to Ramu what had happened. Leaving her with him they had departed, assuring him a search would be undertaken but only in the morning. There had been no one to reproach them.

Ramu had taken no notice of them leaving but had gently washed his daughter's face. He had waited until she was asleep then had fashioned a torch from some old rags and a thick piece of wood and he had gone out into the night.

When Mira had woken she had found herself back at her hut, her daughter curled beside her deeply asleep. For a moment she had been blank not remembering, then it had all come flooding back. Early morning, the remains of her child had been found by the river by some of the village women. Ramu had gone in search of the wolf and was never seen or heard of again. Her sin, she explained to me, had taken both her child and her husband. Relating the story had brought all her suppressed grief to the fore, she looked wilted, crushed and defeated. I felt sorry I had reminded her of the tragedy.

"Why do you still do it then?" I asked her, "if you think it is a sin?"

"It is only with Motilal," she replied, "he provides my rations. I still have Neetu to care for besides which it is only him, there are no others now, and this is not a subject we should be discussing. Come I will walk a little distance with you, they may miss you at the house." We both stood up.

"Mira, have you heard didi...that fat Lalita has taken revenge on Kishore." It was Laxmi, Mira's sister who accosted us on the path as we walked. Stopping in surprise, we waited for her.

"Are you unwell?" she was looking at Mira's face, which still retained ravages of tears as she had cried. Mira shook her head.

"What has happened?"

"Lalita caught Kishore cheating on her, she first got him drunk with that disgusting hooch they sell, then she tied him to the cot." She giggled in amusement, her eyes dancing.

"Who was the other woman?" Mira asked.

"That hussy Rupa, her own sister."

"Rupa? Are you sure?"

"Yes but listen, after she tied him to the bed she poured honey over his private parts and she left him and went in search of Rupa to beat her. As you know, ants find anything sweet.." she laughed merrily and Mira joined in the mirth while I grimaced.

"Did she find Rupa?"

"No she has run away with Raju."

"But he is so old!"

"I know but he works in Bareilly, she will use him then leave him when she has taken as much as she can from him. I better go, it is almost time to draw water. Are you coming?"

"Perhaps a little later, it's still hot."

Laxmi left hurrying to her chores while Mira escorted me home but only after I had made her promise not to disclose where she had found me. We each had a secret we didn't want anyone to know and I knew Mum would have a fit if she knew where I had gone on my own, and Mira's gruesome tale would have had her banning our association with her as well. Another masseuse would have been found and that I didn't want. She talked a lot but her tales were interesting. Village girls grew up early taking on responsibilities of husbands and children at an early age. To her we were adults giving her license to gossip freely. Sitting on the cold floor, the huge bamboo mat with cloth frills suspended from the ceiling with ropes, which worked as a fan, tied to her toe as she rocked it 'to and fro' fanning us. Most often she massaged us with some specially blended oil Gran had mixed. Often we fell asleep with her husky voice droning on and on.

The next day Ivan came to visit, to say good-bye as he was returning to school. I felt sad at his going. We wandered off to the cemetery together. Seating myself under the big guava tree I contemplated for a moment. He stood to the side, gazing off into the distance, his hands deeps in his pockets. He seemed lost in his own thoughts. I felt distracted.

"Ivan will you please kiss me, I want to know what it feels like", I startled myself as much as him with my brazenness but then I had never been shy and if I couldn't ask Ivan I wouldn't be able to ask anyone else, he was the closest I had gotten to boys romantically.

"You've never been kissed before?" he grinned amusedly.

"No. Will you?"

"Come here." I obediently went to him, "close your eyes", he said softly and I obliged. His lips touched mine first lightly then lingered longer, exploringly. Butterflies fluttered in my stomach.

"Do it again," I implored, "that was so pleasant."

"I liked it too," he said gently, and I opened my eyes to smile at him, looking into his eyes I saw a flicker of something, which had the butterflies somersaulting. "Don't close your lips, I'll teach you how to do it properly." He seemed to be enjoying his role of tutor.

This time his lips seemed to melt into mine, his tongue probing gently, the inside of my lips, my gums, and my tongue. His mouth tasted sweet and soft and the kiss seemed to go on and on. Suddenly Ivan pulled away jumping up.

"What happened?" I looked at him with glazed eyes, my face flushed. Ivan seemed to be having difficulty breathing. He laughed embarrassed.

"You're a natural at this, it was getting out of control," he looked uncomfortable.

"Wow you're hot!" he was teasing, but I suddenly felt silly, stupid, and cheap and embarrassed myself further by doing something even worse. I burst into tears!

His arms went around me holding me close, he was laughing, 'silly thing, I didn't mean to upset you, I was just teasing."

"I'm sorry," I gulped, "I behaved so badly, you must think I'm so cheap..." the tears fell faster. The harder I sobbed, the more Ivan laughed.

"Idiot!" he yelled, "you're not cheap, will you stop that damn howling. Your mother's going to have to lock you up, infact a co-ed is the wrong place for you, you're going to create a havoc there.."

All of a sudden I was blazingly angry, "you shouldn't have done it," I shouted at him, forgetting I had initiated it.

"You asked stupid."

"So what, you do everything I ask or what?" I felt more comfortable screaming at him, sniffing inelegantly into the sleeve of my blouse.

"Did I excite you Ivan?" He looked daggers at me and I felt all sunshiny again, obviously I had had some effect on him. Now why should that have been so important? I shook my head in bewilderment. He turned his back to me, not saying a word.

"Will you write?" he turned back to glance at me, I nodded my head and he grinned looking relieved. "Come on, I have to go. Can you do one thing for me?"

"What?"

"Stay away from boys."

"I'll try," I told him demurely, linking my arm with his I walked a little distance with him, waving until he disappeared into the guava gardens.

Winter vacation came to an end with the onslaught of March winds and the warming of the weather. Fallen leaves rose with each gust dislodging the tiny mites nestling under and scattered randomly along with sand that stung the eyes and filled the nose.

The family broke into groups and left by different trains for various destinations around India.

Dad's younger brother Jefferson and his wife Ruth had left with their two children for Dehradun to visit Ruth's parents before returning to Darjeeling. Ida, Noreen and her three children left for Allahabad and Nelson and his family for Lucknow. Florence, Uncle Mac with Glenda and Bobby, Uncle Sunny's grandchildren went to Nainital.

Left behind were Grandpa, Grandma, Uncle Wilfred, Uncle Sunny, his son Donny who had been in some war where he had been shell shocked. He roamed the farm in a world of his own muttering to himself and Zeena, nicknamed Buddi, why we never knew, or maybe because she looked old with wrinkled skin and gray hair even though she wasn't really old.

Six

"Buddi is unique, she has to be, being born in an asylum," said Neville as we sat on the lower berths of the compartment in the train carrying us to Darjeeling.

"Yeah that's why her eyes are like that?" I told him.

"So why didn't Mum do the same thing?" asked Ann who had been listening intently

"What?" I asked her.

"Give birth to us in an asylum, I wouldn't have minded coloured eyes too."

"Yeah and no brain," I said.

"Ofcourse she has a brain, everyone has a brain," she replied.

"But there's nothing in it" I told her, "like yours".

"No different from yours" said Anne.

"At least I wasn't picked from the gutter. Mum thought you looked cute sitting in the garbage bin." She looked at me outraged.

"I wasn't in a garbage bin."

"Then where do you think you came from?"

"From Mum."

"What you think Mum is a buffalo or something?" I screamed while Neville and Roxanna laughed. "You've seen Bess giving birth, you think Mum can do that?"

"No.." she looked hesitant, "so how were you born then?"

"A stork brought me from heaven."

"But I heard you say you were born in Poona."

"That's what heaven was called in those days."

"That's where I was born too."

'Yeah! But like I said, the stork didn't bring you, you were sitting there in the garbage bin, crying your eyes out, Mum took pity on you, she liked your curls so she picked you up all smelly..."

"Enough!" Mum had removed her attention from the Femina she had been scanning for recipes. "Don't fill her head with rubbish, I'm surprised at you."

"Oh leave her alone, they were only having fun," said Dad who had been much amused at the exchange.

Uncle Sunny had related the story, one evening, of Buddi's birth and how she had come to be retarded though no one in the family used that word, 'odd' was what they said.

Gurly his wife had been disillusioned with village life. Not only that, like most women who marry, her life was centered around husband, kids and home. She needed a break, and what better place to visit than Madras where Madge Smith, her old school friend lived. Madge kept inviting her and besides she needed someone to confide in, to have fun with like they had done in school.

"She would smile whenever she remembered the pranks they had played," he had told us. "Yes definitely Madras she had decided cunningly."

All she had to do was to convince him that he would be better off without her for a while and that was not so difficult. He was already tired of her constant complaints, all she had to do was step up the frequency.

"Stewart I'm fed up of the flies," she would say, "the sand is just about in everything. I've had three baths already."

"So don't bathe," he would tell her.

"It's so hot, why don't you put in air conditioning?" she told him one time.

"We don't have electricity," he had replied.

"Then get it, I'm sick of this life. Get electricity."

"It's not possible right now," he had replied calmly. Uncle Sunny was a master storyteller and could hold us entranced with his mimicry.

"Nothing is ever possible...what I'd give for a bed without sand in it, no dust in the house, air-conditioning, shopping in proper shops and I'm just dying for some sea food, sea air, swimming in the sea. What do we have out here, a river with foul smelling embankments, no lights, and no proper toilets? When you married me you never said we would have to live in this God forsaken place..." his voice had been rising in octaves until it screeched shrilly in imitation of his deceased wife.

"Why don't you take a break and go somewhere for a vacation?" he had told her.

"What a wonderful idea, will you come with me?" she had asked him knowing what his reply would be.

"I was sorely tempted to say yes, just to frighten her but being a gentleman I allowed her victory."

"No. Think of somewhere to go and I'll see to the tickets."

"Well Madge has been writing, I haven't seen her in months," she had told him

"Okay go to Madras." He had sounded relieved, which he had been. He would finally have some peace. She had begun curtailing his *shikar* on purpose, getting up to intercept him in the mornings and beginning her tantrums. He had needed a break, he had been waiting for her to go somewhere for a change. He had looked forward to some peace and lots of *shikar*. His eyes had shone in anticipation.

"So we both got our wish you see," he had told us.

Madras, she had found, was hot, humid and deliciously civilized. Madge in good humour had squired her on endless rounds of shopping and restaurant bingeing. Then they had met him, the person who had taken charge of her life and shaped her future destiny. He had been called Baba Santoshi. A thin ascetic man who didn't believe in eating and who had worn nothing but a loincloth, clothes had been so superfluous, like food. Life and death had been overcome. He had been able to control hunger, thirst, and his bodily functions. Sex had been a tool that he used as an aid to rejuvenation, lengthening his life while he shortened the lives of those foolish enough to fornicate with him.

He had created illusions. They had seen what he had wanted them to see. He had hypnotized the skeptics. His devotees he had dredged from those who had searched for an escape from their dreary lives, from loneliness and boredom. He had supplied all their needs. He had introduced them to pleasure, happiness, and stimulation. All who had gone to him had been given a new lease of life. Gurly had been no exception. Her unhappiness had been replaced, her frustration had been removed and she had returned with the firm conviction and the means to control her errant husband.

She had mixed the potion in his cup of tea.

"Stewart, come here, I've made tea." She had told him that fateful day.

"Just leave it on the table," he had told her, absorbed in cleaning of his gun.

"It'll get cold."

"I'm just coming," he had replied and gone to drink his tea after placing the gun carefully on the bed.

"Gurly?" Grandpa had called her and she had gone from the room to see what he wanted while Uncle Sunny had come into the room and picked up one of the cups of tea and sat down sipping it. The wrong cup.

"Leo wants to know if you need anything from Kasgunj." Gurly had returned and seated herself next to him.

"Nothing that I can remember," he had replied. "Now tell me did you enjoy Madras?"

"Oh! I had a wonderful time." She had picked up the tea and had drunk a little while she had told him about Baba Santoshi and the shopping with Madge. By the time the cup had been empty she hadn't been feeling too good.

Temper tantrums had become almost routine but when the frequency and duration had increased drastically and the porcelain and ceramics had diminished in keeping with the outbursts, it had behoven Uncle Sunny to take action, which he had by locking her in the dining room until each bout had been spent. He had never liked the dinner set, nor the tea sets she had been so fond of collecting, if she had chosen to demolish her precious collection who was he to stop her. Probably the hormonal imbalances that normally occur during pregnancy he had thought.

That had been putting it mildly. In lucid moments, Gurly had known she had drunk the tea meant for him. She had never remembered her bouts of violence and she had slyly continued to take the white powder Baba Santoshi had introduced her to. She had liked the sensation to that of flying, sometimes she had flown high, and she had escaped the leaden earth-bound body soaring away on the wind. She had touched the sky, played with stars and sat in the moon looking benignly down at the world. She had been free, free. He had made us laugh with his flights of imagination.

"It's no use pretending, Stewart," Grandpa had told him, "we're worried. Gurly needs professional help. I think you should consider a trip to Bareilly...." And so Gurly had been sedated by the Doctor at Kasgunj and transported to Bareilly.

The asylum had not been what she had expected, actually who could have expected to have been off loaded for bad behaviour to a roomful of unusually sighted people who saw things with a vision not given to normal humans. Normal meant ordinary, natural. Abnormal was extraordinary and that's what she had felt she was. The tantric had been right, a little of the powder and she had been able to fly, she had felt she could do anything. He told us how she had lamented at him, "Why had she sought to include him in the extraordinary powers of perception which she had attained? He was too stodgy, too normal. He was rooted to the earth. He would never be able to fly. She understood the people here, they like her had visions, they saw the other worlds, they were special and if the normal humans didn't understand who could blame them." She would laugh out loud at her insights, he had told us. Some months later Buddi had been born. She had been so excited at the child while he had been nonplussed. She had felt her baby too was extraordinary, one eye blue, one green had confirmed her belief.

One day she imagined she was flying and when they had come to give her lunch she had darted through the open door and jumped off the *verandah*, falling the three stories to the ground. She had broken her neck and had died instantly.

"Wake up! Come on down, time for dinner." Mum woke me from the deep sleep I had fallen into. Yawning heavily I clambered down. Some of the passengers had called it a night and were sound asleep.

One day led into another monotonous day. Dazed flies buzzed lazily waiting to get fed while rolled newspapers waited expectantly for a chance to swat at them. Train journeys were to be suffered not enjoyed. The flies, heat, dust and the unwashed odours from other passengers were borne with long suffering patience. Our favourite past time was staring out the grimy windows at the landscape, which for the most part was very similar, fields of the current crop which at this time seemed to be mustard or wheat, or barren landscapes of mud and scree. Sometimes there were areas of thinly populated trees of an unknown variety and the outskirts of squalid towns and cities and most often the common sight of men, women and children blatantly squatting anywhere and everywhere to relieve themselves. The person who had called India, "one large toilet," had really got that right.

A grunt from the berth opposite disturbed my thoughts and I glanced in irritation at the *dhoti-clad* passenger who spent most of his time snoring. The train was a perfect place to do a thesis. There were the whistling breezy ones, the grunting, snorting ones, the groaning, muttering variety, indeed if one traversed the length of the train the varying snores would have provided enough material to write a paper on. We perforce refrained from rude comments, as Mum expected us to behave circumspectly at all times but a disturbed sleep wasn't the harbinger of a good mood. I found myself dozing off to sleep now. It was soothing to just close my eyes and be deaf to everything. A somnambulist lost in sleepy imaginings, dreaming dreams of a future which were never ordinary but full of the spice which had accumulated from too many readings of adventures and romances and dashing heroes and beautiful heroines who didn't have blonde hair and blue eyes but auburn hair and hazel eyes. And the train was not a train but a luxury liner sailing across some imaginary sea, or the flower filled bower of an exotic garden until sleep overcame afternoon revels and all was lost in deep slumber.

Seven

Darjeeling or 'Dorjee-ling', meaning place of the thunderbolt with panoramic vistas of snow-clad mountains, majestically towering over the valley of pine and rhododendrons, creamy magnolias and silver firs. Clean mountain air lending an unsullied clarity to the wide-open spaces, green hills and thick forests. Undulating hillsides planted with tea, the main trade, with tourism and timber coming a close second. Swirling mists, thick fog, drizzling rain and violent storms, which crashed through the sky on occasions, adding to the excitement of a vibrant land.

Our school was a Methodist Mission with old stone buildings aesthetically nestled in a valley below North Point, peopled by staff and students of various communities and countries, living together in harmonious cohabitation.

Changes had taken place by the time we returned, some of the Anglo-Indian staff had emigrated off to England and Australia. A whole lot of Anglo-Indians had been going over the years in a steady trickle. Dad's own brother, Nelson, had made it to Australia with his family and settled there. Anglo-Indians felt they fitted in more abroad, in westernized countries, than they did in India. They felt their children stood a better chance at a decent life. This was a fall out in their mindset, stemming from their days in the British Raj where they had felt discriminated against when the British rule in India ended. But there were still a lot of our community all over India and it was common to find Anglo-Indians socializing with members of their own community. We too had our own traditions and culture, a mixture of the East and West, which we resolutely adhered to.

This year my teacher was an Anglo-Indian. Tall with black-rimmed glasses he looked down on his pupils sternly and commented on the dire consequences of disobedience and disrespect.

"Looks like Dennis's father," Karen whispered over her shoulder and I looked at

Mr. Morris again. He did resemble Dennis the Menace's father even down to the sharp nose and the way he stood. But later in the day the comradely feeling I had for him vanished as he induced unwarranted punishment and the fact that he was an Anglo-Indian too made me want to disown the community. From time to time he placed students in the corner near the door with the upturned dustbin, an old painted kerosene tin, over their heads while he did target practice using the duster, a square bit of wood with felt on it. After this display of talent, our entire class emulated mice and who could blame us, ringing ears were definitely not to be recommended.

Mr. Morris's wife was the art teacher and she decided to test our knowledge of art by giving us a topic, which entailed us using our imaginations to draw a picture and paint it, giving her an idea of our capabilities. The same topic, "an elephant in a lumber camp" was given to each class. She smiled in amusement at the imaginative depictions of elephants. My modern painting of an elephant, which had three eyes and two trunks, caught her attention.

"An imitation of Picasso Mam, he gave all his images more than what they had been blessed with." I told her.

"Is that so? So you're a reproduction artist."

"Yes Mam, I can do Salvador Dali as well."

Chuckling at my cheek, she retreated to view another budding artist's portrayal, which looked as if it had been drawn while he had been perpendicular to the paper. Patting his head she refrained from comment but I wondered how he had managed to get it so lopsided. But seeing as the boy was admiring his work with fierce concentration I decided not to ask him.

When Mr. Morris had to go away for a seminar I volunteered myself as a companion to Mrs. Morris who didn't like staying alone at nights. Mum decided my elder sister; Roxanna would assist me in keeping Mrs. Morris company and as it turned out that was a wise decision.

The Morris's cottage was in a lonely area of the school estate. It was a residential school where most of the staff members lived on the premises in tiny cottages with pretty gardens. This house had a big garden in the front and a substantial yard at the back. The cottage was a little old with three bedrooms, a living cum diningroom, a kitchen and two toilets. There were two porches, one in front and one at the back, which faced a wooded area of the estate. On the left side of the cottage there was a sharp incline covered by brush, which opened out to a part of a nearby tea estate. The incline was too steep to be negotiable and the right side had a narrow pathway, which led to the backyard partially enclosed by a grassy slope. Anyone coming or going would be visible.

Mrs. Morris was pretty but not glamorous. Her black hair was cut in a neat blunt style, which ended in a wispy fringe on her forehead. She was slim and wore dresses, which covered her knees and high-heeled pumps. When we arrived to keep her company, she welcomed us with a nice smile and bustled about putting snacks on the dining table.

"I've taken out some nice books with short stories," she said, "I thought we might enjoy reading through some of them while we munch. Would you like tea? I'll be making a cup for myself."

"We don't drink tea or coffee, Ma' am," Roxanne replied.

"Some juice then," she said decidedly and disappeared into the kitchen. I looked around the room while Roxanne flipped through the pages of one of the books.

On a corner table was a brass ash-tray shaped like a shoe beside which a photograph of Mr. and Mrs. Morris at their wedding stood in stately splendour in a blue ceramic frame around which roses were intertwined. Her wedding dress clung to her bosom then flowed out from a narrow waist into a cylindrical skirt down to the ground. A wreath and veil trailed from her head and she clung to an enormous bouquet of flowers. Mr. Morris stood ramrod stiff in a white shirt, tie and a black suit. He had removed his spectacles for the occasion but it didn't detract from his 'Mr. Mitchell' look. A vase of cosmos decorated their centre table and two long gunmetal containers stood as sentinels on either side of the front door. A long wooden shelf held a wooden carved clock and two ceramic plates with the faces of Victorian ladies and beside them a mermaid in glass who reclined while she combed her hair. A single painting above the shelf intrigued me.

"What do you think of it?" Mrs. Morris's voice nearby startled me. She came to stand beside me.

"Did you paint it, Ma' am?"

"No, it was painted by a friend of mine. She presented it to me on our wedding day."

I couldn't tear my eyes away from the painting. It was of sea-water with floating fish and sea-weed cleverly blended to form an artistic canvas. Forming a background to the painting was a shadowy face. The face was not clear but the eyes burned and seemed to be watching in a predatory manner, which was quite horrible. One glance at the painting and I had been ready to exclaim on the pretty undersea scenery but the face jarred and I dragged myself away and sat at the dining table.

"Why did she put the face in?" I complained," the painting would have been so pretty without it."

"Face?" questioned Mrs. Morris looking at me peculiarly while Roxanna got up to take a look.

"There's no face in the painting. The fish look so pretty." I ran back to stand beside her and Mrs. Morris followed.

"What face are you talking about?" I looked at her confusedly, they were right; there was no face in the painting. Before I could say anything, there was a knock at the door and Mrs. Morris walked towards it.

"Who is it?" she called out but there was no answer, just another knock, and Mrs. Morris opened the door and stood looking out at an empty verandah. Suddenly she screamed and stepped back, slamming the door shut bolting it.

"What's it Ma' am?"

"What happened? What did you see?" But she didn't answer just stood trembling in front of the door staring at it and holding her cheek. There were tears in her eyes.

"Ma' am?" Roxanna shook her hand anxiously and she turned to face us.

"I was slapped!" Mrs. Morris exclaimed and we looked at her in astonishment.

"But there was nobody there." I replied just as a knock came at the door again. We all turned to face the door while the knocking continued.

"Whose there?" Mrs. Morris finally called in a sharp voice but nobody answered.

By now we were thoroughly frightened and we sat together on her sofa clinging to each other, it was then I told them of the horrible face I had seen in the painting, which had disappeared later. After a few minutes the knocking stopped and we breathed a sigh of relief.

"Let's do one thing," Mrs. Morris said in a whisper, "we'll sleep together in my room. We'll take the snacks and the books and we'll read in bed okay?" We nodded assent and helped her place the plates on a tray and the glasses we carried to the kitchen.

Mrs. Morris did most of the reading as the stories were by Somerset Maugham and it was soothing to listen to her voice until we fell asleep. In the morning calling a hurried bye to her we trotted together in a rush to reach home. Being late for assembly was sure to attract a scolding and be publicly embarrassed in front of the class so in the scramble to be ready, the incidents of the night were pushed to the back of our minds until the evening when Mum asked us how it had gone. We were grateful Mr. Morris had returned and we were not required to spend another night. Mum listened to us with a grim face, then made a sweeping statement, which wasn't very complimentary to Mrs. Morris and told us it was the last time she would allow us to keep staff members company. She didn't believe the face in the painting or Mrs. Morris's slap.

"Maybe she imagined it," Roxanna said while we were getting into bed and the knocking could have been someone who didn't hear her asking who it was.

"But the face I saw?"

"You might have imagined it."

"I didn't."

"You did."

"Didn't" culminating in a pillow fight, which ended with Mum's appearance in the room and us pretending to be asleep.

Mrs. Morris had several more run ins with the mysterious slapper and it became common knowledge that she was weird but I still remained her friend because I didn't think she was lying or imagining things. But I never visited her at home either. I thought something lived in her painting and I didn't want to make its acquaintance again. A few months later a new art teacher took Mrs. Morris' place, a British lady who had a squint and towered over us in colourful attire which looked like she had gone shopping on 'Freak Street' in Kathmandu. Somehow the loud colours which she mixed indiscriminately suited her personality and the colourful beads she wore in her hair, round her neck and in her ears, contrasted nicely with her apparel making it a rather outlandish fashion statement. We admired her jute heels, which added to her height but didn't get her any dates. For some reason the men didn't seem to want to be looked down upon no matter how well packaged the enticement was. With long blonde hair, which hung almost to her knees and baby blue eyes, she attracted a lot of attention. When she taught us new techniques with a paintbrush, we became her ardent fans and happily ran her errands for her. I did enquire from Mr. Morris, Mrs. Morris's whereabouts and he said she had gone to visit her Mother but Mum and Dad spoke in hushed tones of 'a nervous breakdown' and referred to her as 'poor woman,' in sympathetic tones when the topic came up in discussions among their friends.

Nothing disturbed the even tenor of our days, which were filled with learning, in the classroom, on the games field and in the swimming pool. The library opened doors to exciting worlds which I had never dreamed possible and I became a constant visitor to its hallowed portals, exchanging books and scanning its shelves every few days in an attempt to unearth all its treasures aided by our librarian, who seemed glad to have someone to chat to, and didn't mind whiling away a few hours talking about her home in some backwater of Kerala which she said, "had the sweetest coconuts and the whitest sand and where it rained like God had unleashed a dam and was determined to flood the earth until it drowned." We left for our winter vacation.

Eight

After celebrating my fourteenth birthday in Darjeeling, we went to Lucknow to celebrate Christmas, which was a slight deviation from our normal routine in the past years. There were no direct trains to Kasgunj and it necessitated a Lucknow detour from where we could then catch a train on the metre gauge. It was at Lucknow that I was introduced to the excitement of a first boy friend. Clear thinking had turned garbled, the cause, an imitation Elvis even down to the sidelocks, who rendered 'shakin' imitations of his vocal renditions while passionate surges tumbled through my emotions and music played in synchronized symphony. Could that really be me? Who would have thought the aspiring bouncer had developed a taste for femininity? The symptoms were so unbecoming, I felt different, softer, glazed. Definitely,

I have to do something about that silly smile; it seemed not to want to listen to me.

Sightseeing was undertaken in a hired *tanga* and we took a tour of the Residency and listened to the sad tale of the massacre of the British who had been trapped there. I could almost imagine the screams and cries of the women and children as the cannon balls pierced the walls and killed them. The imambaras provided a lighter note to the tour, as did the amazing labyrinth of the *bhulbhulaiya* where, from various vantage points, one could peer down into the main halls and where whispers from five metres away could be heard. The Mughals had steeped themselves in espionage and counter espionage and the waterway they had built, as an escape route was simply fascinating. That night I dreamed of harems and couriers who carried important messages along dark passages, who met emperors in secret and of mysterious women with kohl lining their eyes and clothed in diaphanous fabric enticing men, and silver jewelled daggers which glinted in the moonlight as silently as a life was taken. But they were all dreams, dredged from the subconscious and in the morning forgotten like will of the wisps, which floated away, like they had never been.

Christmas was a kaleidoscope of impressions with dances organized by the Anglo-Indian association and so many new faces. After the midnight mass began the festivities after which we were treated to a huge breakfast and sipped wine along with the traditional Christmas cake and melodious singing of Christmas carols. The *kulkuls* and other homemade sweets were sampled throughout the week. A picnic to Khukrel Park, which was a sanctuary for deers, brought an end to the week at Lucknow. After games, songs were sung to the accompaniment of a guitar, and we were treated to a feast of *biryani* and a combination of *kebabs* and *paranthas*, which rounded off the festivities.

At the Charbagh station, I fell out of favour with my sisters. Our three friends had come along to wish and send us off. I had not met the two whom they had met at the Christmas dance and the introductions were only made now. I think they were just being polite and we sat around chatting for a while. I didn't notice the sulky looks on both my sisters's faces, but once the train moved I was told very categorically that I had been making 'eyes at the guys' and they had been more interested in getting to know me than giving my sisters attention.

"What rubbish!" I refuted their statements, "I wasn't trying to steal your guys, what idiots you are…." But no amount of cajoling could pacify them. For the rest of that day I was treated like an outcast, which suited me just fine as I could bury myself in a book without interruptions. This was my first taste of romance and falling in love. It gave me much to think about. The feelings were delicate and required nurturing for them to blossom fully but sadly imitation Elvis didn't quite allow them to bloom. He didn't write and like the petals of a flower that wither and die when under-nourished; they died a natural death.

The rest of the journey held no surprises but we were much entertained by a singing troupe that climbed aboard at one of the smaller stations. The young girl sang a selection of village folk songs while the old man banged away on the *dholak*. A young boy joined in the song from time to time and the two women with them jingled *ghungroos*, which added to the music. The young girl was a beauty and could have been placed in any beauty pageant.

"*Peda*," said Neville, "want some?" he had spied the grimy vendor and oblivious to Mum's disapproving look was enlisting our support. *Peda*, a round milk sweet, decidedly delicious.

"Don't eat rubbish," Mum warned him, "you'll get sick, come on Rocky stop indulging the children."

Mum was a martinet for hygiene; she had already brought along enough food to keep us well fed for days and thought Dad spoiled us rotten as he was easy prey to our entreaties. The tiffin box which was wooden but had netting on two sides to allow air to pass, was normally the heaviest of all our luggage as Mum packed it to the brim with canned food, boiled eggs, bread, *paranthas*, cookies and plenty of other goodies. In later years I noticed Mum had a special trait. She was an excellent cook and when she was upset, the kitchen was her refuge, she would disappear into her special domain and cook up something delicious. Perhaps that's why Dad provoked her often and in a temper she would exit his presence with a few well-chosen, vituperative words and closet herself in the kitchen. Food was Mum's panacea for all ills and was proffered to relieve bouts of depression or anguish among other ailments, which afflicted us in varying degrees during courtship days or the ending of a marriage.

"You'll do nothing but eat, wait for a bit and I'll take out something, okay only peanuts don't buy the *pedas*." Mum brought me out of my reverie; the argument about *pedas* had been resumed.

"It looks clean," said Neville, he had a sweet tooth and could be relied upon to sample all the sweets that were paraded through the train. Earlier he had already had *revadies* which was a sweet made from seasum seeds and sugar and *gajjak* which also was made from seasum seeds but with jaggery a sweet substance boiling the sugar cane juice.

"Neville, it's definitely not clean, how do you know flies have not sat on it. It's open and besides they roll it with their hands, don't be greedy." He made a face conceding defeat and climbed back into the compartment.

"Are you Punjabi?" the man opposite had been staring in fascination at our family. He was tall and dark with salt and pepper hair and bags under his eyes and he didn't have a chest only a stomach, which made him rather uncomfortable and he had this horrible habit of burping. In some communities burping after a meal was considered polite to prove to the host or hostess that the meal had been enjoyed.

"No Anglo-Indians," Dad replied turning to face him.

"What's that?" he looked quite bewildered, "are you from India?" I was surprised he was ignorant about our community. We were spread all over the country, how could anyone not know of us. Most recognized schools teemed with Anglo-Indian teachers.

"Oh yes," said Dad, "ours is a community just like

Punjabis, Bengali and such. Our ancestors were British, Europeans and so on who married Indians."

"So was your mother or father a Britisher?"

"No, they too were Anglo-Indians, and your foreign ancestor had to be from the paternal side to be called an Anglo-Indian otherwise you're an Indo-European or something like that"

"I've never heard of your community," said the man.

"We're a minority group, like the Muslims and of course there aren't very many of us left in India."

"Are you a Christian?"

"Yes, I'm a Protestant, my wife and children are Catholic." The discussion continued for some time but I was only listening with half an ear. Dad told him how Anglo-Indians spoke English at home and felt comfortable in western clothes and mostly celebrated western festivals but then they also celebrated Indian festivals like Diwali and Holi and ate Indian food like rice and curry and were partial to *chutneys* and pickles. I had never come across an Anglo-Indian woman who was not skilled at cooking or who couldn't keep a good table. In general they kept good homes and were wonderful mothers, and instilling good manners and a high standard of morals were their hallmark. Since Dad had an excellent command of Hindi and having grown up in a Hindi speaking state like U.P he was able to express himself eloquently. I kept thinking about what Dad had said, "A man must have written the constitution," as the discrimination against women was so blatant in the statement, that an Anglo-Indian was defined as being one if the person was of European descent on the paternal side. Seems mothers didn't have equal rights and I remembered school forms, which had a section for father's name and signature but with none for mothers. This was rectified by some schools later on.

Early morning saw us at our destination and amidst a flurry of activity disembarked onto the platform of a surprisingly clean station. Not many stations could boast of being clean but Kasgunj, at that time, could proudly display well-scrubbed platforms where garbage didn't seem to exist.

"Chai Baba," said the tall attendant who always came to meet us on arrival. He was carrying a tray with steaming *khullars* of milky tea. We were all in various stages of our morning ablutions. Everybody referred to Dad and his brothers as 'Baba'; they had been called that as youngsters and were always referred to in the same manner no matter what their age, although 'Baba,' was a term used for young children in general.

The boat trip and subsequent bullock cart ride to the farm were interspersed with us scrambling on and off the cart to break the monotony, while Dad chatted with Uncle Wilfred who had come to meet us.

What a ruckus was created when we arrived. Caesar, the white terrier barked and ran around us in excitement. Old Ceasar had died but Gramps had kept one of his pups sired by a mongrel and he too was named Ceasar and just as well trained. Grandpa and Grandma hugged and kissed us, as did Sunny. Buddi only watched from a distance, it would take her a while to get used to us again. There were more aunts, uncles and cousins to greet.

"Just look at them, how big these girls have grown?" that from Aunty Flo. I should hope we had grown; height sometimes gave an advantage, as did a widened girth.

"Oh my goodness! You've put on weight, Addie," this to Mum who didn't look too pleased with the comment.

"So what mischief have you planned this time?" asked Gramps.

Everybody was talking at once. It was nice to be back to meet them all again. We were delegated to sorting the luggage and the excitement subsided as we left the compound.

The weather was unpredictable, but then who could blame it. Rain would threaten, then change its mind and the sun would dazzle with its bright yellow rays. Who could understand its inclemency?

"The world revolves around men," I complained, "and women are stupid, they revolve around men." I was offended that the Lucknow beau had not thought to correspond after all his professions of undying love, seemed like it had not only died but dropped stone cold dead.

"And animals," Neville exclaimed suddenly, "look at my goat, he became a she."

"That's because you didn't check, it got mixed up with someone else's and you brought home the wrong goat."

"Well they all looked alike…"

"Never mind, she's been giving you a lot of kids, you already have a whole family, your business has grown."

The next day Dad was missing early in the morning. He had gone off at dawn with Uncle Sunny for 'shikar' but they were back at mid-day loaded with pigeons. It was sad to see the dead birds stuffed in the bag but when Grandma and Edene, had prepared a curry from the birds we forgot our sadness and ate with relish.

Then it was our turn, Roxanna and I were initiated into our first '*shikar*'. We walked for miles along the bank of the river until we came to a spot where the fish could be clearly seen gliding through the water.

"Aim for the head," said Dad and then the recoil from the 0.22, which threw me backward despite my straddled legs. I missed, but my sister potted one and Neville a couple more. As the mullet floated belly up, one eye staring blankly, Ceasar dashed into the water to retrieve them one by one. Then we crawled along the bank a little more amidst marshy ground until we sighted the brahmani ducks. We had been warned not to talk, so in silence we waited as Dad went nearer and nearer until he could sight along his rifle and 'bang' they all flew up making a racket with feathers flying and for a moment we didn't know if any had been hit then when the muddle cleared and with us rushing in to investigate a lonely body swished limply on the muddy water. The ducks resettled further up the river and we splattered ourselves while getting closer and were allowed our turn too. The rest of the hunt was spent in shooting pigeons and with bags full, hair mussed with leaves and brush, our clothes filthy with slime but our faces shining despite the grime we prepared to return home. Dad was leading the way through the brush, which were mainly tall tufts of sword grass and which made a formidable screen on either side as we trudged in a single file. His rifle balanced easily in his right hand he forged a path ahead of us. Suddenly he stopped dead, frozen in his track. A King Cobra had been coiled a little way ahead, on becoming aware of us it had reared itself up to almost four feet high staring Dad straight in the eye. Without blinking, shooting from the hip he blew its head off. It had happened so quickly we hadn't had time to be afraid. Leaving the six-foot snake lying on the sand we continued tiredly home. Had it been earlier we might have been discussing the incident with much enthusiasm but weary and worn out we silently marched home lost in our thoughts. I shivered a little thinking how near Dad had come to death. Had it been a little later, the sun would have set and it would have been dark, he might not have even seen the snake but that didn't bear thinking about. At home it became an exciting tale to embellish the hunt with, while Gran amply rewarded us with chapatti, *ghee* and sugar with a liberal helping of thick buffalo cream.

Nine

There was something about the air at the farm that always made us ravenous. We were constantly eating. Fruit, especially guavas were always plentiful and we normally ran around the compound with one or other of the fruit in our hands. The buffalo milk was rich and delicious and Grandma insisted we have it at least three times in the day, mostly we required no urging to partake of anything.

Next day bright and early I crawled out of bed to find Gran. She was seated beside the kitchen chula preparing the tea.

"What shall we do today, Gran?" I enquired of her, I was hopeful she had planned a visit to Chhaoni. I wanted to know if Ivan was home too. The previous day's hunt would be something interesting to relate to him.

"You want to go to Chhaoni?" she paused in her task to look at me inquiringly.

"Oh let's go!" I said with excitement, "shall I get ready?"

"Ask Mummy first."

The day had dawned with a thin mist and the nip in the air was invigorating. Just the weather to take a trip. We could be in Chhaoni long before the mid-day sun began to scorch anything.

Ivan had written to me at school. We had kept up a steady flow of correspondence. He had regaled me with episodes of his antics during the year. I didn't approve of him climbing into the tuck shop and stealing some of its items or him having broken his classmate's nose for calling him a villager but he seemed to be a good student and I supposed Aunty Sarah had been pleased. He had mentioned Chris during his summer break. They had become firm friends and went on frequent hunts. He boasted of his prowess with the rifle and the amount of game they had bagged. I didn't quite believe all of it but I thought he probably did shoot tolerably well. Now I had something to excite his interest too, I hoped he had come for the Christmas vacation. We had no telephones in either of the houses so there was no way to check, I could only hope, and in any case, Aunty Sarah was fun to meet too, probably get some more stories out of her.

Ivan was not around when we arrived, only coming in later, loaded with pigeons, which Chris and he had shot. They divided the birds between them so Chris could deliver his booty to his mother. He was still shy and gave everyone a quick smile before departing.

"Who's that?" asked Gran.

"Ferrier's son," said Aunty Sarah, "the father's a good for nothing, he used to work as a guard on the railway long ago, got into some trouble with the authorities and got kicked out of his job. His mother is hard working, you know her; she's the one who makes your dresses?"

"Sharon!" exclaimed Grandma in surprise, "I've only seen a young boy, I didn't know she had a grown one too."

"Sends them to the village school, but Chris doesn't go, says they don't fit in and I can understand that. You know what the village schools are like".

"Then he's not educated ..."

"He is, I teach him and Gemima. In fact that's what I wanted to talk to you about. I'd like you to invite Gemima over sometime to meet Rocky's daughters. She doesn't have any friends, Chris is the only one she can mix with." I perked my ears at this.

"Whose Gemima Aunty, Sarah?"

"Martha's daughter.."

"Who's Martha?" asked Gran.

"Martha Grimes is supposedly the schoolmistress, but if she even gets in half a days work or teaches those children anything is absolutely surprising. Most of the time she's soaked in the local brew and it's a wonder that Gemima living with her hasn't picked up the habit."

"Doesn't she have a husband?"

"According to Gemima, she never did get married."

"But..." then glancing at me, Gran decided to drop the subject but I wasn't about to let it go that easily.

"Why didn't she marry?" I questioned Aunty Sarah but she refused to say another word busying herself with setting out the lunch and I was obliged to help her.

Eventually I got the story out of Aunty Sarah but that was years later and I had to badger her to impart the information. She only told me because I was trying to find a reason for Gem's behaviour, which had been troubling me, and she explained it as "being in her genes." This gene business plagued me often. We put on weight because it was in our genes. We had dark rings beneath our eyes because it was in our genes and we got cavities in our teeth because it was in our genes. Now Gem's irrascible behaviour was 'because it was in her genes'.

Gemima's mother, Martha got involved with a British Tea Planter and he spent days squiring her around Calcutta, attending all the dances with her at the various clubs, treating her to dinners and lunches at the restaurants and in general having a good time. They became engaged and he bought her a fancy diamond ring, then took her to visit the tea plantation in the Terrai region. It was all very gay and she was impressed with the lavish way they lived, the many servants, the opulence of the bungalows, the club meets for tennis, golf, dancing. The life style was so different to hers in Calcutta where she lived in two rooms and did her own housework, but watching the way the other ladies conducted themselves, she felt she would be able to fit in.

Two months after they had met he told her it was time for him to make a visit to England and with much professions of his love, he left her back in her rented premises and took himself off to England. She woke up one morning to find she was unwell and on investigation by a doctor, she knew she was pregnant. Immediately she wrote informing him and asking him to prepone the wedding. Weeks passed and despite a flurry of letters she received no reply. In desperation she contacted a lady from an adjoining plantation to try and discover his whereabouts. The reply she received sent shockwaves coursing through her. The lady informed her that he had married an English woman in England and would not be returning immediately as he was on his honeymoon. After Gemima was born, she tried to contact him again but she was informed he had been delegated to another garden on his request. Having no option she had then returned to Kasgunj where her father lived. Her mother had died at an early age and her father had remarried. He had been the postmaster at one time and his new wife was an Indian from Kasgunj as well. They were not too pleased when she turned up with a baby on their doorstep but they had not turned her out. Prior to his death, her father had helped her get the teaching job, which she still held, at the village *patshala* but steeped in bitterness and angry at the world she spent what she earned on spirits. Gemima had grown up never having anything not even a mother's love.

Now with no more information forthcoming from Aunty Sarah, I looked to Ivan for answers, "Do you know anything about Gemima?"

"Chris has mentioned her once or twice, they're good friends but I've never met her." We were walking to the tomb.

"Have you come here often?"

"Many times. I've left a lamp and matches hidden near the vault, come carefully. It's a little dark and musty smelling but it's not very scary."

It was my first time into the vault, which housed the graves of ancestors. This time I was not afraid of meeting ghosts and there was nothing frightening in any case. The trap door, which hid the staircase, was a little heavy but since Ivan had taken the precaution of oiling the hinges it opened smoothly. The stairs were made of white marble and although covered in dust were easily discernible. There were shelves with graves with dates and names on them and I went around reading the inscriptions.

"How come there are so few," I demanded.

"I wondered about that, no one has any explanation." He had managed to get the lamp lighting and for a while the odour of kerosene prevailed. "Maybe some of them died elsewhere."

The marble on some of the graves was intricately carved. They looked rather pretty. "I love marble," I told Ivan, running my hand's over the design of birds, "it looks so elegant."

"I'll remember to have a nice gravestone carved in marble for you," he said grinning. "Shall we go and see the rest of it?"

"There's more?" I squeaked in surprise

He nodded mysteriously; there was another chamber further back with more graves. The room had carved marble walls as if it had been made specially. "I was running my hand along the wall, the cool of the marble smooth to the touch when my hand hit a break and I felt an icy breeze hit my hand sending shivers up my arm.

"Ivan, bring the lamp here." I demanded.

He carried it over and we both stood staring at the crack in the wall.

"I didn't notice this before," he said, "perhaps this will go soon, "better if we get out now."

"Put your hand here, there's an icy breeze coming from this …can you feel it?" I had placed his hand near the crack.

"You're right," he said, "I wonder….."

"What? What are you thinking?" He was staring at the wall lost in thought and I shook him to break him out of his reverie, "what are you thinking, tell me." my voice was echoing eerily in the chamber.

"We need a torch, this lamp is not enough, come on." He grabbed my hand and began pulling me towards the stairs.

"What happened, is something wrong?"

"Are you coming or do you want to be here alone until I return?"

"Where are you going.."

"To get a torch from home," he said impatiently, "wait here". He left me unceremoniously outside the tomb and darted off towards the house.

It took him half an hour to return and I was debating going after him as I had had my fill of sitting in the hot sun staring at the fields.

"Come on," he said, "let's go down, I've brought some things to eat and a bottle of water." He handed the bottle of water to me and we made our way inside again. I couldn't help glancing around and holding my hand to my nose. The smell was damp and vile. I hoped nothing was rotting still.

We took turns at peering through the crack with the torch and our excitement grew as we could just about make out a sort of chamber behind the wall.

"How do we go in, there must be a way?" said Ivan. He was shining the torch up and down the wall in an effort to discover some clue to an opening."

We banged all along the wall but the crack didn't widen and we almost gave up. Ivan and I were both avid readers of adventure stories and had grown up on tales of the Hardy Boys, 'Enid Blyton and the Famous Five'. It was only to be expected that we would immediately think there must be a secret lever which could open up the room to us but no matter how hard we looked we found nothing and our disappointment was acute as we sat and thought over the problem. Ivan didn't seem to have a problem with the odour in the chamber and he sat and finished off the biscuits and cookies which he had brought with him with his appetite in no way impaired.

"Have you ever fallen in love, Ivan?" I asked him. I was thinking of my short-lived romance in Lucknow and what must have been romances among the people who lay buried here. I was trying hard to develop a look of nonchalance. I didn't want to admit to Ivan I didn't like the vault.

"Sure," he replied, "I fell in love three times this past year."

"Did you do it with any of them?"

"Do what?" he opened his eyes wide at me.

"Well you know.." he was grinning widely. I told him about the incident where we had peeked through our neighbour's chappard from the top of their wall. Ivan collapsed with laughter. "You didn't," he spluttered.

"We did too, and you can't tell anyone."

He gave me his solemn promise.

"It looked so silly," I told him.

"It's not really, you know."

"How can you say that, you've not done it."

"But I have," he said a wicked grin lighting his boyish face.

He told me how he and some of the boys in his dormitory did it on a regular basis with the Mali's daughter.

"She was always hanging around the school and watching us guys," said Ivan, "Amit was the first with her behind the toilets. She was already quite experienced, boy she really knew how to make us...." He glanced at me and grinned

"Make you what?" I enquired, "how sick, all of you with just one girl." But Ivan dropped the subject refusing to discuss it further especially since the image it conjured of him in such a preposterous exercise with some faceless female jiggling up and down made me explode with mirth, which I explained to him between bouts of hiccups. He solemnly informed me I needed to be committed, but I could see he was amused too.

"One thing I can't understand," Ivan said, "why humans pretend not to care when they care desperately. I was interested in my maths teacher's daughter, she studied at a different school and every time I tried to express my feelings for her she would behave in a weird manner, in fact she made fun of me to her friends, one of them told me."

"Girls are normally afraid to show their feelings for fear of being taken advantage of, are you sure she was interested in you?"

"Why couldn't she just be honest like I was?"

"Fear of rejection I suppose or fear of showing herself as weak. Take Mum for instance, she cares so much for Dad but does she tell him? No, she points out each and every fault instead, believing it would make her weak to admit she needs him. Honesty seems to be a dirty word in relationships. Truth makes you weak, pretence is preferable to being open to ridicule or rejection."

"Fear is difficult to dispel I suppose," he said thoughtfully.

"It also ruins relationships, destroys confidence and makes a mess of everything."

"Let's get Chris to help," said Ivan changing the subject, "and we'll break the wall. It can't be more than a slab thick, it's marble, and it shouldn't be too difficult to break through." We were back to pondering the wall.

"What if Aunty Sarah or somebody else finds out, you'll be in big trouble."

"Whose to know, unless you blab…"

"I won't…" I began indignantly and he pulled my hair. "Okay I know you won't. Will you wait here? I'll go call Chris and get some hammers or something." I shook my head and followed him out. I was prepared to wait but not in the vaults.

He was back in a relatively short time with Chris or else it seemed short since I must have dozed for a while leaning against the tree which afforded me some shade. They had brought a chisel and hammer as well so I presumed Ivan had told Chris about our find.

"Hi," said Chris smiling at me and we all trooped down to the vaults once again.

"I was wondering," I said, "supposing someone comes while we are down, won't they hear the noise?"

"Nobody comes here," said Chris, "the villagers are superstitious and don't normally pass this way, they are afraid of ghosts." His accent was atrocious, guess he was more used to conversing in the local dialect than in English but I didn't comment on it. Surprisingly they made an aperture in a short time and when Ivan could fit through we went in one by one.

I was the last to go in and passed the lamp to them so that we could look around. Ivan was holding up the lamp so that the room was lit up and as I straightened I could see the wall behind him and screamed in fright so that he almost dropped the lamp "What the.." he shouted, spinning round and Chris gave a chuckle at our shock. The portrait hung on the wall was full size and so life like it was quite possible to imagine the woman in it to be alive. Now that we were in, the air didn't seem to be so cold and it didn't smell as musty either.

"Wow, the *Begum* was beautiful."

"It's not the *Begum*", said Ivan, "she's wearing a gown," he had always been rather astute and observant, "I hardly think the *Begum* wore western clothes."

I had to agree with him.

"Who is it then?" asked Chris.

"Must be some ancestor," said Ivan in puzzlement. He was staring in fascination at the portrait and who could blame him the woman in it was a real beauty. She could very well have been a seductive heroine straight out of a steamy novel, with her flaming hair that curled down to her waist and her green eyes framed by long lashes. She was wearing a set of the most magnificent rubies encircled with diamonds around her neck. Her sharp features gave her a proud look as she gazed back at us in disdain. Probably didn't much like the artist who painted her, I thought, or maybe that was her habitual expression. But the artist whoever he had been had really been excellent, he had captured her on canvas in a most lifelike manner.

Chris was the first to tear his gaze away from the portrait and this time it was he who gave an exclamation, "By God! Look at the size of the thing."

"What?" we chorused, then looked towards where Chris was pointing. Another grave and this was not just an ordinary one. It was enormous, also made of marble but with no markings on it except for an olive wreath, which had been carved on the top. There were no embellishments like the others had, just a plain marble box of great size. Highly intriguing! We ran our hands over it and Chris and Ivan counted hand spans to get an idea of its length.

"It couldn't be hers," I ventured, "I don't think she could have been that enormous." Ivan and Chris didn't think so either. When nothing further was to be discovered from the grave, Ivan once again turned his attention to the portrait.

"I wonder who she is, maybe Aunty Sarah will know."

"You can't tell her, she'll get angry about the wall. Chris what are you doing?" He was sitting on top of the grave banging his feet against the sides. "You can't sit on a grave."

"The dead don't complain ...what are you fussing for anyway?"

"It's sacrilegious," I retorted.

Suddenly the lamp went out. Once again I screamed. Ivan switched on the torch, "the oil must have finished, let's go before the batteries run down too."

Grandma was ready to go home.

"As usual, you keep disappearing, come on say goodbye to everybody."

I ran around hugging the various cousins, aunts and uncles, then scrambled up into the bullock cart. Ivan and Chris ran behind the cart for a little distance, then stood on a sand pile and waved until they could see us no longer.

Halfway home, Ramsai stopped the cart and we watched a mongoose and cobra fight. It was simply fascinating. The cobra was losing the battle, its head was getting bloodier but the mongoose was very young and we could see she was tiring. From time to time she would dart into the bush and then return to the fight.

"What is she doing Gran, why does she keep disappearing, the snake gets time to recover when she does that." I was getting anxious for the mongoose.

"She eats something," said Gran, "that prevents her from dying from the snake's poison. There the snake is almost dead, shall we go.."

"Oh no! Gran please," so she let me watch but I was not to get out of the cart.

This was wonderful entertainment but for Gran and Ramsai it didn't hold much interest. Most of the land was covered in brown sandy soil with rough grass growing in clumps all over. Cobras and other snakes were plentiful. Many people died from snakebites. Women were more susceptible as they slept in *charpoys* out in the compound in hot weather and their long hair hung off the cots. It seemed the snakes used their hair to climb into the cots and bit them the moment they moved.

A few days passed before Ivan came to Manota on his own, he brought me up-to-date on his findings.

"Chris and I have made a further discovery, we found the tunnels."

"You didn't!"

"Yes, we did," he said proudly, we were sitting in an old guava tree scoffing the fruit. The pink flesh contrasted nicely with the green skin of the guava I had just bitten into, "are you going to eat that or stare at it?"

"So where are they?"

"Guess?"

"In the vaults….I bet."

"How did you know, Chris told you?"

"I've not met Chris again.."

"His girlfriend then.."

"No, just a guess, everyone has looked in all the other places, it had to be there."

"Remember that chamber with the portrait?"

"Mmm"

"We decided to take the portrait out and ask Aunty Sarah who the woman was. The opening to the tunnels was behind the portrait, so we had to put it back. There were stairs leading down, then a sort of rough landing and you could go right or left. The left tunnel has all caved in; we could go only a little way. That's where the breeze seemed to be coming from. The right one seems okay but still.. It's simply fantastic, it's got the same brick walls and ceiling only the floor is still earth. I think I'll be an engineer and build tunnels just like these. There's a whole network underground, I'm going to explore them all."

"Don't you go in there," I advised Ivan, "it could cave in over you and you'd get buried."

We've already been part of the way in some; I just have to know where it comes out. I don't know how much it's ventilated. Some parts the roots of brush and trees have come through there are rats, we'll wear gumboots next time."

"There must be other slimy things down there too. What about that grave, whose do you think it is?"

"My guess would be Bhimsen, he was the Colonel's right hand man, from all accounts he had an impressive size." When animated, Ivan was actually handsome and I studied him noticing the growing maturity in his face. He had the typical features of our family, specially the nose which although sharp, curved a little to the end. In fact he looked a lot like me apart from his hair, which had lost none of its brightness. His duck tails had long been subdued into well ordered curls which Ivan kept a little long as it was the rage among the boys to sport shoulder length hair, they thought it made them look 'hep'. Neville too was sporting a longer length despite Mum's demands to chop the locks off. I had to admire Ivan's curls, my own hair grew straight below the shoulders and despite valiant attempts with Mum's rollers, I was never able to master the art. In later years, however, I was introduced to the step cut which once set with rollers could make a better show than Ivan's own curls.

Ivan and Chris undertook the exploration of the tunnels as a serious task. They planned in advance, discussing how they should go about it. They wore gumboots to afford them protection from any hidden reptiles and scorpions and armed with torches, batteries and an assortment of food and water negotiated the passages, which had not caved in. It was a wonder they didn't get lost in the tunnels but it seemed Ivan had the idea of carrying a can of phosphorescent paint and they painted a big line along the wall as they walked. But ofcourse they couldn't penetrate too far as mostly all had caved in and they met with walls of rubble which paid to their explorations. I heaved a silent sigh of relief, roaming through underground passages inhabited by creatures who preferred living beneath the ground was not my idea of fun. I soon forgot about the tunnels. Gemima came for a visit and we became good friends. Gemima was a year older than me and the same age as Roxanna but she looked like a child with her brown hair tied back in a ponytail. There was nothing exceptional about her except her eagerness to please. She was much of a height with Roxanna who stood five feet nothing in her socks. Annie and myself had outgrown Roxanna in both height and width and she was resentful that now we passed our clothes down to her instead of receiving hers. Both she and Gem were petite and although we crowed over our height then, in later years I always wished I had her slim figure, which never ran to fat and had her looking much younger than her years while we battled away with the bulge.

I marvelled at Gem for braving the countryside alone and coming almost daily to meet us. She was an avid reader and had a fancy for the Mills and Boons books, which Roxanna had graduated to. She could finish one a day and would come back to get another until our store was exhausted. Then we introduced her to Taylor Caldwell, Alexander Dumas, Georgette Heyer and Alistair Maclean which were my preferences and which I had discovered in Gramp's store.

I had an admirer. Chris whose hormones had gone into overdrive shadowed my footsteps and turned up in the most unlikely places. Far from being annoyed I found to my surprise I enjoyed the attention until I noticed the hurt Gem tried hard to hide.

"You're in love with him!" I exclaimed.

"Rubbish" she was vehement but her eyes looked tearful. We were sitting in the cemetery undisturbed except for the flies, which buzzed around us investigatively.

"Why don't you just admit it, really Gem I'm not interested in Chris, it's just I'm not used to guys giving me attention and I was just seeing what all the shouting was about."

"I wish he would stop treating me like a kid sister and see me differently." She said miserably, "he doesn't have eyes for me at all, the way he looks at you, anyone would think you were a princess or something." I laughed at her woebegone face.

"Well make him take notice."

"How can I?" she wailed, "I'm nothing to look at, I wish I looked like you or Roxanna."

"Don't be nuts, we'll have to think of something."

"But don't you dare tell him, it will be worse to have his pity."

"I know, I feel the same way..." she smiled at my disclosure.

"It's Ivan isn't it?"

"He treats me the way Chris treats you and I want him to notice me differently, so there, we're exactly in the same boat." We giggled at our plight.

"This is so ridiculous," I said, "come on. Instead of sitting around moping let's go and play seven stones or something."

That vacation Gem and I suffered the pangs of unrequited love and in doing so drew closer together bolstering our pride and honing our pretence of being gay, suffering together. We became regular correspondents when I returned to school and was highly entertained by Gem's letters which regaled the pranks she and Chris got into and specially Aunty Sarah's methods of instilling morals in them both which had little effect on either, as neither of them believed in a supreme being or were inclined towards religion. Chris's mother prayed, according to Gem, but Chris himself had the firm belief as did Gem, that there was no God. If indeed He did exist, they felt sure they would not have been in such sad economic circumstances. No amount of arguments could convince them otherwise, and since at that time, I was not particularly interested in changing their viewpoint, the topic was dropped with common consent. Aunty Sarah, ofcourse, persisted in her efforts but without much progress. They soon learned it was easier just to listen to her quietly and when she didn't incite a flurry of arguments, she took it for granted that her scriptural teaching was having some impact.

Since Chris and Gem lived in the village they were privy to all sorts of stories, which she passed on to me. Gopal, the headman's son, fell in love with Maya, the washerwoman's daughter. Their castes were different and it was unimaginable that their parents would agree to their union. They decided to elope and one night Gopal stole money from his father and went to the meeting place they had arranged. Maya didn't come to meet him; cold and anxious he waited until early morning then sadly went home to face the ire of his father who had discovered the money missing. Later from gossip, he was able to learn that Maya was absent from her home. He became worried and began to make inquiries. When his father heard the news, he too questioned his son closely who broke down and confessed that he had intended to elope with her but she had not come to their meeting place.

The washerwoman's sons began to spread the rumour that Gopal had disposed of their sister and when villagers heard that he had not been home that night they too suspected him. The police took him into custody. He languished in prison for six months before they released him on grounds of insufficient evidence. Maya was never found and no information about her ever came to light. There were many theories that the wolves had got her or she had been kidnapped by dacoits but what actually happened to her was anybody's guess. Gem secretly believed the washerwoman's sons were the culprits. They might have killed her and disposed her body somewhere just so there was no stigma on their family.

After Ivan returned to school that year, Chris brought Gem to see the secret room and the portrait in the tomb but it was only later he disclosed his knowledge of the tunnels to her. The secret room in the vault became Chris and Gem's favourite place. Here they could hide from the world and pretend they lived in some grand old style. Gem wove fantasies, which they enacted to keep themselves occupied. I wondered that anyone would want to stay buried in that chamber but it was a place, which they felt was their own, and where nobody could spy on them or make fun of them. It was amusing for the village lotharios to follow Gem and make suggestive remarks which had Chris up in arms ready to do battle on her behalf and at their homes the atmosphere was not conducive to happiness.

Often he had had to skip his meal. His father retaliated nastily even to twisting his arm when he came in between his parents squabble. He was prone to violence and Chris was always afraid his mother would get hurt. Later he would have to make himself scarce till his father's anger had cooled. Whenever his father had been specially abusive Chris would answer him back. His mother knowing Chris would not be spared sent him off urgently, pleading with him to be careful. She promised to save food for Chris but often he had to remain hungry for hours. Gem, when she knew he had not eaten would sneak him some of her own food not that there was much in their larder either but still something was always available.

Chris and Gem were oddities. Chris was not related to us or perhaps he was in some distant way since most of the Anglo-Indian families who lived there were related in some way or other as they had all inter-married at sometime or the other. Chris had the red hair and green eyes, which was a throw back to some Muslim ancestor so it was most probable that he too was related. He looked a lot like Ivan in fact, and Ivan had always theorized that Chris's ancestors could have been from the concubine's line. Well at any rate Chris's family was very poor. They owned no land and lived in rented premises on the edge of Chhaoni. Like most Anglo-Indians at that time Chris's father had worked on the railways as a guard but he had for some reason or other become an alcoholic and had soon been kicked out of employment. It was common to hear Anglo-Indians being bitter at their plight, the Britishers had put them into all the administrative posts which allowed the British a platform of good governance and their loyalty had been their trade mark. The posts and telegraphs, the armed forces, the railways and other government manned operations were their forte as most were educated and hard workers, yet when India gained independence, they made no provisions for them.

They were not accepted in Britain as being too Indian and they were not accepted in India as being too British. In India, upper caste Indians began to take over the posts they normally held and most of them were left redundant, without any means to support themselves. The women too faced discrimination in a different way, they didn't cover their faces or heads as other communities did and they adhered to the western style of dressing. This more than anything else ensured that they were regarded as loose charactered and without morals.

Chris's father was bitter that he had been summarily dismissed without a hearing and his frustration was taken out on his long-suffering family. They subsisted on the meager earnings of his mother who was the dressmaker for the Anglo-Indian women who were partial to wearing dresses and skirts. Every month someone would place a few sewing orders with her just so she could have a little earning. Every month farmers like grandpa would send them some rice, wheat and fruit whenever they remembered. Chris was sent to the village school to study, as there was not enough money to send him to an English medium school in a city. He had a younger brother who was too small to attend school so he played with the village children his fair skin and red hair in sharp contrast to the brown skins of the other children.

Gem was Chris's best friend and she too studied at the village school. She was in a worse state than Chris. Her mother taught the children at the *pathshala* for a mere pittance which she received from the government. Mostly she was in an inebriated state and hardly managed to teach them anything. She spent most of the day moving around in a stupor while

Gem did the work around the house. She was behind in her rent but the landlord taking pity on Gem didn't evict them. Chris was Gem's champion and often fished her out of scrapes with the village children as they teased her unmercifully especially as they grew older.

Ivan fascinated Chris. He spoke English so well and always seemed so well turned out. Ivan had the advantage of a good education and a well-ordered family life. Chris envied Ivan his education and his fine home. Ivan for his part was not impressed in any way with the way he lived. If he missed not having parents he never showed it. Ivan was bored with playing childish games with his young cousins. When he met Chris he intrigued him. They were more or less the same age so it was only natural that they started spending time with each other. Ivan was fond of adventure and managed to get himself into a number of scrapes much to the chagrin of Aunty Sarah who was his guardian. But no amount of scolding could repress his naturally high spirits. Before long they took to going for shikar together. Ivan taught Chris how to shoot and to play various games, which Chris never even knew existed. Chris was a misfit. His family was too poor to socialize with the other Anglo-Indian families and they were not villagers so they couldn't fit in with the villagers either. He and Gem always felt like outcasts. They longed to belong and their longing only increased their hopelessness. When Ivan brought Chris into his world for the first time he was given a taste of what it felt like to be accepted.

Ivan was smart and a good shot. He taught Chris to shoot as well and it was common to see them trudging home, their bags filled with game and Ivan's dog, an indeterminate breed, running alongside them. Chris was always invited to partake of all the meals and he did so with relish much to the amusement of Aunty Sarah. She had been horrified at first when Ivan had befriended Chris but when she got to know him she undertook to atleast see that he had some decent clothes to wear. The manner in which she proffered the clothes was done so skillfully that Chris, who had his own brand of pride, was able to accept them without feeling he was at the receiving end of the charity.

Gem hated Ivan. Chris had abandoned her for the time being with his newfound friendship and she was envious that he seemed to have almost become a part of Ivan's family. She was lonelier than ever and waited with exasperation for Ivan's holidays to end so she could have her Chris back. At first Chris had felt guilty at abandoning Gem and he had thought to introduce her to Ivan too but then he had been afraid that Ivan would not accept her into their circle, her being a girl, so he had dropped the idea.

Ivan was generous and when he discovered that Chris's family were eating better since he had begun taking him on *shikar* he gifted him an airgun for Christmas. Chris who had never owned anything so exciting in his life had literally jumped with joy but he never did take it home. He kept it with Gem for fear his father would get his hands on it. Gem was only too happy to be its custodian and when Ivan was away would go into the jungle with Chris and help to flush out game. Pigeons were his main targets but he had to get quite close to shoot them, as the range of the gun was not very powerful. Later, when Chris showed Gem the secret room, they hid the gun along with all the knick-knacks they found on their various jaunts. Chris's father found another way to torment him. He would fling out the game, which was being prepared in a rage, he didn't want Ivan's charity even if Chris had done the shooting, he wanted none of it. Between father and son a wall of hatred was growing, a cauldron of simmering anger and rage built through humiliation, which festered. Chris learnt the hard way to take taunts silently, to hide his feelings because he knew, should his father get an inkling of his real feelings he would torment him mercilessly but more than that his mother would bear the brunt of his anger. His mother did her best to be the buffer between them but she too knew it was only a matter of time before it erupted and she lived in dread of that day.

Aunty Sarah didn't let matters end there, however, she had Chris come over to her house to study. She insisted on teaching him and she loaned him a number of books to study from. One day during one of her difficult lessons, Chris told her about Gem. Well being big hearted, Aunty Sarah asked Chris to invite Gem over for the lessons too and being of a hospitable nature it was simple to insist they share her lunch as well. Gem soon began to lose her waif-like nature and began to fill out. She looked more like a girl rather than a skinny boy. That was the year we met Gem too, the year I was fourteen.

The summer brought about a change in Chris and Gem's relationship. His boyish infatuation was replaced by something more lasting for Gem, her yearning to be noticed differently met with success. They were closer than ever now, they were also more worldly wise. They longed to get out into the world, to change their lives. They talked and dreamed of a better life but with little hope to change things, their dreams stayed just dreams. Now that they had glimpses of a life they knew they could fit into, the one they lived choked them with its futileness and in despair they clung to each other more than ever. It was inevitable that their relationship, which so far had been a childish bonding, should now progress to something deeper, more in keeping with their maturity, which they were fast attaining.

"You're getting big," teased Chris, "you won't fit in to your clothes soon."

"Aunty Sarah gave me a dress Chris, should I wear dresses, what do you think?"

"You in a dress? Goodness imagine you...." then as he noticed her downcast expression he smiled, "wear it Gem, it will be nice to see you looking like a girl for once."

The effect was not what either of them expected. The dress clung to Gem's figure in all the right places and as she gazed at herself in the mirror she was astonished that for once she actually looked pretty. On Chris, the effect was quite different. In recent weeks he had begun noticing strange urges and a deep restlessness. His longings were for something, which he couldn't understand nor explain. Now looking at Gem he suddenly understood what he had been feeling. Her femininity in the dress made him realize that the feelings that had sprung to life only recently were centred in her and the fact that she was almost a woman. He was in love, and Gem who had reached maturity at an earlier stage and had confessed her love for him to me, recognized that the understanding she had come to earlier was only now growing in Chris. The knowledge made her shy and her face suffused with colour she turned her head away from him.

Chris didn't know how to proceed. This wall had suddenly grown between them, for once in his life he was tongue-tied. Seeing his predicament made Gem laugh and the ice was broken.

"You look like the cat got your tongue," she laughed, "aren't you going to say something to me?"

"You're awfully pretty Gem," said Chris.

"It's just the dress," said Gem shyly but her heart was singing and she gazed back at Chris openly adoring.

Aunty Sarah noticed the difference in their relationship immediately and insidiously introduced chapters on morals and behavioural codes into all the lessons. Her favourite were quotes from the Bible and often she would make them read scriptural passages which she hoped would induce them to behave in a prudent manner.

Ten

In later years Gem and I would laugh at the stories she had told them. Although my family didn't visit them very often, I managed in between studies to make a few trips to visit them all. Aunty Sarah was especially glad to see me and thought it good that I had befriended Gem. We still exchanged confidences and while her love for Chris was reciprocated, mine for Ivan had sort of metamorphosed into a lasting friendship. With Gem too, the friendship deepened and we became closer than ever. Never having been out of the village she was eager to discover everything about the rest of the country as well. Her thirst for information had me answering question after question until sometimes in exasperation I would tell her to "shut up" and she would march off to her home. Mostly we enjoyed being together and wandered around the fields, in the gardens or down to the river. We experimented with all kinds of makeup and would have Aunty Sarah in splits of laughter when we came out wearing various hues of eye shadow and lipstick. Chris's reaction was something else.

"You're making Gem look like a tart," he grimaced once, and I saw the down cast expression on Gem's face. She had wanted to impress him but instead he was being scornful.

"Why can't you mind your own business?" I yelled but Gem ran off and washed the whole thing off.

Thereafter there were no more makeup sessions, the transition had already begun, we were leaving our childhood behind. The childlike connotations of curiosity were being rapidly replaced by new interests, new subjects to delve into, a whole new world to explore where boys were no longer just boys but a different species all together. This was the time to be introduced to new loves and the pain of apartheid of giving life a whole new meaning. Where choices were diverse, not just which dress to wear or which sweet to take but the charting of a future, of new experiences, new friends, new thoughts, of bodily changes which pleased or irked according to circumstances. New perspectives, new dreams, where fathers were no longer laps to be sat in or mother's soft and cuddly but long lectures which emphasised 'dos and donts'.

Gem's Mum developed cataract and her duties in their home increased tenfold. Most often she was unable to attend Aunty Sarah's classes and when she discovered the reason, Aunty Sarah informed Gem that an eye camp had been organized at Kasgunj and Gem could have her mother's eyes operated there. She had just turned seventeen.

The camp was crowded with people who had come from neighbouring villages the incentive to attend being the fact that all treatment was done free. Gem met with one of the doctors who examined her mother's eyes and he promised that he would take a look. He seemed interested in Gem and questioned her on her family background. The next few days saw him showing more than a normal interest in Gem who couldn't help becoming excited at his attention. It was the first time she had come in contact with a man who didn't live on the poverty line, who in fact screamed wealth with the way he dressed, the opulent car he moved in and the diamond ring on his finger. His attention made Gem feel attractive and intelligent. Her experience of men was limited to Chris and Chris's father. She had no notion of how to deal with such a man as this doctor; it was all so new and stimulating.

Two weeks after they had met, he invited Gem to dine with him at the modest hotel he was staying at and she accepted with alacrity. From among her mother's stored clothes she retrieved a red dress, which had once been fashionable and Chris's Mum alter it to her measurements.

"What are you going to do with this?" she had asked Gem. "There's nowhere to wear such a pretty thing."

"I just like to dress up sometimes auntie," Gem had told her and she obligingly altered the garment but she was sad that Gem had nowhere to go in such a fine outfit.

Chris had smiled when he had seen the dress thinking she would one day wear it for him but Gem had given him an impish grin and run off home. Feeling a little guilty at her deception, she had thought to cancel her date but the lure of a new experience with a man whom she thought good looking and kind made her think better of such a gesture.

That evening she had gone alone to Kasgunj, the dress carefully concealed in a plastic shopping bag along with a lipstick, which she intended to use. Her one complaint was the old sandals which she had no choice but to use and which didn't quite suit the dress but not having any money to buy another pair, she had polished the offending shoes as best she could and had set off for the hotel where she was to meet Anil Sharma.

Anil was thrilled that Gem intended to take such trouble for her date with him and had made the suggestion that they dine in his room so she could change and get herself ready, and also it would lend her the necessary privacy so she did not become an object of the other occupants curiosity. Gem had agreed.

The dinner had been a success as Anil, experienced with women, had Gem laughing over his stories. Anil was not very tall but he had even features, which were pleasant to look at, and a crooked smile, which lifted the corners of his mouth. More than looks he had the gift of the gab, and he had built a picture of a fascinating life in Delhi, a fine house, a variety of shopping which drew pictures of a life vastly different from hers and there had grown a hunger in her to be part of the picture he painted. In her excitement Gem had drunk a little too much of the wine and the heady liquor had proved her undoing.

"You're adorable," he had told Gem, "so innocent, but I'm going to change your life irrevocably, I'm going to help you with the transition from child to woman and you're just going to love the experience." Gem had not answered she had been somewhat inebriated.

Recognizing Gem's uninhibited condition, he had taken advantage of it to introduce her to the art of sexual intercourse. As Gem described it in graphic detail, "when he kissed me it was nothing like the ones Chris and I experimented with, while he kissed his fingers were doing something pleasurable with the nipple of my right breast, and then he pushed me on to the bed and his hands were all over me. He aroused such sensations with his tongue and his hands. It was like nothing I have ever experienced, one moment I was ready to scream as he entered me and then a strange sensation filled the whole of me and I felt so wonderful I wanted to cry. I didn't want that feeling to go away, I wanted it to go on and on..." Gem didn't have to think about it, she decided she had enjoyed the experience thoroughly and when he kissed her again, she had participated with much enthusiasm and with a fiery passion, which had probably made Anil feel their roles had somehow become reversed and Gem was not a novice any longer. Over the next few days Gem had met him often and their meetings had been steamy episodes of lovemaking which both had enjoyed to the full without thought for any consequences. During one of their sessions Gem had brought the subject of marriage up.

"It's not possible," he had explained to a stunned Gem, "I'm already married. I'm a Hindu Brahmin, you wouldn't be accepted in my family." Gem had already dissolved into a flood of tears distressing him and he had tried to pacify her by telling her he loved her but that he couldn't help being already married.

"I don't love her," he had told Gem, "but I am married to her. In our community we have arranged marriages, we marry the women our parents choose. I also have two daughters, you have to understand, I can't marry you."

He had explained to Gem how family ties were important to him and that after receiving dowry from his wife's family he was not in a position to leave her.

"But I'm not leaving you," Gem had said, "can't you take me with you? I promise I won't be any trouble." He had shaken his head sadly.

"It's not possible, dear girl. Look I will return tomorrow, but we'll keep in touch and I promise we'll meet again."

Chris hadn't been able to understand Gem's mood when he had met her. She hadn't seemed interested in the old haunts, in roaming around with him. There had been an air of aloofness, which had puzzled him, but thinking it must be some girl thing troubling her, he hadn't pressed for an answer.

Gem wrote relating the preceding events and I wrote back telling her she had been very foolish. A man she didn't know had enticed her and she had fallen for the whole gambit. What upsets me more were Gem's declarations. She insisted she had enjoyed herself tremendously and if the opportunity presented itself, she would indulge herself again. There was an overtone of defiance in her letters which didn't bode any good and I was troubled that Gem seemed determined to take an unconventional course which could only end in disaster.

My fears were well founded as the next letter I received told me of her flight to Delhi. He had written telling her he had arranged for her to be his daughters's nanny, her most pressing duty would be to teach them English. Excitement at getting a job coupled with the fact that she was going to Delhi with all expenses paid had her in seventh heaven, not so Chris who couldn't reconcile himself to being without her. Gem did not disclose her intimate relationship with her employer and although a little suspicious as to how the job had come about, he had to be satisfied with the explanation of having met him at the eye camp and impressed him with her suitability to be his children's nanny.

Gem's life in Delhi had her crowing with delight. Her letters were filled with hours of shopping and dining out and picnics to the park with the kids and her favourite past time, movies in the movie halls which she had never dreamed existed, but some parts of her letters I didn't like.

"His wife is a typically conservative woman and not very pretty," she wrote, "he spends most nights in my bed, the room has a connecting door to the nursery where the children sleep. She doesn't suspect a thing. In front of her we behave with such decorum, he never looks at me and hardly ever speaks to me. I think I would have made an excellent actress. And his lovemaking has become so intense. He's so skillful he makes me want more, I get desperate if I can't have him near."

I told her she was behaving in a highly irresponsible and immoral manner;

"What you're experiencing is not love, it's sex and lust

and you are becoming addicted." But all remonstrance fell on deaf ears. She wrote again telling me I was imagining misfortune where there were none and morals were for those who could afford them. She felt an illicit relationship gave quite a different interpretation to a relationship. For one thing it was exciting, the constant thrill of being on the verge of discovery added to the stimulus coupled with the fact that it was forbidden increased her enjoyment. Like Eve who disobediently sampled that which was forbidden, so in continuity our insatiable appetites for the unattainable leads us on intrepid paths and if it means breaking the rules. Why not, the enjoyment is all the more for having been stolen.

"That's why marriages fail," she maintained, "the adventure gets crushed by that respectable institution where responsibility is a key word. Its all very well for those who revel in being prime examples of marital bliss, but what about those who bow down to convenience and live their lives in stifled suppression of their own desires and emotions, who live subdued by circumstances and obligations?"

She was vehement that man should not always be in subjection, freedom should reign supreme.

I argued that this would lead to lawlessness and widespread disturbance, but she insisted that the spreading maladies of depression and discontent would be dominated by a race of healthier individuals as being free would take away the spice from following the path of the forbidden and when something can be obtained without the ingredient of danger it loses its desirability and is no longer coveted.

I tried out Gem's theory on my Professor of literature and she replied very firmly.

"Marriage is a necessary institution," she said, "for the continuity of procreation to stem licentiousness which if left free to propagate would in all likelihood put paid to morality. It is necessary to combat the evil of free reign of expression, to bind people to follow the set norms so that the evils of society are suppressed for the betterment of everybody." Who could argue such a statement but I carefully wrote it down and sent it to Gem in the hope it would change her radical thinking.

Gem's elation didn't last very long. A few months later, she found out she was not the only one he cheated with. I discussed her predicament with Ivan and told him Anil was a worthless human being who preyed on young women.

"If a person is happy in a marriage, he won't seek another relationship," Ivan replied. He normally championed the men while I took the part of the ladies. He had come on a brief visit to Darjeeling on an errand for a senior lawyer for whom he did clerical work while also studying for his bar exams.

I was trying to figure out why the man did what he did. Ivan thought it stemmed from being unhappy with his wife.

"You mean his illicit cavorting?" I asked him.

"Whatever you want to call it... extra-marital affairs," he stressed.

"Obviously something had to be wrong for one partner to stray."

"In this case he's oversexed," I told him. Ivan laughed aloud. "I think he just gets enjoyment out of doing it," I continued, "and he likes doing it with different women. Gem is terribly unhappy about it.'

"She's stupid." Ivan was annoyed that Gem had abandoned Chris and gone chasing after a man who treated her so disgustingly. I was surprised Chris had never introduced him; Ivan might have been the one to change her way of thinking. He had formulated a picture of Gem as being unfeeling and rotten.

"Don't be so hard on her Ivan, she's so confused." I defended her, after all he didn't know her but I did.

"Try getting some sense into her then," he said irritated. His concern was Chris and what he would feel if he ever found out.

I sat quiet thinking about Gem, I had no excuse for her behaviour but perhaps it could be explained.

"There's good and bad in all of us," I told him, "but sometimes we become unbalanced and confused and the bad aspect predominates. The whole world is made up of opposing influences and no matter how hard we try to pretend that all of us are only good, we cannot deny the existence of our 'otherselves,' our alter nature. Gem will come to her senses and she'll return."

"I hope you are right, for Chris's sake at least, he mopes around such a lot."

Ivan had a deep interest in psychology and he liked to delve into human relationships and see if he could analyse the reason for the disagreements or why people stayed together.

While discussing the aspects of good and bad and trying to discover why Gem did what she did, he told me about the theory proffered by an eminent psychologist who had written that each of us have both masculine and feminine qualities inside us and it is these opposing sexes which drive us to either cling to a person or drive them away and these two forces were the culprits for our behaviour. If we are feminine then we have an inner masculine self and if masculine, a feminine self, which unconsciously becomes the role model for the person we fall in love with and when that person doesn't live upto our role models then we are disappointed and the relationship fails.

It was an interesting theory but it still didn't give me an idea how to extricate Gem from the situation she was in. She had to want to leave but as yet I had no clue how to convince her. Erotic love had seemed the antidote to her limited existence but instead of alleviating, her circumstances had plunged her into another kind of suffering. But as it turned out I didn't have to convince her, the man showed himself to be totally depraved when he expected Gem to participate in a threesome with himself and another woman. She drew the line at that and returned to Kasgunj a much wiser person.

"He was a master at using women," she told me, "and we women in our emotional foolishness allowed him to do so. I wasn't the only one he used."

"When will women become wise and sensible," I lamented, "men don't centre their lives around women, their careers, their lifestyle are more important. A woman is a part of their life but not the focus of it."

"Well that's how they were made," said Gem, "a man is conditioned to provide for the family, so his primary aim is his livelihood. A woman is conditioned for reproduction therefore her primary aim is the mate. That's the difference."

I looked at Gem in astonishment. "That's an amazing insight. I guess that's why women focus so much on relationships, though now with the changing world, women have begun to focus on careers as well and if she's into a relationship, she doesn't allow it priority. Women are evolving too, but the degrees of their emotions have remained the same. A man is naturally promiscuous while a woman would want to hold on to the one she has if what you say is true, then he has to be the mainstay for her existence, providing for her and the kids."

Being honest and not wanting to deceive Chris who loved her such a lot she told him the truth and expected to have him condemn her but he surprised her by reacting differently.

"So that's what you were up to," he growled his voice tight with anger, she had just finished relating her sordid tale "I wondered how you had got the job, how could you, I thought you loved me." The pain and anguish in his voice was more than Gem could bear, she ran to him wrapping her arms around him.

"I do love you Chris, that was something else, it was not love." Pulling her hands from around his neck Chris slapped her. They were both stunned by his action and they stared at each other in hurt and bewilderment. Hesitantly she reached for him again, the slap had not harmed her, what hurt more was the look on his face, the betrayal he was feeling, and she wanted desperately to comfort him. Then Chris relented and pulled her to him holding her tight. He wanted the pain he was feeling to go away too and when she began to kiss him, the dam of pent up emotion burst and he took her with a force that ravaged them both but dispersed the anger like nothing else might have done. Gem was relieved and exhilarated at the same time.

"With Chris it was like I was burning in a ball of fire," she told me, "he consumed me so completely, I literally melted, I felt one with him. I'll never leave him again. I enjoy this so much."

There was no conforming Gem; she was a law unto herself. What I admired most was her frankness. She lived life according to her own code where her feelings were the pivot to her conduct. I could not condemn her. She was the antithesis of all the things we had been taught, but I believed she was truly liberated, she felt no shame or guilt in her actions, she was free. Who, in our world can claim to be free, we are bound by convention of one kind or another, by social strictures, by rules and regulations, by behavioural codes and morals. Gem bowed down to nothing, she believed only in herself, and I envied her this belief, at a time when we were just beginning to have confidence in ourselves she had already forged ahead and while we were taking our time growing up, Gem had already attained maturity.

Eleven

Meantime Grandpa got bitten by a snake and died. It was all very dramatic. He called out to Grandma to give him his tea, when she handed him the mug he said her name and died. It was a shock to Grandma, she never did recover and then she was diagnosed with cancer. She joined him sooner than we expected and I do think she was glad. She had no will to live after he was gone. All the chemotherapy and medication simply had no effect. It was a sad time for everyone and Manota was never the same again. With them went the family gatherings. Hardly anyone ever came to visit now. We still made it back during the winter vacations but the spark was missing. Manota had become silent. Uncle Sunny was in his own world, Uncle Wilfred no longer seemed gay, he missed Grandma, only Buddi remained the same although I think she missed Grandma too but since she couldn't express herself we didn't really know.

Until the time Uncle Sunny was alive, the farm was intact and although he was an indifferent farmer at least he saw that Uncle Wilfred and Buddi were well fed. In all families there runs a thread, which is of a darker hue, sometimes, the black sheep of a family. Our black sheep had a heart dark as coal. His second wife, Mercy was as brown as the bark of a tree and just as rough. The year Uncle Sunny died, his younger brother Cyril and his second wife came to stay, although how she ever came by the name Mercy puzzled us, she was the most unmerciful person I have ever met or hope to meet in this life. Uncle Wilfred was kept on short rations thereafter and without the knowledge of his family was turned out of the only home he ever knew. Not able to make a living and unable to find a way to contact his brothers, he died of starvation. Buddi was not starving but neither was she being well fed. She was given a little food for doing all the menial jobs around the house. Then Uncle Cyril sold a portion of the house to Shaitan Singh, cut down all the guava trees and sold the wood off. He left after ruining Manota taking Buddi with him. Nobody was ever able to locate where he took her to as he and his wife simply disappeared and were never heard of again.

His children in Delhi would impart no information about him, claiming ignorance. It was a sad time for all. We went to Delhi to get information out of Uncle Cyril's daughter.

"Look," whispered Roxanna, "she's strange," I looked at the lady who had opened the door to us. She was plump with frowsy hair and glasses. Thick, black rimmed spectacles, which she didn't look through but over.

"Yes?" she inquired of us.

"We're Rocky's daughters, may we come in?"

"Rocky? Oh! Come in, come in.." we were lead into an untidy hall piled with odds and ends of papers and boxes to an even more cluttered living room which had some strange odour. Clothes were strewn on chairs and a thick film of dust coated the furniture. Mumbling to herself, she unceremoniously dumped the bundle that was on the sofa onto the floor and bade us be seated. As we gingerly complied, seating ourselves on the edge of the couch I glanced down and it was then I saw her socks. One was pink, a rather nice soft baby pink and the other sock was black with yellow stripes. I dug Roxanna in the ribs and indicated she take a look at the socks. We almost erupted into giggles but couldn't help the smiles.

"So how come is it you girls are in Delhi?"

"We came to find out if you know where your Dad is?"

"Dad?" she looked at us thoughtfully, "what has he done now...come on tell me?"

"He's taken Buddi off somewhere, we want to know where he is." She was already shaking her head.

"I don't know and I don't particularly care. Dad always was a law unto himself and he only remembers us when he needs money."

"But don't you know where he is now? Would it be possible to get a message to him?"

"Look girlie, I don't have any information but you leave your address, when he contacts me, I'll let you know, okay?"

"Could you give us your phone number, we can ring to find out?" She heaved herself out of her chair and looked around, it was as if she was seeing her apartment for the first time.

"What a mess, I'm a nurse I just don't get enough time to do anything, would you like to have some tea?" she glanced back at us and we smiled at her and declined.

"No really, we have so much to do still."

"Okay here's the number," I handed her our address and number which Roxanna had written down and we took our leave. No calls came to inform us Buddi's whereabouts. Quietly and sadly she had exited our lives. For a long time afterwards we didn't visit Manota.

A search was initiated. The conditions of the institutions, which housed mental patients, were appalling. Filth was everywhere. The odours of urine and the smell of unwashed bodies seemed not to be noticed by the inmates at all. Not all wanted to allow us in only checking their registers to see if she was listed but with the aid of a few palmed hundred rupee notes which Dad had thoughtfully kept handy, we got access to their wards. Some patients didn't seem to even know that they were alive, they sat in corners and looked blankly at the walls, they had been in those circumstances for years and with nothing to look forward to they took no interest in anything. They looked so pathetic, unkempt, frail and hopeless. Looking into their eyes was like looking deep into pools of emptiness as they patiently waited for their sojourn on the earth to end. We were glad Buddi was not among them. We drew a blank at the institutions around Uttar Pradesh and Delhi. She had truly disappeared.

Twelve

I wrote to Aunty Sarah and she replied often as did Gem but Ivan was busy practicing law and his letters became few and far between eventually stopping all together. Our lives were changing too. School days were over, there were new goals to attain, new lessons to be learnt, new loves, new adventures.

One year in Calcutta made a big difference. I wrote to Gem, "It's sultry and exciting. We visited the marble palace with friends. It was so beautiful. The nightclubs are groovy and Pam Crane, the crooner has a sexy voice. We went to the docks and ate prawns, which were simply huge. If you saw the new market and all the people that walk around in it, you'd go crazy. I like the flower market best, especially the roses. Wish you were here!"

Gem replied, "write some more, I almost feel as if I'm there, you are so lucky. I'm madly in love with Chris and Kasgunj. Aunty Sarah is well but having some trouble with her eyes. I read to her sometimes. Thanks for the magazines, I've learned to sew from Chris's Mum and I've made a patchwork skirt, which looks really great. Wish you were here!"

I didn't wish I was there. Growing up held it's own fascination. When it was time to leave college, the days took on a different hue. New acquaintances, new friendships coupled with new environments, which slid us into experiences of a different kind. Gem and letters to her and Aunty Sarah took a back seat. I was moving forward into a different world; ambition was of a different kind. Relationships with new people dominated and before long I too was thrown headlong into that emotion which is much sought but which leaves one feeling dispossessed of proper sense and where impulse seems to predominate. Romances were becoming a major event in my life but so were fears of taking the wrong decision of making a wrong choice. Besides which I hadn't come into contact with men of my own community apart from family and becoming a part of a family whose ways, religion, traditions and culture were different to mine made me hesitate to take the next step. All my illusions of relationships and partnerships were undergoing change. My mind and my heart didn't seem to be in synchronization. My heart was pulling in one direction and my mind another with its rationalization and logic and putting up barriers to what my heart wanted.

On the whole, Anglo-Indians had made great strides in rehabilitating themselves, those left in India were able to establish themselves as being well educated and cultured and most were doing well in their chosen fields, be it business or profession. Many had established themselves as educators and populated most of the Anglo-Indian and English medium schools as teachers and administrators. Their tradition of being loyal and hard workers were maintained and they were most often chosen over their wholly Indian counter parts when a choice was deemed necessary. Not to say there weren't the odd few who couldn't quite make it and were forced to live in straightened circumstances but this too was true of all communities and so it came as a surprise to face discrimination in this day and age but I suppose sometimes the remnants of an earlier period would rear its head and put to shame the progress that was so often bragged about. In heated moments, I was referred to as a "dingo" which was the derogatory term applied to Anglo-Indians by certain individuals who thought themselves to be superior. Dingoes in actuality are Australian prairie dogs and I suppose the term was used because many Anglo-Indians had emigrated to Australia but how and why it came to be used for members of our community quite escapes me.

To top it all, Aunty Sarah, my long time mentor, decided she had enough of the earthly existence and quietly slipped from the world, which had in any case, lost most of its appeal. The loss of sight put paid to her revels into the fantasy worlds woven by authors, her only consolation being Ivan, who had excelled himself and become a lawyer with his own practice in Delhi. Despite all his entreaties, she would not budge and one night she passed quietly through into the other realm. As she had lived so she went with the minimum amount of fuss, stately to the last; every inch the lady. I became the proud possessor of English hats and hat boxes and numerous books which she had selected to be given to me but it didn't quite make up for not having her around, and not receiving her well written mail and the snippets of information she constantly imparted.

Gem's letter informing me of Shaitan Singh's invasion of Manota was another shock but was the perfect solution to a sorrowing heart. A remedy was necessary to oust the sorrow and required something more than the comfort of soothing words. I resolved to undertake the expulsion of the present unworthy occupants and with determination set off to Kasgunj to achieve my goal.

Thirteen

Chris was having a hard time of it. His father's temperament was getting worse and worse. His mother bore the brunt of it as she would try to hide her meagre savings from him, but if she didn't part with the money for the local moonshine, he would beat her severely. Chris tried his level best to protect her and in the bargain would get beaten by his father as well. One day trying to protect his mother, Chris hit his father over the head with a shovel. He fell down and didn't get up again. At his mother's urgings he ran away and hid himself in the vault. That was the only place he knew where he could hide. That's where Gem found him.

"The police are looking for you," she said, "he's dead, you hit him too hard".

"I don't care," Chris had said stubbornly, "he was rotten.."

"I know," Gem had replied soothingly, "your Mum told them the whole story but they still want to question you.."

"What should I do, Gem?" he asked her.

"Stay here, I think it will be safe...I'll bring you food and some clothes, a blanket to sleep on, it's cold in here," she replied.

"But I can't stay here forever.." Chris said.

"No you can't, but...I don't know what's going to happen Chris, we just have to wait a while."

Chris nodded in agreement. He had tried hard to hide the tears from Gem but she had known and in her own way had tried to convey her sympathy to him. She had been certain that although he had pretended not to care he had still been remorseful over what had happened. That had been his father after all, Chris had feelings for him and to be the cause of his death had lain heavily on him.

In the meantime, Manota was seeing unusual activity. It had become a den of thieves, a hideout for murderers, and robbers who conducted their business without a thought for the hapless people they robbed. Little did Uncle Cyril know what nefarious activity he was plunging Manota into and if he did know I doubt whether he would have desisted in ruining the place. It didn't belong to him, so why should he concern himself with taking care of it. His only aim was a quick buck and this he achieved easily. Shaitan Singh was a dacoit and he easily persuaded Uncle Cyril to sell the house for a paltry sum of six thousand rupees. He had a band of the most awful men. Manota and the fort like house was ideal for their purposes, who would look for them in so respectable an establishment, rightly they thought themselves safe and the high walls which afforded a clear view of the surrounding countryside, with only a single look out, could give them a fair warning of approaching danger and they could escape from the door near the stables which led directly to the village. There was sufficient space to stable their horses and other cattle, a strong room for their loot, it's a wonder our ancestors didn't turn in their graves. Their main targets were the rich businessmen who travelled from Kasgunj to Agra and surrounding areas. Sometimes the trains were targeted too but apart from the villagers who were too poor to be worth looting they managed to keep themselves well occupied and busier than bees with their practiced profession, if one can call robbing a profession too.

Their source of information on rich travellers mainly came from their friends and relatives who worked in the banks and hotels and whom they bribed lavishly with some of the spoils, so with such accurate information they never missed a target and before long the pucca dillan was full to overflowing. From time to time, a few of his trusted men and himself would undertake a journey to Delhi where the goods were disposed off and the money shared out among them. Contrary to expectations, they didn't indulge themselves in wine, women and song. Wine definitely, the local brew supplied from the village, but not women, their own wives and children lived with them and to all intents and purposes it resembled a normal village household with rather more than just family members.

No one making a visit would think otherwise. Dancing women were the only entertainment at festival time but mostly they maintained low profiles. They had several run ins with the police but were always able to escape easily. The police were never able to establish where the dacoits hid or perhaps they really didn't want to locate their hideout. As it is, they were always short of men and the *hawaldars* were mostly family men. Chasing dacoits with outdated weapons all over the countryside was definitely not their cup of tea, it was preferable to pretend ignorance.

Since none of the family members thought to visit at that time, they felt themselves to be quite safe. But they hadn't reckoned with Chris.

Chris was getting bored with being cooped up in the secret room. Sometimes when it was dark he would go out for some fresh air but he was always afraid of being seen. Gem's visits were awaited anxiously but she couldn't come very often for fear of being followed and giving his hiding place away. Besides the village was ripe with rumours of a doghead who had come down from the mountains and taken residence near the village. The people were afraid to move out after dark for fear of being a victim. Chris was afraid for Gem too. Probably a wolf being mistaken for a werewolf which supposedly existed in the middle ages and were called dogheads. The tribe had dogheads and wore cloaks of fur subsisting on a diet of flesh, like cannibals and lived in caves in the mountains. Whenever something unexplainable happened in the village superstitious stories would do the rounds. Whatever it was in reality, Chris didn't want Gem to take any risks. When Gem wrote about the werewolf that was haunting the village, I informed her that St. Christopher had been a werewolf too but after he had converted to Christianity he lost the animalistic side of him and became a normal human. People who travelled a lot prayed to St. Christopher to protect them on their journeys. I told Gem to do the same and nothing would attack her but she scoffed at the idea of prayer. She showed my letter to Chris who was battling a bout of depression and he looked at her his eyes bright.

"I've thought of something, bring me a torch and a whole lot of batteries," he had told Gem.

"Why? What you gonna do with it. I hope you're not going to go out in the nights, it's not safe," she told him.

"I've an idea, Gem, I think I will go to Manota. There's nobody living there now. I will be safe there..."

"I'm scared Chris, it might be too dangerous, please..." she had pleaded to no avail, Chris had been adamant. He had insisted that she get him the torch and batteries. He had been determined to go.

"Can I go with you too, please I'd like...." He cut her short;

"No, Gem don't insist, I don't think it will be too safe.." but she had flown into a rage, "I knew it was dangerous, I don't want you to go there," she looked at him with tears drowning her eyes. "You're all I've got, why the hell are you so stubborn?"

She had jumped up in fury and he had grinned at her teasingly.

"Did I tell you how cute you look when you're annoyed?"

Gem had wailed and thrown herself at him and they had both sprawled backwards onto the floor.

"I'll get you the torch and batteries if you let me come with you," but Chris refused.

"It will be difficult you returning alone, I won't feel comfortable." She had pleaded but his mind had been made up and she had to concede defeat.

"It's getting late Gem, bring some food as well." He had called after her.

Gem had run all the way back home. The sun had already set and she knew it would get dark soon. Chris's mother didn't ask why she had wanted the torch but had refused to part with money for the batteries. Finally Gem had decided it was easier to take a few litres of kerosene oil and some rags to Chris and they had fashioned flame torches with a piece of wood which Chris felt would serve as well, infact better. Anxiously Gem had watched him disappear into the night.

Chris's journey to Manota had been uneventful. He had discovered Shaitan Singh in residence with his men and their families. It had taken him the better part of the night to return and exhausted he had lain down to sleep wondering if Gem would come. She hadn't come that day or the next. Wondering how to get word to her, he had decided he himself had to make the trip to the village to apprise her of the fact he had returned and was in need of sustenance. Gem came in the afternoon on the off chance that he might have returned and was contrite he had been left with no food. She fetched food and water, spending the night while he told her what he had found at Manota. The next day Gem made inquiries and told him all she could discover, Shaitan Singh had apparently bought the property. He asked Gem to write and let us know what had happened. Chris was sure we were ignorant of the facts and this was true, no one had thought to inform us of Manota changing hands.

Fourteen

Chris went back to Manota. "Shaitan Singh," he called, standing beneath the wall. He had to squint as the sunlight dazzled the eyes. His red hair was concealed beneath a cloth turban, which he had soaked in water before the long trek.

"Kaun?" Shaitan Singh looked down at the figure he didn't recognize. Several men, women and children peered over the wall. A dog barked from further along.

"I've come to meet you. I have something I want to discuss."

"Come up," he said briefly.

He seated him on a *charpoy* in the cool of the *verandah*. One of the women poured water from the *chattie* and offered it to him. He had drunk thirstily before returning the glass.

"I want to join your gang," Chris said bluntly and Shaitan Singh had stood somewhat agitated.

"What gang?"

"Look let's not pretend," Chris had said boldly, "we both stand to gain from this. You know I'm wanted for the murder of my father and if I didn't have good intentions would I have come and placed myself in your hands?"

"What do you want?" he asked him.

"I want to join you, I want a share, like the other men, you can trust me," Chris said.

Shaitan Singh had silently contemplated Chris while his men had squatted in groups, eyeing Chris intently.

"How do I know you won't betray us?" he asked him.

"Because I'm wanted by the police just as you are, would I go and place myself in their hands? You're an outlaw, so am I, that makes us brothers."

Shaitan Singh had nodded his head, what he had said had made sense, he could see the thawing in the faces around him. Chris had been accepted.

Chris couldn't resist temptation, for someone who had so little; it was only natural that he should now feel that this was his golden opportunity, the only way to rid them of poverty. The road ahead seemed clear and he looked in anticipation to a new future where finally the dust of their old existence could be shaken and they could begin afresh.

When Gem found out what he had planned she was horrified. "If they ever find out you plan to have them captured, they'll kill you Chris. Please, please be careful."

"They won't find out," he assured her.

"We have a way now Gem, our future is guaranteed, but

don't tell Mum just yet, I still have to figure out how am I to loot them and then leave that here."

"We'll have money soon Gem," he told her although he wasn't very confident that he could make it happen but he didn't want Gem to see that, "we can leave this place, go somewhere far where nobody will find us," he told her.

"My Mum's sick Chris, I won't be able to leave her just yet...but you could take your Mum and brother and go. I can come later, when my Mother is well."

"No!" He insisted.

"But Chris.." she tried persuading him.

"No, Gem, everyone here knows we are inseparable, aren't the police already harassing you to tell them my whereabouts? If I go without you, they will put you under tremendous pressure and they will have you watched....perhaps they watch you even now...are you careful...Gem?" he had been anxious that she might have been followed.

"I thought of that too...I always make sure I'm not followed, I'm scared Chris...what's going to happen to us?" she wailed.

"We'll get through this Love...we'll wait till your Mum's well.." he hadn't been as confident as he sounded but Gem had seemed pacified for the time being. They had snuggled down together under the blanket. For some nights Gem stayed with Chris returning home only in the early mornings. Shaitan Singh in an expansive mood had provided them with a small chappard where they had had a measure of privacy from the inquisitive eyes of the families billeted there.

Fifteen

While Chris ran about with the dacoits, Ivan had come home to Chhaoni. The stone Buddha head was a surprise. It couldn't have been anything else. Who would have thought a few hundred years after it had been buried the soil would startle labourers by disclosing a tiny portion and humans being naturally curious, would, true to form, dig further to uncover that which had been hidden. How it came into existence buried in that exact location had archeologists fantasizing on a new venture of uncovering a Buddhist civilization they had not thought existed until this discovery. Government departments couldn't quite dampen their enthusiasm despite delays in permission, after all it had lain there for a few hundred years, what did it matter if it lay a few more months cosily buried in the soil and after all it was better to stretch out the time of making decisions.

Haste makes waste, was the motto of Government departments and the employees adhered strictly to this rule and emulated the slowest moving creatures on the earth which were their role models. How better to conduct their laborious work which took months in the pondering and more months in the execution, with small delays of files being misplaced and the unimportant details of money changing hands before the just as mysteriously misplaced, mysteriously appeared again. All part and parcel of the well oiled process, which was a marvel of innovative planning and execution almost perfected by finely honed thinking and skills of organization.

"Two hundred only," said the Patwari, "Sahib, everything is so expensive nowadays, even sugar for the tea..." he sighed meaningfully, looking at Ivan with soulful eyes which couldn't quite hide the avarice lurking there. The Patwari was the village babu, incharge of the land documents.

"I know, I know," Ivan commiserated "make it a hundred."

"Hundred and fifty."

"Done!" said Ivan promptly and the little old man smiled his oily smile disclosing rotten teeth disfigured by pan stains.

"Ofcourse there's my boss, another three hundred would help him to put his signature to the forms, you do understand, his signature is very important without which it cannot be forwarded. Did I mention that the clerk has to take it to another department, only fifty rupees and the official who stamps it, perhaps rupees hundred would help him speed up the process..." he trailed off sadly, "we try to help everyone, we work so hard."

"Five hundred," said Ivan parting with the money, which disappeared immediately, he placed it on the table.

Suddenly genial the man bellowed "*Chaprasi*, lazy fellow, don't you see we have a visitor, where is the tea?" then in a confiding tone he spoke aside to Ivan, "it is very hard to get good help these days, the *daftaries* don't work well but what can we do Sahib, we do our best with whatever we are given." Nodding his head, Ivan tried hard not to let his amusement show. The man cleared his throat, then said timidly, "Oh yes, there is a small detail that I forgot to mention." He shuffled the papers on his desk briskly while Ivan waited. "This figure in this column has to be changed."

"Changed?" Ivan raised an eyebrow.

"Yes, it's a matter of a small percentage, ten percent to be exact....ofcourse we could leave it as it is but it may take some time, you understand?"

"How long?" Ivan questioned frostily trying hard not to let his irritation show.

"Six months, maybe eight, I try my best but there are so many others, you do understand.."

"Yes, yes, alright I'll add the ten percent."

"I'll give you a new set of forms. If you can bring it in tomorrow, I'll personally take the file for the signatures." His eyes gleamed happily. "Don't worry Sahib, all will be done. Just three days, I give you my word, just leave it to me."

Ivan leaned back against the back of the chair he was sitting in and smiled in relief. Thank God that was over! Sipping the tea, which surprisingly tasted good he surveyed the office he was sitting in. Dust swirled in the rays of the sun, which penetrated the old shutters. Cobwebs hung from a ceiling which had once been white but which now had deteriorated to a dirty gray. Green paint peeled from the blistered walls along which piles of dusty papers, files and registers stacked haphazardly gave the room a cluttered appearance. Amidst the paper chaos the clerk sat comfortably, his thin frame hunched in the wooden chair, his round glasses perched on his broad nose as he peered short-sightedly at the papers on his desk. Wouldn't do to let the Sahib see how little work he had. Pretending a show off business, he sent the peon ferreting among the dusty papers dislodging some more of the dust motes, which rose in spurts before settling back again.

"I'll return tomorrow," said Ivan hurriedly getting to his feet, "thank you and namaste!" he called as he went out of the door.

"*Namaste! namaste!*" the clerk called happily, relieved he could now get back to his important routine. "Fool!" he shouted at the peon, "what are you fiddling with the papers for?"

"But *babuji*, you said…"

"Never mind, never mind…I wish to rest now." Within a few minutes, settled comfortably in his chair, his snores permeated the office. A lone fly buzzed happily in synchronization with the whirring of the fan. Against the frame of the door, the peon drowsily nodded, drugged by the heat and the days, which dragged in monotonous regularity.

Sixteen

Renovations on the house began next, the modernizing of the toilets especially. He intended to spend more time at Chhaoni now that he had taken on two more associates in his law firm. He missed the freedom of the old days, the *shikar*. "Wonder what Chris is upto" he thought, "must pay him a visit, haven't seen the guy in ages."

When Ivan learned that Chris was wanted for the murder of his father, he was more determined than ever to pay his family a visit. Chris's mother welcomed him warmly,

"Why Ivan, how smart you are.." she smiled at him.

"Nice to see you Aunty...how are you'll managing..."

"We're fine Ivan, Gem has taken over the sewing, everything's alright, really."

"Gem?"

"You haven't met Gem?"

"No, who is she?"

"Chris's girl, Martha's daughter, the poor child has had a hard time of it. Martha's always ailing. It's a pity she won't stop drinking that local rubbish. It's not fair to Gem... she never complains you know. What will you drink Ivan, can I offer you a cup of tea?" She smiled at him.

"Tea will be nice. Who's Martha?"

"She's the local school mistress but if she even attends two days of school or teaches those kids anything....I think the Inspector is going to have her replaced and who can blame him. It's Gem I worry about."

"And Chris?" asked Ivan, "where has he gone?"

She shook her head sadly, "he's in trouble Ivan, my boy is in trouble. He was just trying to protect me...Jim was always a brute. He's a good boy...never hurts anyone." Her worn face creased with the worry of years screwed into lines of pain. Ivan pitied her, she looked so despairing.

"I know," said Ivan, "perhaps I can help him, I'm a lawyer you know, I can get him proper counsel."

She looked at Ivan hopefully and he tried to reassure her, "Chris will have to stand trial but if you will let me help I'll do my damnedest to get him off with a light sentence. Aunty don't cry...please..." but she could not stop the tears.

Chris's brother came in while Ivan was trying to console his mother. He was a young lad now but still with his mop of red hair,

"Hi Ivan!"

"Hi!"

Chris's brother, Stevie was more comfortable in the local

dialect (a mixture of Hindi and Urdu) "so you must have heard about Chris, I'm personally glad he took out the swine."

"Steve.." his mother admonished.

"You always liked to pretend he was okay but he brought you nothing but grief."

"Enough, Ivan doesn't want to hear you talk nonse.."

"It's okay, thanks, this tea is good."

"What do you do Steve?"

"Nothing much, just hang out.."

"My children never did stand a chance for anything" and Chris's mother was crying again. The futility of their whole lives depressed her often, especially now when she thought of Chris.

Suddenly Ivan was confronted by a slip of a girl with light hair and even lighter eyes. She had entered the room like a whirlwind and stood confronting him, her fists clenched. She looked like a child but he could see her figure was fully developed. She shouted at him now, "what did you do to Aunty…why have you made her cry."

"I haven't done.."

"Aunty…what did he do.."

"Gem, Gem it's Okay, this is Ivan…Chris's friend, he's a lawyer, he wants to help Chris."

"Ivan? Oh."

"Hi.."

"Go away," said Gem rudely "you can't help him, besides we don't know where he is.."

"I think you do," said Ivan quietly, "I really can help him, I want to help him."

"There's nothing you can do, he's run away and I don't think he's coming back, what can you do anyway except get him hauled into jail...please go back to your fine house and leave us alone...you don't belong here..."

"Gem! Why are you behaving like this? He's Chris's friend.."

"Fine friend," scoffed Gem and stamped her foot.

Ivan was surprised. Gem seemed angry with him for some reason. He was sure she knew where Chris was but she wasn't going to tell him.

"I think we should tell Chris that Ivan is ready to help Gem.."

"Auntie!" Gem was trying to warn aunt not to say anything.

"No Gem. Let Chris take the decision, he cannot stay hidden forever. Ivan, we'll get a message to Chris, I'll let you know what happens."

"Alright," said Ivan standing up, "just tell Chris I'll do my best for him. I won't let him down. Nice meeting you Gem..." he said sardonically and she had the grace to blush, colour diffusing her face. Ivan laughed to himself as he waved at them.

"Why were you so rude to him Gem? It's just not like you."

"I know but I never liked him, he would come home and Chris would become a different person...I just couldn't stand him."

"Well we need him now, he can help Chris, speak to him this evening...see what he says." Gem nodded her head.

Chris had thought about Ivan a lot when Gem brought him the news much against her will, she had not wanted to tell him but fearing he might see him on one of his nightly forays and then get angry at her for hiding the news from him, she thought it better to disclose it to him herself. She told him that Ivan was serious about helping him although she herself had misgivings about getting him involved.

"But I think it's just what we needed Gem," said Chris, "I've been thinking Ivan might be the right person to tell about Shaitan Singh and his men, if he gives the information to the police..."

"But Chris, then he'll know you're hiding there, he might not be pleased, he might tell the police about you.."

"He's not like that, he won't let me down." He hugged Gem. He knew her dislike and mistrust of Ivan stemmed from neglect.

"Forget about the dacoits Chris, we've got troubles as it is, let's not add to them."

"I'll feel safer if they were safely locked away...besides I have a plan to take their loot, if we are to use it, it would be much better to be rid of them...don't worry about it Gem, I'll think of something." He was kissing her, pressing his body close and Gem forgot about Ivan as she responded to his lovemaking.

Ivan was dreaming, the woman in the portrait was trying to tell him something. He reached out to her and she would step back a little, just out of reach. Again he stretched out his hand to her and she moved away. She was trying to tell him something but he didn't understand....

He woke in a bath of perspiration. Moonlight was filtering in through the open window; there was slight breeze. A soft sound distracted him, there it was again, something came through the window and fell on the floor with a soft thump. Cautiously he got out of bed and tiptoed to the window. A man was standing beneath the window ledge, his face clearly defined in the moonlight for a moment before he slipped into the shadows again. Ivan recognized Chris, he went downstairs and unbolted the door and Chris slipped into the house.

"Sorry to disturb you....I had to wait until nobody was around."

"Come to the bedroom," said Ivan, "we can talk there".

Chris nodded and they went along the corridor and seated themselves on the bed.

"I don't want you to think even for a minute that I'm going to give myself up Ivan, but I need your help on something else."

"Look Chris, I can really help you, we'll try and get you the minimum sentence and..."

"No!" Chris interrupted, "I'm not here to discuss that, I know you'll do your best but even one minute in jail will simply kill me...I want you to help me in another way..."

Seventeen

The village had never seen such excitement. The police had come in jeeps silently in the night and without warning. They had then proceeded to Manota on foot and surrounded the house. Both entrances had been sealed tight. It had been a short and bloody battle between the dacoits and the police. Chris having had prior warning of the impending capture had made himself scarce.

"Thanks Ivan," said Inspector Chauhan, "these guys have been a constant thorn in our sides for so long. By the way, you never did tell me how you came by the information?" Chauhan had to call in reinforcements from Agra. They had arrived the same evening when the capture had been planned, so nobody had advance information.

"As you know Manota is part of our family property, we

have some loyal people in the village, I was bound to get the information."

"Well, I suppose the chap didn't want you to give his name, they were much feared around here and it was almost impossible to get anyone to talk." Chauhan stroked his moustache, which curled at the ends. He was very proud of this appendage. He felt it gave him stature although how he thought a moustache could add height to his portly figure was never clear to anyone. "There's something else I wanted to talk to you about," he said now, "our families have known each other for years," he paused looking at Ivan.

Ivan nodded his head, he half guessed what was coming, "you have a friend Chris, I don't suppose he has contacted you, has he?"

"Actually, that's what I wanted to talk to you about too," said Ivan, "what are you going to do about Chris?"

"If we can find him, he'll have to spend some time in jail and he'll have a trial. His mother has given a written statement and so has his brother and a few of the other villagers who saw what happened. It's a clear case of self-defence. He can get himself a good lawyer."

"I'm a lawyer," said Ivan, "I'll see to his defense, but first we have to find some way of making him give himself up.

I had written to inform Ivan I would be visiting and hoped he would be in residence but not knowing whether he would be there or not, I decided it better to take accommodation on arrival at Kasgunj. I had little idea then how I would rid Manota of its unappealing occupants apart from informing the police, but I wasn't too certain of getting much help from them. I had spoken to Dad but with his busy schedule in the school he was unable to get away, he advised me to wait until he could get free, but that was the last thing I wanted to do. My only hope seemed to be Ivan and with that in mind, I had written a letter and then without waiting for a reply set off for my destination.

In the meantime, Ivan went to see Chris's mother. He found her helping Gem at Gem's house. Gem's mother had died; they were preparing her for burial. Some of the village women had offered to help. Ivan was sorry for the girl who looked at him with large teary eyes made red by weeping.

"Please allow me to take care of everything.." he offered.

Gem was glad to hand over the arrangements to Ivan who assisted by Steve, had her mother buried with as little fuss as possible. A few of the villagers attended out of curiosity and some because they felt sorry for Gem but that was all. Chris's absence was noticed by all but none commented on it. Later Ivan told Chris's mother what the Inspector had said and she said she would try and get Gem to change Chris's mind but she didn't promise anything.

Ivan was busy for a few days so he didn't go to see Gem immediately but when he did he told her to stay at Manota. Chris would be able to stay there too, quite safely. The police were satisfied that there was no loot to be found and they assumed the dacoits had hid it some other place. Chris had never told Ivan that he had looted the dacoits. He had hidden it all in an aperture of the tunnels, which had been blocked up as part of it had caved in. So Ivan too thought the dacoits had a different place for their loot.

It was three days later that he decided to go at night to the vaults and talk to Chris. He had sent a note to Gem by one of his servants to tell Chris to meet him there in the secret chamber. Armed with a powerful torch and a *lathi* he went to the tomb. For at least fifteen minutes he stood silently in the shadows and looked around to make sure that no one had followed him. The villagers were superstitious and mostly they avoided this area, so he didn't have any fear of them being around but still, he thought it prudent to check.

The portrait as always fascinated him. He marvelled once again at the beauty of the woman. Unconsciously perhaps, it was because of her he had never married. He had dated plenty of women but they had all fallen short of his ideal.

Chris was not there. The room was empty. He waited for almost two hours but Chris never came.

The next morning Ivan went to Manota. Gem was not there either. Nobody was around. While returning to Chhaoni he went to Chris's mother's house. There was no answer to his knock. Gem's house too was silent. He questioned some of the villagers but nobody knew anything. Sometime, perhaps while everybody was sleeping, they had all left. When they had gone or where, nobody knew.

Eighteen

On arrival at Kasgunj, I had been directed by one of the porters to the Raja's palace, which had now been converted into a hotel. The present Raja, Govind Hari Singh Aditya, was an environmentalist and he had all the rooms with running hot and cold water by using a *gobar* gas plant. The town too had changed considerably with many hotels and new dwellings all along the roads. It was teeming with life, the sights and sounds reminiscent of other cities of India. The vegetable vendors, the hawkers with their *thela gaadis* brimming with plastic, brass, copper or aluminium ware. The flies were happily savouring the uncovered dishes at the wayside food stalls, the rickshaws neck to neck with opulent cars inching over the road and jamming the traffic, while impatient scooterists yelled expletives and wove their way in between narrow spaces and unsuspecting pedestrians were jostled and pushed to make space for yet another pedestrian. And the dust mingled with the exhaust and coated everything with a film of greasy grime. This was progress, the small town had changed to a city and the increase in population and pollution made certain the transition could be deemed effective. Only the sweetmeat shops had not changed. Thickened buffalo milk was still sweetened with a white powdery substance and served in earthen *khullars*, which were used in place of glasses, and the *rabbari* was still as mouth meltingly delicious. I have heard it spoken with authority that Kasgunj can boast to make the best Indian sweets in Uttar Pradesh and if my opinion were solicited; I would have to agree with them.

Ivan soon got news of my arrival and insisted on me moving to Chhaoni. I was installed in Aunty Sarah's old room which brought back memories of wonderful times which were made more wonderful by a remarkable woman with a large heart and a sharp mind who could turn the words of Browning and Keats into magical symphonies and David Copperfield and Charles Dickens into the main course of a sumptuous meal.

Later, Ivan related the events which had taken place at Manota, the capture of the dacoits which lost none of its spiciness in the telling and then he told me about Chris's predicament and why he had put Gem to stay there after her Mother's death.

"That way she and Chris could have been together safely until something was settled about his case." Their disappearance concerned him greatly. He worried about them.

"I can't understand it," he said, "where could they have

gone and how," we were having dinner together on the verandah.

"Since Chris didn't want to give himself up, he probably persuaded them to go away with him."

"I made inquiries at the station, they didn't buy any tickets, nobody seems to have seen them."

"It's only three hours to Agra, perhaps they went by bus."

"I didn't think of that," said Ivan, "you must be right, I'll make inquiries tomorrow."

When dinner was over, Ivan poured himself a brandy and came back to sit near me.

"I've been thinking", he said, "I was wondering if Chris had anything to do with the disappearance of the dacoit's loot."

"Why haven't they discovered anything?"

"I was talking to Inspector Chauhan today, and he told me that Shaitan Singh had given a statement that their loot had disappeared from a locked room. Infact it seems they keep disrupting the central jail fighting among each other. I have a feeling Shaitan Singh's days are numbered."

"You think Chris took it?"

"What other explanation could there be. Chauhan thinks Shaitan Singh has stashed it somewhere but I think it's Chris. There couldn't be any other explanation for his disappearance. Tell me, would his mother and brother go with him without any means to live, and Gem?"

"You're right," I grabbed Ivan's arm in excitement.

"Hey!"

"I'm so glad for them Ivan...I hope it's true. I hope they have the loot. Look what their lives were like, they had no hope for anything living here, now they have a chance at something decent."

Ivan was thoughtful, "Yes...I see what you mean, you liked Gem, didn't you?"

"She's a nice person."

"What about your relationship?"

"Another one which didn't quite make it, I think I'm going to be an old maid and infact I like living alone."

"People need each other," he said, "if they were really honest they would admit they are co-dependent. A woman needs a man just as he needs her. Those who say they can be happy living alone are lying, it just means the natural urges have been suppressed and they can pretend to themselves that they are happy alone." I made a face at him. He was so right but I preferred to pretend for the time being and he smiled at my non-reply. We left it at that and I left Ivan smoking on the verandah and went to bed.

The next day Ivan took me into town with him. My trips to Kasgunj these days were far different from the earlier ones. Ivan had a jeep and we crossed the river via the aquaduct, which was as imposing as ever. We had an invitation to lunch at the Raja's residence. He wanted some advice from Ivan on his land matters.

The palace sprawled over half an acre. An old brick building still retaining some of its grandeur with well kept gardens, patterned in squares, lush green lawns, a breath of fresh air among the arid landscape mostly denuded of any greenery due to excessive construction.

Govind Hari Singh, neatly turned out in a safari suit, met us at the entrance.

"I'm taking you for lunch at the hotel's dining room," he said, "I have a surprise for you, there is somebody I want you to meet."

"Somebody? Who is it?"

Govind just laughed, "Patience, you'll soon meet her."

She was a surprise and had Ivan gasping. I thought she looked familiar but I couldn't place her, I wasn't sure if I had met her before.

"This is Alaida Patricia Dunn," said Govind, "she has come all the way from Coleraine."

"Coleraine!" I squeaked and glanced at Ivan who for some reason seemed to have been struck dumb.

"And these are your Indian relations Ivan and Charl," Govind continued with the introductions. "Come let us sit, then you can talk."

"Relations!! Are we related?"

Alaida laughed softly. She was beautiful, her pale skin almost transparent, with a light dusting of freckles, auburn hair and eyes like emeralds. She was slim and very tall, almost as tall as Ivan who was a good six feet. She spoke with a pronounced Irish accent, a lilt to her voice.

"Maybe we're not," she said, "but some of our ancestors were the same. I'm a descendant of William Gardner and according to Goveend, you are too," she emphasized the 'ee' in Govind's name drawing them out.

During the meal she told us she was a student of history and when she had found some old family papers pertaining to William Gardner, his career in the army and his advent to India, she had decided to see the place herself. She had done some research and the story had fascinated her. This trip was to try and discover whatever she could. Her travel agency had booked her into the Raja's palace and when she had begun asking questions, Govind had met her himself and he had told her about us.

"I'll take you to his tomb," said Ivan and I looked at him. All this while Ivan had not spoken a word, he had only stared at her and I had noticed she had become a little uncomfortable under his gaze. I had been puzzled by his behaviour; he normally never behaved in such a rude fashion.

Alaida seemed glad he had finally spoken, "I should love that, infact I'd be glad if you could tell me everything you know."

"All in good time," smiled Ivan, "would you like to come and stay with us a few days? It would be a novel experience but I must warn you, apart from a decent toilet, it's a little primitive."

She looked excited, "Oh, I'd love that.."

"An authentic village experience," I added.

"Ivan, you were behaving very strangely," we were speeding over the roads in his jeep suddenly he seemed in a hurry to get home.

"I could hardly believe my eyes!"

"What!"

"It's her,"

"Who?"

"Don't be dumb," he said brusquely, "didn't you recognize her,"

"Recognize who.."

"Alaida"

"I haven't met her before."

Ivan looked at me in exasperation, "the portrait, in the vaults, now do you understand."

"The vaults? Oh my gosh! Are you sure?"

"Yes, I've looked at it so many times, that's why I couldn't speak. I just wanted to go on looking at her. She's so beautiful." He sighed, "do you think you could get the house spruced up for her.." he looked at me anxiously, "I shouldn't have invited her to stay, she won't enjoy it."

"She was thrilled to be invited, stop being stupid, you've done up the house, I think she'll enjoy the experience."

"We'll get some more help from the village tomorrow.."

I laughed at him and he grinned at me, "I feel like a teenager again."

"And I know why." I gave him a knowing look and Ivan avoided my eyes, but he was smiling. We were both well out of our teens, but from the look in Ivan's eyes, he seemed to be experiencing symptoms of a teenager. "Did love at first sight really exist?" I wondered, as we seemed to fly over the roads on our way home.

Ivan brought Alaida back with him the next day; we were seated on the verandah sipping the fruit punch I had made earlier.

"Tell me how he met his *Begum*," said Alaida, she spoke with a soft Irish brogue.

"The story is rather famous, it's been mentioned in several books as well. He was sent to negotiate a treaty with the Princess of Cambay and while he was in the *durbar* a curtain was pulled aside and he caught a glimpse of the most beautiful black eyes in the world. She was veiled as was common for most Muslim princesses and he could only see her eyes. That's how he fell in love." Ivan was laughing, "like a fairy tale don't you think."

"That's not the whole story," I interrupted, "he couldn't concentrate properly on the treaty after that and the girl was bold, she allowed him to look at her a second time and he was hooked. He demanded her hand from her father with whom he had been negotiating and was pretty offended when her relations refused his proposal. Well, they thought about it again and I'm sure he must have used some gentle persuasion as well and since he was the ambassador they changed their minds and promised her to him but then all didn't go smoothly. There was trouble at the court and they had to flee. This is where he built his palace and where you are sitting now, is part of what used to be the Turkish baths."

Alaida was thrilled with the story, "he's such a romantic figure, there aren't men like him around nowadays," she glanced sideways at Ivan who suddenly became busy fiddling with his cigarette lighter and I looked at him in surprise. Had I made such a remark he would have jumped down my throat by now.

"There might be some romantic ones around but most men, in my opinion are too afraid to admit their feelings openly for fear of rejection. It's not that there aren't any of the Colonel's type around but that they don't have his type of courage."

Alaida was laughing, "I do think we're going to get along wonderfully!" she exclaimed and Ivan smiled at us a glint in his eye,

"Shall I make myself scarce if you are going to go on a male bashing spree?"

"Not at all," she smiled sweetly at him, "what do you do Ivan?"

"I'm a barrister, I don't really live here much, my practice is in Delhi but I have two partners who run the show when I'm away."

"And you?" she turned to me smiling, "this fruit punch is very refreshing..."

"At the moment I'm footloose and fancy free but I work for a tea company. When I'm ready I'll think of something else to do as well, what about you?"

"As you already know I'm a student of history but I also work part time in the library back home. There's no tea grown here or is there?"

"I don't live here," I grinned at her, "I live in Darjeeling that's where the tea is grown and where I work."

"Ofcourse!" she exclaimed, "Darjeeling tea."

"Alaida," called Ivan, "what sort of place is your family home? Is it a sort of castle?"

"It's reminiscent of a castle without actually being one and the estates are quite substantial. My uncle has a hard time maintaining everything."

"What about your immediate family?"

"My parents were pretty old, they passed away within a span of a year or so. It's almost four years since I lost them. I live with my uncle now."

"I'm sorry, you must be missing them a lot."

"Actually, they got me when they were pretty old already and I was basically closer to my nanny than my Mum, but still, I do miss them even now."

"I'll take you to see the tomb and the family vaults later," said Ivan, "tell me about Coleraine…"

"I'll just check on how lunch is coming along," I said and moved off to the kitchen leaving them to continue the conversation.

We made plans during lunch to take Alaida to see all the sights and to visit Manota as well.

"But I want to do it that way," she insisted, she seemed to be enjoying the simple Indian food, especially the *makki rotis*, "I want to go over the river in that ancient boat, I want to pull the rope and I want to walk the five miles to Manota or go in a bullock cart. Please Ivan, it will be a new experience for me, I'm really excited…"

"It will be hot and dusty," warned Ivan. "I'll see what I can do about arranging a bullock cart."

"I'll pack us a picnic tomorrow," I said, "I wonder what state Manota is in."

"I can't believe there's been so much excitement around here, this is really material for a book…you must write it all down…this is …Oh I'm so glad I came," she said.

"That's an idea, I think that will be my new project and if Manota's in any shape I think that's where I'll ..."

"You're staying here and no argument." Ivan interrupted me, "you can do your writing here in a nice civilized way, Manota won't be fit for you to live in it yet. We'll do something about that later, okay?" I had to agree with him, I had forgotten about the toilets.

"So shall we take a walk to the fields, I'll show you where the Buddha's head is first, then we'll go to the tomb. Or, if you prefer, you can rest now and we can go later.."

"No, I'd like to go now if it's okay with you...I'm simply dying to see it all. It's all so different here. Thanks, the lunch was delicious, I've eaten so much but I'm already looking forward to dinner.." this had us all laughing as we strolled into the courtyard.

"We'll need hats," I said and went back in to get some straw ones, which were always kept handy.

The portrait had Alaida spell bound. She could see the striking resemblance to herself and we stood staring at it speculating who the woman could be.

"I do look like her...it's amazing! But I don't think I have her look, she looks so cold, a little venomous, I wish there was some way we could find out her identity... "

"I thought it might be the artist she wanted to murder." We all laughed at that.

"I was dumbstruck when I first saw you, I could hardly speak."

"Oh Ivan, I thought you were just reserved."

"I thought the cat had got Ivan's tongue, he was behaving so out of character.." our laughter echoed in the vaults startling us.

"Maybe the clue to finding out who she was lies with you Alaida?" I said thoughtfully

"Me?"

"Yes, you could go through old photographs of your ancestors, do some research, that sort of thing."

"I see what you mean....yes...there just might be a chance.. now you've given me a project to do.." we smiled at each other.

Early morning, before the sun was up, Alaida saw us down by the river; a well-stocked basket being carted along by Ivan and a jerrycan of water a weight in my hand. A thin mist hung over the river, giving it an eerie look. The old boat rocked gently from its moorings and we climbed aboard.

"The bullock cart will be on the other side," said Ivan, "Shyamlall's son will have got hold of one."

There was a nip in the air and I was glad I had thought to put on a windcheater. Ivan and Alaida were wearing jackets and were oblivious to the cold. We climbed into the boat and Ivan pushed it into the water before getting in. He had removed his socks and shoes so that they didn't get wet. Taking hold of the rope, he and Alaida began energetically pulling on it hand over hand. It was grimy with the dust and dirt of other hands and damp from the river but they didn't seem to mind its condition. The mist swirled about us and when we reached what I thought was the middle, it seemed to get thicker and I had difficulty making Ivan and Alaida out.

There was no fear of us getting lost as the rope was tied at each end of the width of the river to a strong post and by pulling on the rope we would reach the other side unless by some misfortune the rope gave way or the post broke, but that seemed a dim possibility so I sat wrapped in my own thoughts while we crossed the Kala nadi. I supposed the water being blackish in colour had given it its name. It was a tributary of the Ganga and divided Kasgunj and Chhaoni from Manota and other villages.

Ivan began singing in his deep baritone, "Ten green bottles, standing on the wall, ten green bottles, standing on the wall, if one green bottle should accidentally fall, there'll be nine green bottles standing on the wall..." Alaida joined him in the song and their voices floated out over the river.

We reached the other side and I was glad to climb out of the boat, sitting astride a damp piece of wood was not my idea of fun.

"*Kaise ho*, Munnalal?" Ivan greeted the turbaned man sitting on his haunches beside a bullock cart. The bulls shook their heads at us, their cowbells clanging loudly in the silence. Munnalal showed his white teeth in his brown face as he grinned on seeing me,

"Rocky Baba's daughter?" he asked happily and I smiled back at him and nodded in affirmation. He said he remembered me as a kid and I supposed it was possible as we had spent a lot of time roaming around in the gardens.

The roads were still the same sandy stretches, lined on either side by tall screens of sword grass. Time had stood still here; the countryside was unchanged. The fields of mustard were soon visible as the sun began its slow journey across the sky, as were the fields of barley and wheat. I sat opposite Ivan and Alaida in the cart and dozed as the cart moved steadily, the cowbells ringing in my ears. Alaida was wide eyed looking around her. When I glanced at Ivan, he was watching her, a slight smile on his lips.

When I woke up we were almost at our destination and I looked around in surprise. Ivan and Alaida were laughing at me.

"Sleepy head," he said, "you were sleeping like a log and you were catching flies.."

"Indeed I was not," I exclaimed indignantly.

"Your mouth was wide open and you were dribbling like a baby," he teased me.

"Look at the poor graveyard, it's all overgrown, what a state it's in!" I was distressed to see it so unkempt. We had our own family cemetery where Grandpa, Grandma and Grandpa's parents were buried alongside a few other immediate relatives.

"We can get it cleaned up," said Ivan. When we entered Manota, the roofing on the stables looked in need of repair and the big door which lead to the village leaned drunkenly on only a single rusted hinge. We climbed out of the cart and walked up the slope to the house. Alaida had not said a word until we entered the courtyard.

"It's modelled on an English fort," she said, "the design is the same as some of the castles in England and Ireland, this is on a smaller scale ofcourse."

"A miniature," Ivan smiled, "well, our ancestors were English, so I suppose they brought a little of England with them. I surmise they probably copied their English homes to make them feel more comfortable. The one who built this was Tandy the third son of Stewart William Gardner who was the grandson of the first Baron of Uttoxeter. Come on, let's go in so you can see the whole thing."

Alaida stared in awe at the house. It was not what she had expected. Built in the courtyard style, the inner portion resembled more a Greek amphitheatre than an English castle.

"Good Lord!" she exclaimed, "it's so unusual, look at those round Roman pillars, those stairs....Ivan this is so impressive."

"I expect it is, trouble is we've gone so used to seeing it all the time, we hardly notice anything out of the ordinary. There's still no electricity, or running water." He warned her taking in her flushed face surrounded by a mass of curls which had escaped the tight French knot she had scrunched her hair into. Alaida grinned at him in delight.

"I would have been disappointed if it had electricity or running water, this is more authentic. Baths with well water, oil lamps," she hugged herself in glee, her eyes twinkling, "a decent toilet would have been divine I don't think I would have quite enjoyed going out to the fields or the chamber pots." we laughed together. "I'm so excited," she said, "it's still like it was a hundred years ago, this is so wonderful."

Ivan smiled at her enthusiasm. "The Gods had smiled on him the day he met Alaida," he thought, he couldn't believe his good fortune.

"Come on, I'll show you inside," she followed him up the tiered stairs along the verandah and into the living room, further back to the dining hall, the store, the back yard where one could look down on the livestock and granaries and the enormous wooden door connecting the village. Back out into the compound, the wall from where she could see a vast expanse of the plains stretching as far as the eye could see. In the fore-front the graveyard was dotted with marble headstones and thereafter, trees and more trees.

"Are you hungry?"

"A little peckish actually though I ate such a huge breakfast."

"It's the air, it makes you want to nibble all the time. I remember as kids we were always running around with something or other in our hands.

Our feet sank into the sand, which still filled the compound. Grandpa had filled it with river sand when we were little as he thought it would keep us occupied building castles in it. But it was no longer clean like it used to be; dog's dirt, the pellets of goat excreta and bits and piece of paper lay strewn about. The place looked what it was, neglected, abandoned. Only the tall round Roman pillars of the verandah and the imposing staircase leading up to it were as before but the rooms were dirty and dusty, the walls in need of paint. Pigeons were nesting in the rafters of the roof and their droppings were everywhere. But for all that, it still looked grand and I could see Alaida was impressed.

"It's badly neglected but you can still clean it up and with a coat of paint it will look grand again. What's this?" She was staring at the chulas in the kitchen.

"That's the stoves which were used to cook on, it's a typical village method. Certain things are still primitive. If you want to go to the loo, we'll have to go in the fields or behind some bushes."

Alaida's laugh was contagious and we couldn't help laughing with her. The *chatties*, which used to contain fresh water for drinking, were still in their places on the verandah but with nothing in them. All the books, weaponry and other knick-knacks, which used to be in the store, were missing as were the antiques and most of the furniture. Nothing worth anything had been left behind and I was saddened to think of the loss of priceless heritage pieces which had passed onto God only knew, whose hands.

Ivan was talking quietly with Munnalal. I surmised he was making arrangements to get the place cleaned up. Then we trooped down to the well and after allowing Alaida to try her hand at drawing water, we sat in the shade of the old beyr tree which didn't seem to be bearing any fruit anymore and had our lunch. In between bites of the sandwich, Alaida wanted to know more about the family history.

"Did you know the Colonel, William Linneaus, had his own cavalry regiment, the name was changed later to Second Lancers but for a long time they carried his name. They were famous and decorated a lot especially during the Gurkha and Maratha wars. He was instrumental in the signing of a treaty between India and Nepal where Nepal ceded some land in the Kumaon area to India." Ivan was peeling an orange.

"His sons also married Mughal royalty, and one of them had two wives," I added.

"Do you have the family tree? I'd like to have it too," her eyes were shining, she seemed to be enjoying herself and Ivan gave her a fond look handing her the orange.

"I've got it somewhere around or what was put together by Aunty Sarah, but I can't vouch for it being absolutely correct."

I told her about the recent claim for the title from the descendants of the first son, "but everything is little muddled, nobody knows the whole story, we all grew up on a diet comprised of bits and pieces," I sighed, "the old people who knew it all have passed on and there's not much in writing." Alaida was curious about how we had acquired the land and I explained about the *'daihege'*, which came with an Indian bride and the Zamindari system and how the customary revenue was paid to the government after being made proprietors of the land. This system was abolished when India gained independence and a lot of the *Zamindar's* land was taken over by the Government which coupled with vices such as gaming, lost them a considerable amount of their inheritance.

The sun was too hot yet to make the journey back, so we reclined on the *dhurrie*, which Ivan had thoughtfully brought along and in no time at all we dozed off. When we woke, the heat had abated and we were surrounded by a crowd of young grinning children, who had come to look at us and especially to stare at Alaida who fascinated them with her reddish hair. Alaida was just as fascinated with them and had them smiling while she clicked their vivacious faces. Ivan threw a handful of coins beneath a tree to distract them and in their scramble for the coins they forgot all about us and we were able to leave.

"Some of them had such cute faces!" exclaimed Alaida; she had been busy with her camera. The whole trip had been dotted by Alaida stopping to take photographs. Two nesting pigeons on the ruins of what used to be the stable roof had also come into their share of the limelight as Ivan had climbed into the feeding trough of the stable and shot them for her. We laughed at the vanity of the birds who had looked at the camera complacently not at all disturbed by their pictures being taken. One would have thought they were so used to facing the camera everyday.

Nineteen

The days flew by and we had exhausted ourselves in remembering the history of our famous and infamous ancestors. Nature had done its work with Ivan and Alaida and that cherub, cupid could be blamed for hitting his mark accurately for once and not allowing his arrow to go astray. We were discussing their wedding.

"It has to be in Coleraine," said Alaida, "at the family home, my uncle would never forgive me if it was held anywhere else. You will come won't you?" she was looking at me anxiously.

"Of course she'll come," said Ivan, "you wouldn't want to miss seeing Coleraine and besides, I'll take care of all the expenses, I want you there."

As always he had read my mind but I knew I still had to have a serious talk with Ivan. Knowing she had to be up early to catch the train to Delhi, Alaida went off to bed. Ivan was to accompany her all the way to Delhi and see her off at the airport so I motioned for him to keep sitting.

"If you're immigrating Ivan, what's going to happen to Chhaoni?"

"You can check on Chhaoni and Manota as well. I'll make sure there's enough money for its maintenance."

"What are you going to do about a living when you are in Ireland, are you still going to practice law?"

He sighed deeply, "that's the only thing that's bothering me, I guess I'll have to take whatever job I can there until I redo some bar exams, then I should be able to continue practicing. There's lots to work out still but don't be anxious, we'll sort everything out....come on, off to bed, you're looking half dead......and thanks again, you did a wonderful job here with the meals and everything," he ruffled my hair and gave me a hug.

"See you in the morning..." I was indeed tired and bed seemed absolutely inviting. Tomorrow the house would be silent. Aunty Sarah's books had been screaming to be read. I could now use the time to read, there was going to be plenty of that soon, perhaps I would make a start on my book too. The prospect of going to Ireland...my head hit the pillow and I was sound asleep.

I was running along some sandy beach, my hair streaming behind me in the wind, the sea was sparkling beside me while I ran and ran. The sand and the sea were endless and I didn't seem to be tiring. In the distance was a castle, which was covered with vines and branches of trees, there was somebody, peering at me but I couldn't see her. I just knew she was there and I had to reach her but no matter how fast I ran I couldn't seem to make any progress. The castle beckoned but I couldn't reach it. I woke with a start. The sky was beginning to lighten; I lay in bed listening to my heartbeats. The dream had been so vivid, what had brought that on, I wondered. The sounds of the birds intruded and I knew it was time to get up. Ivan and Alaida were leaving for Delhi and there was a lot to be done.

Alaida was coming out of Ivan's room, her hair long and lustrous, her negligee almost transparent. She smiled at me unashamedly. "He's simply fabulous, I don't know what I'm going to do all these months until he can join me."

"Alaida, do you think Ivan will fit in there, you've seen what India is like, will he adjust?"

"It's not that different really, he'll be okay and besides he has me." She yawned, "you worry too much you know, we're marvellous together, everything will be magnificent." She entered her own room and gently closed the door. I had sensed a little irritation at my question. Was I being paranoid? I wondered, why did I not feel comfortable with Ivan going over to Ireland? It was stupid to allow these feelings which disturbed me, to take precedence. I felt despondent; perhaps I just didn't want to lose Ivan. I would miss him but this move was inevitable, I would have to adjust too and in any case we didn't see each other often and we could still correspond.

At the station we said our farewells, "Don't discourage

Ivan about moving," Alaida said gently, "I sense you have some doubts about all this and I don't think you are too happy but it will really work out fine, please be positive."

"I'll do my best and don't worry, I won't put any spokes in your way, I want Ivan to be happy."

"You're a dear," said Ivan hugging me, "and we are going over together so you can help me adjust before you leave okay?" he was grinning boyishly. The happiness on his face dispelled my misgivings and I waved back as the train moved out of the station.

Ivan was a civil suits lawyer and he had been disillusioned with the idea of marriage until he met Alaida. I hoped he would be happy with her, it had all been so sudden.

"I'll never marry," he had said once to me, "I've seen enough of what couples get up to, either their behaviour drives them to drink or drugs, then to abuse and the partner retaliates by divorcing them, some of the details I get are pretty gruesome."

"But not all marriages are like that," I told him, "I've got friends who are happy and then what about our own family members, there's examples for you there."

"Sometimes they've known each other for years but still they torture them, treat them in some inhuman fashion, it's all so depressing. People live together for years and instead of treating each other with respect they treat each other in the worst possible manner and the strange thing is they justify their behaviour instead of admitting to their wrongs, this is what really astounds me."

"Well Freud did explain that, our conscious mind sets up blocks which allows us to rationalize or justify our undesirable behaviour while suppressing the motivation which led to it, so justification is a lower instinctive behaviour in humans."

Ivan was smiling. "I'd forgotten how you keep poking your nose into each and every book you come across. I've got this case where the husband battered the wife and the parents want me to make her leave him but she insists on going back. How do I convince her. She keeps making excuses for him, says he promises to change if she stays with him."

I told him to tell her that by staying with him she was making him believe that she accepts his abuse. "Are there any children?"

"Two, a girl and a boy, " he replied.

"Well that's the best lever to use, ask her if she realizes that by staying she's going to lose the respect of her children. According to statistics boys who have an abusive father become abusive adults and daughters become victims. She's giving them role models. Her only option is to leave and make sure the children understand that being beaten is not acceptable. She has to set an example."

That was one case that he was never able to resolve. The woman went back to her husband and Ivan didn't know what happened until a few months later when her parents came to him again and told him that their daughter was back home again but crippled for life. He had thrown her off their second floor balcony and her spine had been damaged. They wanted Ivan to get the husband to pay for her treatment but the fellow had disappeared taking their children with him.

I was to return home to Darjeeling when Ivan returned from Delhi and would visit again during the holidays. In the meantime we had a lot to do to get organized for a visit to Ireland. Ivan's papers would have to be processed once Alaida sent the sponsorship letter. Thereafter I could apply for a tourist visa.

He arrived at mid-day the following day. I had been expecting him and he was glad of the hot food, which was awaiting his arrival. As we sat down to our meal, I told him I wanted to visit Manota once again before I left.

"We can go tomorrow," he said "and then I will arrange your tickets".

"It's Diwali today, will they burst crackers in the morning as well?"

"Perhaps, but it shouldn't interfere with the route we have to take. We'll just have to be a little careful near the villages. I hope you're not going to insist on going by bullock cart again." I laughed with him.

"You can drive me, it will be quicker."

In the evening we sat outside listening to the noise of the crackers as Diwali was celebrated in Kasgunj. From time to time the rockets lit the sky and burst with a distant bang.

"We'll have to get a reliable person to stay at Manota or someone might encroach on the property". I agreed with him.

"Maybe one of the old servants could be kept as the caretaker," I told him. He yawned, nodding his head.

"I'm for bed," he said, "we should leave early. Incidentally, guess who we met on the train to Delhi?" I shook my head at him, I couldn't think of anyone.

"Steve".

"Who?"

"Chris's brother and it was really pretty bizarre, he's changed himself tremendously."

"Is he doing well?"

"I wouldn't call it that," he said dryly, "he's what we call a *hijra*'"

"You're joking." I was shocked to think that Steve had become a *hijra*.

They were eunechs (transvestites, impotent men who dressed themselves as women) clean shaven and who applied cosmetics to improve their looks, and danced at weddings and other occasions. There were stories told about them, that when a child was born in a family and if they suspected the child had their leanings they would visit the house and demand the child be given to them and if refused they resorted to kidnapping the child at an opportune moment.

"How did you meet him and what is the news of Chris and Gem?"

"They met with a group of these people on the train from Agra to Delhi, you were right they did take a bus. He told me that these people convinced him he was one of them. When they reached Delhi he doesn't know how it happened but he got separated from Chris and the rest of them. After that it's a blank, he found himself with these people and he says he's really happy for the first time. He didn't try to find Chris or his mother, he doesn't know where they are." I stared at Ivan in horror.

"Was he dressed in women's clothes?"

"A sari actually, he looked right somehow."

"Didn't you try to help him."

"He didn't want any help, he was on the train with a group of them, they travel without tickets and nobody dares say anything to them. "He puffed at his cigarette contemplatively, "Steve didn't looked doped or anything, he seemed sort of contented. When I met him before, he looked sort of frustrated, this time there was definitely a change in him, he looked contented."

I stared out into the night thinking about what he had just said. Human beings were so complex. Why would a normal person be happy with that sort of life? What made humans do the things they did. I could only hope that Steve did belong in that community. If he didn't and had been forced into that, it just didn't bear thinking about.

"Did Alaida meet him too?"

"Yes, she was fascinated with him, they had a pretty heavy discussion on *tantrics* as a matter of fact."

"Tantrics, don't tell me, were there any on the train?"

"No, but he told her where one of them could be found in Haridwar."

"I hope you told her horrible they are, I've heard some of the terrible things they do."

"She went and met one of them at some *ashram* in Delhi just before she left." Ivan didn't look at all happy.

"Ivan how could you have allowed it?" He just shrugged his shoulders.

"She didn't tell me. I went to my chambers to meet with my associates; she went on her own. I only found out about it afterwards. Come on, we can talk some more tomorrow. We have to get up early." He stood up and smiled at me. Sighing tiredly, I followed him in.

Twenty

Coleraine located on the coast of Northern Ireland was filled with scenic charm immediately capturing our imagination and our hearts with its beauty. There were over twenty miles of sparkling coastline and thirty miles of navigable river. The countryside was breathtaking, especially the cliffs of its coasts, the lovely sandy beaches and the even lovelier woods. The University of Ulster in Coleraine was renowned among the Universities in Ireland.

"This is where I study too," said Alaida. We were being conducted around the campus and she proudly showed us her favourite places, especially the library.

The next day she took us to dine at the Causeway Coast and we indulged my craving for seafood while Ivan sampled the salmon which was delicately flavoured with sauces and pronounced it excellent. I was impressed with the Giant's

Causeway with its array of hexagonal basalt columns and our guide related tales of ancient Irish Giants giving us a sample of craic or Irish wit. It had taken Ivan seven months to be accepted for immigration, I had almost changed my mind about accompanying him for his wedding. But Ivan would hear none of it, he had insisted I come. He wanted to have at least one member of his family present at the nuptials. Now I was glad he had been insistent. The Irish were warm hearted and entertaining and the scenic beauty had already captured my imagination.

"It's simply wonderful, Alaida, you're so lucky to live here among so much beauty." "Yes, I know what you mean, and it's only when one is away from the place for a while that he realizes it's beauty. If you grew up here, like I did, you tend to take it for granted." We climbed into Alaida's Volkswagen to return to her home.

"We can do some water skiing one of these days too, I hope you are enjoying yourself."

"Oh yes," I replied quickly but Ivan said nothing, he had been quiet for most of the trip, I resolved to speak to him alone, something was troubling him. He was staring out at the landscape and pretty as it was, I didn't think it required such fierce concentration. Alaida too sensed something and glanced at him in puzzlement.

"When do we get to see the church," I asked her and she smiled at me briefly before turning her attention to the road.

"I thought we'd go to mass there tomorrow... you'll be able to see it then."

"Are you Catholic?"

"Yes, what about you?"

"I am but Ivan is Methodist."

"Oh.." there was a little confusion on her face, it was not strange that Ivan had mentioned nothing to her about that, he normally never discussed religion and in any case they had such a short time together it wasn't possible to know everything about each other. Perhaps that was what was troubling Ivan.

"Ivan," I looked at him, "you're very quiet."

He sighed and turned a tired face towards me, "Sorry, I'm not good company right now, just feeling a little out of sorts." He looked apologetically at Alaida, "I hope you won't mind if I don't come along on the trip tomorrow. I'd like to spend the day with Patrick instead." The disappointment on Alaida's face was plain to see but she smiled at him.

"You rest and spend the day with Pat, there'll be other days." Patrick Dunn was her uncle but he insisted we all call him by name as Alaida did.

We were due to visit the L-shaped Rathlin Island with its 175 different species of birds. It was strange that Ivan was so disinterested in the trip. Something was obviously bothering him. He didn't make an appearance at dinner either so I went up to his room to find out what the matter was. He didn't answer my knock so assuming he was asleep I went along to my own room.

"Did you speak to Ivan?" Alaida poked her head round the door of my room.

"Come in," I smiled at her. She looked like a kid with her plaited hair.

"I spoke to him before dinner, I don't think it's anything serious. He did manage a slice of toast and a cup of soup."

"Maybe he's caught a bug or something, he was looking awful this morning."

"He said he wanted to discuss something with you," she paused contemplatively "I don't know why but I get the impression Ivan is not telling me something...you won't hide it from me will you?"

"There's nothing Alaida and I'm sure he'll tell us both what is bothering him tomorrow, don't worry about it."

"I can't help worrying you know," she said softly as she left the room. I switched off the light and climbed wearily into bed. It had been a full day and I had to admit I couldn't help worrying too either. Perhaps we would have to call in a Doctor to see what ailed Ivan.

Alaida's home was a beautiful Manor, which took one back to the Elizabethan era with it's grand piano in the hall, the intricately woven tapestry and the gilt edged mirrors which seemed to be in every room. A broad staircase with long gallery connected the wings of the house on the upper floors. Each bedroom seemed of greater size. The sprawling gardens were well kept and had a variety of flowering plants which enhanced the beauty. Adjoining the Manor was a wood, which Alaida had confessed earlier she spent a lot of time in.

The next morning I decided I would have my talk with Ivan so I went across to his room and knocked on his door. There was no answer, thinking he might not have heard as the doors were solid oak, I knocked more loudly and when I didn't get a response tried the knob and the door opened under my touch. The sight that met my eyes gave me a shock. Ivan was lying on his bed his arms by his side palms facing upwards, his eyes were closed, a slight smile on his lips. He looked to be fast asleep and sitting on a high backed chair near his bed was Alaida, her long hair falling to her waist, looking back at me calmly, her eyes were strange, they had gone almost dark with some emotional intensity. An array of candles were lighting at the foot of Ivan's bed and some more at the headside. The room was full of smoke and the perfume of incense. It seemed like some ritualistic ceremony was taking place. I was filled with a sense of foreboding, it was bright daylight why did they have candles lighting, something wasn't quite right here.

"Alaida, what's going on...Ivan?" I called as I came into the room but Ivan didn't wake.

"He's sleeping she said softly, isn't he lovely." I looked down at Ivan, he did look peaceful perhaps I shouldn't disturb him but I still felt uneasy. The silence was unnatural.

"He's too still," I murmured then reaching out a hand I placed it on his forehead. It was cold to the touch and suddenly Alaida was there knocking my hand away.

"Don't touch him," she screamed, "you can't touch him."

I stared at her in horror, her teeth were clenched, her look venomous. Ivan didn't wake despite the noise and I looked down at him in puzzlement.

"I had to do it..." she whispered into the silence and immediately a cold dread filled my heart, I touched Ivan's hand, but he didn't move, I shook him, Alaida had returned to her chair and was sitting placidly, a complacent smile lighting her face. I wondered if I had imagined her expression of a few moments before.

"Ivan, Ivan...Ivan wake up, what has happened to Ivan...Alaida we need a Doctor," I shouted.

"There's no need to call anybody, Ivan's dead," she said emphatically as I stared at her in disbelief then suddenly she was shouting, "I had to do it, I couldn't let it happen all over again, I had to do it..." she fell down beside the bed weeping.

"I grabbed her shoulder and shook it hard, "what did you do, what..."

"I put it in his tea..."

"What did you put in his tea? Please you have to tell me..." the tears were rolling down my cheeks, I didn't want to look at Ivan, this couldn't be happening, this was some kind of a nightmare, this was not real. Kind, humorous Ivan, my dear friend what was happening here? I shook him desperately. For a moment I thought I must be in some kind of dream, then Alaida's Uncle Patrick came into the room.

"What is going on?" his voice was sharp as he stared at each of us in turn. I was practically hysterical.

"He won't wake, she's done something to him!"

When the Doctor came Alaida was sedated and he told us what we already knew, Ivan was dead. Patrick and the doctor conferred together after which a few calls were made and an ambulance came and took her away. I continued to sit near the window in Ivan's room until Patrick insisted I go to my own room and rest, but rest I could not. I sat near the window staring into space. It must have been hours later, when Patrick came to speak to me.

"I'm sorry," he said quietly, running his hands through his white hair, "all this has not been fair to you, I do apologize."

"Please...I just have to know, did she tell you?"

He was silent for a while, and then he said I think you deserve to know the whole story.

He told me how after her parent's death in a car crash Alaida had begun hallucinating. He had taken her to a psychiatrist and she had been put on some medication and she had improved for a while but then one day, he found her in her Grandmother's room dressed in some old dress staring into the mirror. She didn't know who she was, she claimed to be "Isabel," her grandmother. She was institutionalized for a time for dissociative disorder, but had recovered.

"What is dissociative disorder?"

"It's when a person takes other identities and believes themselves to be a different personality than their own."

"You mean like split personality?"

"Yes. Something like that."

"When did all this happen?"

"That was almost four years ago, she's been perfectly normal since then, I don't know when it came on again."

"Can I ask you something?"

"Please.."

"Does Alaida look like her grandmother? "

"Yes, each generation of women has had that red hair and green eyes, yes she does look like her grandmother and her mother."

"Then you're Alaida's maternal Uncle, her mother's brother?" he nodded his head in assent.

He rang the bell and asked the maid to bring us some coffee. He had insisted on me having some food and we were seated together in the small lounge. The house was full of old furniture, it didn't seem beautiful anymore, dark and menacing somehow or was it just my imagination but everything seemed gloomy in keeping with my mood. The tapestry of gold and blue was offset nicely by the deep maroon carpet. The room seemed larger than it was as an antique mirror ran the length of one wall. In other circumstances I would have been entranced with the grandeur but at the moment all I could think about was the demise of Ivan.

"What did she use?"

"Some sort of drug," he said quietly, "they took the tea cup to test what's left of the liquid, did they have a fight, a quarrel of some sort, do you think? Didn't she tell you anything?"

"She kept mumbling, something about not allowing it to happen again...It just didn't make any sense." We were both quiet wondering at the words.

"I'm so sorry," he looked apologetically at me, "I wish I had known she was into a relapse, we might have prevented the tragedy, this is all my fault." He looked so worn and tired, I felt obliged to reassure him.

"It's not your fault Patrick, I think Ivan sensed something different about Alaida, he didn't seem very happy yesterday, I wanted to ask him but I never got a chance. Do you think I'll be allowed to see Alaida, I need to talk to her? She seemed so normal yesterday."

"I'll arrange it...but now I think you need to get to bed

and rest." He got up and walked towards the house and I followed suit bidding him good night. I had a lot of thinking to do and I didn't know if I could sleep but still, bed seemed the best thing.

I woke in the night shivering. There was something needed to be done, something had happened...then I remembered and the tears came, hot and scalding and I cried until exhaustion set in and I could cry no more. But sleep eluded me, unanswered questions were going round and round in my brain, what had made her do it? Why? I wished I had had a chance to talk to Ivan, I had not even said goodbye...what foolishness, I didn't know he was going to die. Alaida had seemed so normal, how could she have done such a thing? The questions bounced around in my head but no answers came. Then I had an idea, suppose Ivan had kept a diary, perhaps there would be some clue among his things. Opening the door I ran along the corridor and went into his room. His body had been removed to the morgue and the doctor had given a death certificate but I was not sure what he had put as the cause of death. Patrick had insisted there should be no scandal and no police but I was not of the same mind. I resolved to speak to him about it.

I stood for a moment hesitating then I put on the lights. I searched among his things but found no diary, there was nothing. His cigarettes lying on the dressing table looked so ordinary, ready waiting as if he would enter and pick them up, the tears threatened again so I turned to run from his room back to my own when I saw it. Near the door was a niche in the wall, the diary was lying there, a pen stuck between the pages as if he had been writing and put the book there when he went to answer the door. I stood shivering holding the diary; I felt close to Ivan, there was something he wanted me to know. The sky was already beginning to lighten when I returned to my room and finally fell asleep.

When I awoke the next day, it was well past noon. After bathing and readying myself I went down to the dining room. The house was quiet as usual, there was never very much noise in any case as Alaida's uncle lived alone. He had never married and was a professor in the University of Ulster. I wondered if he had gone there but then I saw him, his back to the house sitting out on the lawn.

"Good afternoon," I said politely as I came near and he looked up.

"I hope you slept well," he looked at me anxiously, "I've got permission for you to see Alaida tomorrow, and since they've removed Ivan to the morgue, I thought we'll have a quiet funeral tomorrow morning if you like."

"Yes, that'd be fine. I need to ask you something...how did you know she had used some sort of drug?"

"I asked her what she used and she said she had put the drug in his tea. Ivan was not feeling very well that morning she told him she had added some herbs to make his stomach well. He drank the whole cup."

"How did you get her to talk?"

"I just asked her questions and she answered all of them happily. She seemed proud of what she had done, it was easy to get her to talk." He sighed despondently, "she looked so normal, it's so difficult to believe what she has done."

We were silent looking out over the garden. I knew I had to tell Patrick what I had discovered but I wondered if he would believe me. Ivan's diary had been a revelation. He had written of Alaida's meeting with a tantric at Haridwar. She had been fascinated by the man who had introduced her to the black arts. The man had performed some tricks of changing some items into jewellery, which he presented to Alaida, and she had become a sort of devotee of his. She had returned to India a month after leaving and had lived at his ashram at Haridwar where he had taught her something of the tantric arts. Tantrics have never been constrained by morals; they explored realms far beyond mortal comprehension. He had taught Alaida about poisons and drugs and she had smuggled in some of the powders he had given her. He had many women who were slaves to him and he controlled their minds with the drugs he fed them. They believed he was supreme and did his bidding, no matter the cost. Tantrics indulge in the dark activities whereby they use darkness to find light. They familiarise themselves with the dark aspects of human life especially related to death so that they are able to dispel pleasure and pain or desire and disgust. Ivan had been horrified to discover Alaida resorted to the use of drugs from time to time. She claimed they made her think clearly. Their disagreement had been on this issue and her continued interest in the black arts.

"Come, let's have lunch, you've had no breakfast and I thought it would be better to let you have a good sleep." I smiled at him, he was trying hard to be hospitable and really. It was not his fault that his niece had gone insane, but I knew no matter how hard I was trying to suppress the feeling, I was blaming him a little for Ivan's death, after all he should have warned us she had not been right earlier. Yes there was a little resentment, but the information I had culled from Ivan's diary made it clear how she had become unhinged. If she was on drugs as he had written, I knew I had to impart the information to Patrick. He took the news without surprise.

"I felt there was something different about her when she returned from India this time, but I thought it just might be the fact that she was in love and anxious to see Ivan again. You said Mage drugs, what do you mean by that?" The whole idea of Hindu *tantra* and Mage drugs was repugnant to him not to mention outlandish. He looked confused and revolted.

I explained to him about the Mage drugs used by the tantric priests, one of which was called AUM which was a mixture of RNA, heroine, cocaine, LSD and an extract of hemp. The heroine was supposed to rid the mind of anxiety, the RNA would stimulate creativity, the hemp and LSD would work to instill joy and the cocaine to stimulate the mind to do things. The resultant effect sometimes made a person go insane. It was only the tantrics who could imbibe the mixture without ill effects. With Alaida's history of mental illness and having tried the drug, this could very well have been the cause of her going over the edge.

"She probably used some kind of poison given to her by the tantric, on Ivan too. I think you should read his diary, it will give you an insight into what was troubling him." Patrick nodded his head dazedly. He didn't look like he believed any of this.

Ivan's funeral was scheduled for early the next morning but I asked Patrick if he would take me to the morgue for one last look at him. I still couldn't quite believe he was really gone and I needed to look on him one last time before he was encased in a coffin. The journey to the morgue was a silent one, each of us occupied with our own thoughts and I didn't notice any of the countryside. I was thinking of Ivan and our journey was over. He had kept joking on the plane and humouring me with his imitation of an Irish accent. His eyes had sparkled with laughter and he had looked as if he had no cares in the world. I had even remarked on how young he looked, "If you go on in this fashion," I had said, "You'll start looking younger than Alaida and then people will think you're her son. How about giving me the secret of your rejuvenation."

"Try a little love." He had joked.

They say love is akin to hate, I thought, had Alaida somehow confused the two?

How ironical he had come all the way to Coleraine to die. On our arrival he had been so enthusiastic about the place, marvelling at its beauty and he had made a remark about being pleased at the opportunity to stay, little knowing it would come to pass but differently from what he had imagined. Alaida had come to meet us full of excitement, their future had seemed so bright, they had seemed so right together, she had seemed so normal, who would have thought that eight days later she would do such a horrible thing. What had warped her mind, what had triggered her relapse, was it only the drugs?

We had reached the morgue, a solid stone structure, which looked cold and forbidding. There was nobody in the lobby but Patrick seemed to know his way around and led me to an office with a steel desk and well stuffed chairs without arms. Two thick registers sat solidly atop the desk behind which an enormous man overflowed a chair which looked in danger of collapse. His cheeks were red and round as apples but one look into his bright blue eyes made me forget his girth and his precarious perch. They twinkled merrily and seemed out of place in so somber a location.

"So what can I do for you?" he enquired cheerfully.

Patrick gave Ivan's name and the nature of our visit and he tried hard to suppress the twinkling of his eyes but to no avail, obviously death didn't affect him in the same manner it affected us and had it not been so solemn an occasion I would have done my best to discover the secret of his merriment. Death and life seemingly amused him. I thought of the tantrics who had the same belief that life and death were the same but where they overcame death by controlling the dark areas of life, he seemed to control death by laughing at it and infusing its darkness with light.

With mammoth effort he unwound his enormous frame from the chair and rolled out the door motioning us to accompany him. We followed his way to a room opposite his office.

On a concrete slab in the centre of the room a body was laid out covered from head to toe with a white sheet. Beside the slab a steel trolley had been placed with various instruments, bottles and brushes. Holding the sheet by the ends he uncovered Ivan's face and stood back so we could look on him.

He looked so serene. A facial muscle twitched and I stood paralysed. Had I imagined that? Gingerly I stretched my hand to touch his face. It was still cold. Feeling chilled, I turned away while his face was covered again. Latently I had discovered this love for Ivan, which had lain dormant, now I understood my discomfort at Alaida and Ivan's relationship. I was plagued by this see-saw emotion which somersaulted the heart and sent it thudding and rampaging through the stomach which jolted in surprise at such fierce upheavals signaling the brain in astonishment as to why it was under siege, revolted at being so rudely assaulted, plunging to the depths causing the sensation of suddenly having lost altitude in imitation of an airplane dipping and in defense, the surge of adrenaline which further destabilises the system with an onslaught of rushing nervousness leaving one dumbstruck as to all the unprecedented havoc. Who could have thought such a small word could cause such agitated reaction. The rapid descent from such a height to rude reality sent me reeling and only time now could assuage my grief and dry the silent woebegone tears that poured in my heart incessantly. I was devastated by this knowledge. I hadn't realized I loved Ivan such a lot. I stood stricken until Patrick finished speaking to the gentleman then followed him out to the car. The drive home was just as silent as the journey to the morgue had been. When we reached the manor I retired to my room to wallow in misery and cry unashamedly and in between bouts of hysterical weeping I thought of the fat custodian of the morgue who sat cheerfully in his office quite untouched by the serious nature of death and whose blue eyes laughed out at the world seemingly amused at some secret joke. I wondered if all Ireland was peopled by lunatics and I couldn't help smiling at the thought, and the tears dried of their own accord until I felt presentable enough to show myself below the stairs again.

That afternoon, I was allowed to see Alaida. The doctor arranged for an attendant to be present, he said she was not stable yet but he had her on medication. It would take her time to recover.

"And then what?" I questioned him, "will she have to stand trial?"

He shrugged his shoulders, "that is not my area of expertise."

I resolved to speak to Patrick on this, I didn't feel in a charitable mood. Why should she go scot free, Ivan had lost his life. I wanted to see her punished. Her uncle obviously had influence from the way she had been whisked off before the police had a chance to question her. I didn't think Patrick would be too happy with my train of thought.

The attendant motioned me to follow him and we went along a corridor until we came to a door behind which was another corridor where we turned right and then a row of rooms with the doors closed. I had imagined the hospital would be depressing with dark corridors and dingy rooms but instead the whole atmosphere had been bright and cheery with plenty of light from the high windows. He opened the door to the second room and I followed him in.

Alaida was in a room which was all white, the walls were bare, the sheet which covered the mattress was white, there was no pillow. There was nothing in the room except the bed and it was fixed to the floor. The window had bars on it and she was standing near it looking out. She turned when the door opened and I entered the room.

The attendant stood just near the door after carefully shutting it. The doctor had insisted that I not be alone with her, he claimed she was unpredictable. This was part of the Coleraine's Health Care which stretched over miles of ground. The gardens, which I had come through, were well kept and buildings well maintained. A number of other patients had been in the corridors and out on the lawns with nurses and doctors and attendants hurrying to and fro. The mental section was a little segregated. An attendant had come with me after I had signed in at the reception and spoken to the doctor. Now I stood facing Alaida who looked pale and distraught, with dark circles under her eyes.

"You have to get me out of here," she said tears running down her cheeks, "I'm not mad really, please you will help me won't you?" she was pleading and I couldn't help pitying her. I supposed they had put her on some kind of medication.

"Why did you do it Alaida?" I asked her softly.

She stared at me for a moment blankly, the tears drying in her eyes; "He was going to leave me, just like the first time." She didn't seem to mind answering my questions.

"The first time?"

"Yes. William was going to leave me again he was going to India, this time he had to die before he could go back. Yes.."

the expression on her face changed, became almost sly, "he cannot go away now, he's going to marry me..." Then suddenly in fury she ran at me and the attendant stepped between us. I had forgotten he was there, he caught her hands and while she screamed he struggled to control her while motioning with his head for me to leave. The last sight I had of Alaida was her face that contorted with rage and looked horrible. As other attendants ran to assist I turned away. Her beauty seemed to have shrivelled in that moment and she had looked so old, like some horribly wizened old woman, a caricature of herself.

What was it that changed people, was mental illness so terrible? I knew I should be compassionate towards her, who knew what she suffered, what went on in her mind. But there was no compassion within me yet. I was angry and upset. Ivan should never have died, nothing now could bring him back, and I couldn't even like her.

When I reached the house, I related all that had happened to Patrick. He watched me quietly, he could tell I was angry.

"It's not fair," I told him, "you're to blame, you should have warned Ivan she was insane."

"That's not fair to me," he said gently, "I didn't know she had had a relapse or that she was taking drugs. If Ivan knew why didn't he tell me, we could have got her some help, or for that matter how did he allow her to get involved with this tantric business. I don't think I'm much to blame for the whole damn thing."

"Well, you should have told him she had been in an asylum earlier too." I said lamely, he was right Ivan had known but had not disclosed any of it to us. I was angrier with him than with any of them. What puzzled me was how he drank the liquid from her hands if he felt she was behaving strangely. Had Ivan had a death wish, was he so much in love with Alaida that he didn't care if he died or not, or was it because he couldn't bear the change in her?

"It's so strange, she referred to Ivan as William and she said he wanted to leave her like before. Obviously she was hallucinating because of the drugs, but who is this William she thought he was?"

Patrick looked at me thoughtfully, "tell me what was the name of our common ancestor, wasn't it William?"

"Yes but who does she think she is now?" I looked at him in bewilderment, "do you have any clue as to what might be going on in her mind?"

For a moment he stared out over the lawn, "I think I'm beginning to piece all this together. There's a story her grandmother used to tell her, about her great grandmother. It seems she was this William's cousin and she fell madly in love with him and although he had feelings for her too, the fact that she was so closely related made him refuse to even consider marriage with her. Rather than let it go any further, he took himself off to India and he never did return." He paused for a while and I waited silently for him to continue, a slight breeze ruffled my hair and I could smell the fragrance of the roses, which came wafting on the breeze. We were seated outside on the lawn, having an after dinner drink. The lights from the house threw shadows around the garden in patches. I couldn't see Patrick very clearly as he had chosen a seat a little in shadow, then he continued, his voice soft, "she waited, hoping he would return but instead she received a letter from him informing her that he had married an Indian. It left her devastated, and for a time, her family were worried that she might do something drastic but she recovered and swore one day she would have her revenge. Only late in life did she finally marry a man she had known from young. She only had one daughter."

"The portrait," I said, "that's who the portrait is of."

"I don't understand," Patrick was leaning forward to see me better, "what portrait?"

It necessitated me telling him about the vaults and the portrait we had found there.

"My God! That's it then," exclaimed Patrick, "it all fits together, "Helene was the name of the lady, and when my niece first began this split personality syndrome, she seemed to think she was that Helene and would lose her temper and behave irrationally when anyone called her Alaida."

"So perhaps it was the portrait which triggered her relapse, she thinks she's that woman," I exclaimed.

"What do you mean? How could..."

"It's hanging in her room here," I told him, "Ivan brought it over as a wedding present since she liked it so much." Patrick was standing in agitation.

"How is it that I knew nothing about it?" "You were not here when we arrived. She was so excited, she had it hung in her room immediately." I followed him as he went into the house and took the stairs two at a time. When I got to Alaida's room, he was standing staring at it. Alaida had it hung facing the bed and the woman in it looked back at us, her expression was one of contempt. Now I could understand the expression. That was the look of a woman scorned...well she had her revenge, she had told the story to her daughter and her daughter had passed it down to hers and the last generation, a sad, mixed up child was the victim of that hate and an innocent man lost his life in a demented moment. No wonder the portrait had been walled up in a separate room.

Then suddenly Patrick spoke startling me, "she sent him this portrait as a wedding gift, a constant reminder of her hate. I'll have it removed from this room and destroyed before Alaida returns."

Patrick was called downstairs to attend a telephone call and I continued down the corridor to my room. His voice calling my name had me hurrying to the landing, he sounded urgent.

"Ivan's body has gone missing from the morgue," he shouted, "I'm going there to find out the details," and he disappeared out through the front door leaving me staring in astonishment.

Who would want to steal Ivan's body? I sat on the stairs in confusion. I didn't understand how everything could keep getting worse. Ivan's funeral had been scheduled for early the next morning. Now we didn't even have a body. The situation had become preposterous. I collapsed against the banisters hysterically laughing until tears streamed down my face. I was glad the domestic help had not come to investigate and crawling on all fours I somehow managed to get myself to my room. I didn't think I had sufficient strength to even stand.

A loud knocking on the door had me awake in a moment and shakily I sat up in bed as the door was tried and found open. Patrick came into the room switching on the light from the switch near the door. The sudden illumination had me screwing my eyes in distress.

"They found Ivan," he said excitedly and my eyes flew open taking in Patrick's dishevelled appearance. Uncermoniously he sat himself on the bed.

"Ivan's in the hospital, they're keeping him under observation. He might have pneumonia." I stared at him wide eyed. He closed his eyes tiredly rubbing his forehead and yawning.

"Patrick," I said urgently, "are you feeling okay?" I was wondering how to deal with him. I didn't have much experience dealing with people who went over the edge. He opened his eyes and looked at me and suddenly began laughing and I cringed away in fright wondering what to do.

"Oh dear!" he exclaimed contritely, "I am sorry, I'm just so tired. Ivan's not dead...don't ...don't dear child. Don't look at me like that it's true, he's in the hospital, he's alive! He wasn't dead in the first place. The drug Alaida gave him gave him the appearance of being dead but he wasn't really..." I don't remember the rest of the conversation. I must have blacked out because when I came to Patrick was bending over me anxiously. He sat back relieved.

"I seem to be going about this in all the wrong way. I gave you a shock...I'm sorry." I found my voice at last.

"Is it true about Ivan?" he nodded his head.

"I'll take you to him in the morning." Patting my hand he stood up and stretched.

"I'll fill you in the details after I've had some rest." Smiling at me he left the room shutting the door softly behind him.

Ivan had what people who run around naked in the cold on a winter night catch, pneumonia and was confined to the hospital under close observation. Bugs under a microscope are given more elbowroom. Doctor Carmichael who attended him was intent on trying to discover what the drug he had ingested was, while Dr. Alban who looked vague with her rimmed glasses, which fooled most of her patients, probed his mind digging to the depths to uncover the darkest secrets of his mind.

"What a waste of effort," Ivan remarked, "the deeper she digs the more blank spaces she finds."

"Blank spaces, don't be funny, hasn't she hypnotized you yet?"

"Oh sure she's very hypnotic I can't take my eyes off her, do you think she'd go on a date with me?"

"Be serious Ivan, what has she discovered?"

"Oh only that I'm smart and a good catch and she likes my brain."

"Oh, so she tasted it, did she?"

"Yeah, and there was absolutely nothing in it, sorted of melted on the tongue something like that special sweet they make out of beating milk in the early morning, what's it called?"

I was sure he had recovered especially when I saw him peering down the neck of one of the nurse's uniforms.

"So what did you discover?"

"Discover?"

"Mm, down her dress."

"Oh" looking sheepish, "I could do with a nice pair of pillows like that."

"Ivan, you are the limit."

"No really I'm within limits, they expect it."

"And a crass.."

"You're relegating me to the portals of ordinary mortals, I've just returned from being in the tomb, resurrected you might say."

"You weren't dead idiot."

"Sure, now I'm an idiot what's the difference anyway, I almost was."

"Well it's not the same and if you don't shut up you soon will be."

"What? Is this the tender love and care I get for coming back just so you don't cry?"

"Oh you …you better rest."

"Rest? Haven't I had enough of that already? Wow it was cold in the mortuary.."

"Oh Ivan.."

Patrick had searched Alaida's room and found the packets and potions she had locked away in her dressing table. They had been taken away for testing. Ivan told them about a Mage drug, which induced the symptoms of death, used by tantrics but none of Alaida's store revealed such a one. There had been other artifacts as well which had been unearthed from her closet. We wondered how far into the black arts she had indulged.

Seemingly she had used the entire amount of the substance which Ivan had taken, as the drugs in the teacup had elicited insufficient amounts for testing and it was not among the other substances. Speculation was rife and Ivan became something of a guinea pig until he recovered from pneumonia and was discharged from the hospital.

"What did it feel like?" I asked him when we were alone, "do you remember anything?"

"If you think I can reveal anything about a near death experience," he said, "I have to disappoint you. I was conscious the whole time but in a sort of black void. I was desperate to get through to you to let you know I was alive. I was afraid of being buried." He took a deep breath and I looked at him horrified, he must have truly suffered. I shivered to think of what he would have felt had we actually had the funeral.

"Why did you drink the stuff from her, weren't you aware she wasn't in her right mind?"

"I knew," he said sadly, "but I didn't think she would want to kill me, I still think she loves me." There were tears in his eyes and I reached out to squeeze his hand in sympathy.

"I know what it is she used. It's called; acrima tenebris, its an alchemical preparation made from lead salts, nightshade and tears of people in sorrow. According to what I read about it, by distilling and consecrating the solution on a Saturday, it will become filled with the powers of death and darkness. It can be mixed in food and drink and will induce stupor followed by apparent death. Most often the victim is buried alive as it's extremely hard to tell if the patient is alive."

"But you were cold, doesn't a live person have warmth."

"The drug freezes all the bodily functions, so the body becomes cold just like when a person dies."

"Have you told the doctors?" Ivan shook his head.

"I don't think they have open minds on our tantric stuff. For them Alaida is a drug addict and insane and I had a near death experience and that ends the matter, besides I think it's better if we don't discuss this too much. Patrick is not too keen to disclose any of the tantric business and I agree with him." I nodded my consent

"Will you come home?" I asked him and he shook his head.

"I'll see this through, she's going to need me."

"Ivan don't, please I'll feel better if you come back."

"Poor baby," he said gently, "you've had a tough time of it. We'll discuss this later, okay. Just enjoy yourself now and we are going to have a good time." He smiled at me determinedly.

He had always been stubborn but so was I; after all doesn't love give one the freedom to melt the fortress of fear? I refused to be defeated before I had even begun, I intended to live life with colour and beauty and make love every moment. As Omar Khayyam said:

'Ah make the most of what we yet may spend,
Before we too into the dust descend.
Dust into dust and under dust to lie,
Sans wine, sans song, sans singer and sans end!'

Twenty One

Doctor Linda Evans regretfully informed Ivan he could not visit Alaida yet.

"But I must," Ivan insisted, "I might even be able to help her get well".

"That is not what I feel," she told him, "infact she may have a relapse. In any case most of the time she's sedated. You do realize, it's not only a mental disturbance, it's drugs as well and with withdrawal symptoms it's not a pretty sight". Ivan looked at her in annoyance but she just gazed back at him calmly. Her eyes were gentian blue with thick lashes and her skin like creamy magnolias. She didn't look anything like what we had expected Alaida's doctor to look like; she looked a cover girl. She had a way of observing people from the corner of her eyes and when she did look right at a person one had the impression she was seeing much more than what one wanted her to.

"It's no use glowering at me like that and by wasting my time insisting, you're not helping Alaida any."

"What the hell, why do you doctors think you know it all. Surely a few minutes with her won't hurt?"

"Ivan, we've wasted enough of her time, come on let's go." I stood up and Ivan turned and stormed out of her office.

"I'm sorry doctor," I apologized, "he's not always like this." She smiled at me.

"Do you always do his apologizing?"

"Not really, he's not normally so foul tempered."

"Will you come to see me some time alone, I'd like some information from you."

"Sure I'll do that."

"Okay I'll give you a call." Smiling a goodbye I left her office.

Ivan was pacing up and down outside.

"Apologizing for me?" he didn't look at all contrite. "I'm not giving up, she can expect me again soon."

"She's right, you know, seeing you could trigger a reaction

which might affect Alaida adversely."

"I don't believe that, I just want to see how she is."

"You're too stubborn, Dr. Linda knows what she's doing. Come on, let's go."

Ivan began spending time on gathering information on Alaida's disease. Far from being upset with her he wanted desperately to have her cured. Dr. Linda didn't seem to mind his endless questions giving him much of her time. More and more I was left to my own devices and Patrick seemed to think it was his duty to keep me entertained for the duration of my stay. There was something about Patrick that was very endearing. He looked much younger than his years and he had a gentleness that coupled with his old world charm made him very attractive. I found myself falling under his spell. Walks in the woods, sailing, dinners, lunches, dances and hours of conversation.

"Why didn't you ever marry, Patrick?" I asked him one evening as we sat sipping tea on the manor's front lawn. His eyes crinkled in amusement as he turned to look at me.

"I wondered when that one was coming. There was a lass with whom I was very much in love, she died the year we were to marry."

"How did she die?"

"Leukemia."

"I'm so sorry," I said gently, "it must have been very painful losing someone you loved in that manner."

"That it was dear."

"There was no one after her?"

"Not until now..." he looked deep into my eyes and I

realized he was not jesting. He looked so serious. I jumped up hurriedly running my hands through my hair, which was in disarray with the breeze although it had cooled my flushed cheeks.

"Sit child," he said softly, "I won't embarrass you further, I didn't mean to blurt it like that."

"I'm not embarrassed, just a little flustered, I didn't expect you to say that." We smiled at each other.

"I know I'm too old for you but I guess a man can dream…"

"You're not old! I mean that, all this time I've never once thought of you as old."

He laughed, "you're just being kind", but I shook my head.

"I really meant that," I didn't think of Patrick as old.

"There's something so childlike about you and yet something so worldly wise, I couldn't help myself you've had a powerful effect on me."

I had wanted to discuss Patrick with Ivan. He had been showering me with more than just flowers but Ivan seemed to be avoiding me and spending more and more time with Linda.

"Please Patrick, could we not discuss this right now, I need time to digest all this, I need to think."

"But I think yourself has known all along haven't you?"

"I had sort of suspected," I murmured. I had known his feelings were not exactly fatherly but what I wasn't clear on were my own feelings. I looked at him with mixed emotions. There was a lot to like in him but..

"Is it still himself?"

"Who?"

"Ivan lad."

"I don't know..." I said hesitantly, wondering just how transparent I had been. "I just know I'm furious with him, he's hardly given me any time, he seems to have forgotten I exist."

He sighed unhappily, "I noticed, he seems all wrapped up with Dr. Linda. Look I don't want to pressure you but I do think I could make you happy and in time, perhaps, you could learn to love me."

"Patrick.."

"I know there's a big gap in our ages but," he laughed shyly, "I love you enough to cover that gap." I smiled at his eager expression and wished with all my heart I didn't have to hurt him.

"You've made me feel so special all this time and I wish things were different..." I trailed off lamely, relieved when we were interrupted.

Ivan rushed on to the lawn in excitement while we looked at him in puzzlement.

"I have some news for you, Linda and I are getting married," he blurted beaming at us looking so pleased with his announcement while we stared at him in open mouthed astonishment. This was too sudden. Unable to control my emotions, I jumped to my feet and fled in horrified confusion, rushing the flight of stairs to my room, bursting into tears the moment I was safely inside.

Why couldn't I have loved Patrick, why had it always been Ivan? I sobbed inconsolably into my pillow when I felt a gentle hand stroking my hair. I had not heard him enter. The rhythmic strokes soothed and after awhile I felt calmer but I didn't turn as Patrick quietly left the room. My open reaction must have hurt him deeply yet he had come to comfort me.

"Why didn't you ever say anything?" Ivan had entered and as was his way gone directly to the heart of the matter.

"I don't want to discuss it," I wished he would leave the room.

He sighed deeply, "you're the last person I wanted to hurt."

"Go away Ivan," I said "I don't want to discuss it, I'll be alright soon, I always am."

"I know," he said softly, "but I'm not going away till I know you're alright."

"What an idiot you are," I got up angrily, "do you think just because I'm dying for your love I'll do something stupid, get real? I've got more brains than that," he was laughing.

"That's more like my girl."

"I'm not your girl," I retorted, "you never once looked at me as a woman and I've done nothing else but love you for years and years..."

He hugged me to him, "if I had known I would never have looked at anyone else."

"Rubbish, I've always been this good friend, this dependable person to discuss everything with, this...this faithful dog.." Ivan was laughing at my disgruntled expression.

"I just wish you had opened your mouth, why didn't you ever say anything."

"What good would it have done me, there was always some idiotic woman occupying your life...oh go away Ivan, I look a mess and I want to be alone."

"I can't leave you in this condition," he was looking at me anxiously.

"Yes you can, I'm fine, only I won't stay for your wedding...now go away."

"Okay I will," he said quietly, "I'll miss you at the wedding, but I hope when you've recovered sufficiently, you'll remember you're the best friend I've ever had and I care a lot for you and then I want you to return." He walked towards the door.

"You can bet on it, I'll return, I'll ruin your marriage and have a passionate affair with you, so don't think you're safe," I said spitefully as he left the room grinning widely, then ducked back again with a parting shot.

"You could always be my mistress..." I flung my shoe at him and he hurriedly left slamming the door behind him.

Twenty Two

"That is how I left Ireland, Chris."

Chris was shaking his head looking at me. "Ivan was daft to ever let you go." I smiled at his words, keeping silent as we strolled in the compound enjoying the cool night air. The sky was clear and star studded. I could smell jasmine and something else; an earthy fragrance, which I suddenly realized, was Chris's aftershave. The crickets were out in full choir, singing their delight to be alive, serenading the neighbourhood, harmonizing with the cicadas buzzing their own melody. An owl hooted in the distance, the sound haunting, reminding me that out there the night creatures walked, stalking their prey. I glanced at Chris, he was lost in thought, was it of Gem he was thinking? I sighed deeply.

"What is it?" he asked quietly, "that was a deep sigh."

"I was wondering if you were thinking of Gem, I wish she was here."

"She is here," he said softly, "a part of everything, up there in the stars, in the whisper of the breeze, can you smell the jasmine? She loved its fragrance, I feel her near....I think of her often and it's as if she's here...I think she is happy, I am where I want to be."

"When you left here, what did you do?"

"We went to Agra first. It was the first holiday I had ever had. Steve was so excited. We hired an autorickshaw, Mum was the experienced one, she knew where we should go, what we should see. When Dad was in service, he had been stationed there once; she was familiar with it, though she did say it had changed a lot. I've never seen Gem so happy. We were just so glad to be alive!"

"Ivan felt you had taken the dacoit's loot, he did try to find you."

"Was he upset?"

"I don't think so, it was just his analytical mind, he likes tidy endings, he wanted to know if you'll were alright."

Chris's eyes crinkled at the corners as he smiled, "It was Ivan I was worried about. I felt if anyone found us, it would be him and I wasn't entirely sure he would do the right thing and turn us in."

"I doubt it, whatever he may be, he was always loyal. Look at him with Alaida. He didn't marry her but he is monitoring her treatment and making sure she is all right. For a time, I actually thought Linda was purposely keeping Alaida from getting well because she was determined to keep Ivan and her apart but Patrick told me it was all my imagination and in any case, she is getting well now."

"You correspond with Ivan?"

"No. I'm not sure what I feel now but I'm giving it plenty of time. I get all the news from Patrick."

"Is he still hoping you'll change your mind?"

"Yes, but he's just so sweet about everything. I love his letters."

"Are you thinking of going back for a visit?"

"Not right now."

"Will you stay a while?"

"Do you want me to?"

"Yes, in case you haven't noticed, it's pretty lonely…I'll take you to Kasgunj to visit two old ladies, I think you'll enjoy them.

"Who are they?"

"You never met them, did you ever wonder where the Christmas cake and all those baked goodies came from?"

"To tell you truthfully I never really thought about it, these old women, were they the ones who supplied all that?"

"Yes and they're quite interesting characters, I make it a point to visit them whenever I go to Kasgunj. We never had money to buy from them when I was a kid but every Christmas they would faithfully provide a whole cake to us. Ofcourse they were not so old then."

"You had a really sad childhood, Chris. I wish it had been different for you."

"I had Gem," he said quietly as if that made up for everything and perhaps in a way it had. She had been everything to him, his laughter, his tears, his joy! After they left Kasgunj they had wandered, finally settling in Delhi where Chris had gone into the transportation business in partnership with a man who had a flair for business. His money had more than tripled. He had even learned to drive a truck and sometimes accompanied his lorry drivers on their freight trips. It was at the nursing home where Gem had died that he had met Munshilal Adhikari, our family lawyer, whose wife was having their eleventh child and he had told Chris that the house and lands were for sale. Chris had lost no time in purchasing the property. He told me how he had Adhikari settle his case too. A lot of money had changed hands before he was able to actually take possession of Manota.

"Gem made friends with a Scottish lady, it was she who refined our language. How is it you never told me my accent was so lousy?" he accused.

"I didn't have the heart to disillusion you, at that time you thought you spoke so well."

He laughed, "I did wonder later on if you had secretly laughed at me."

"We did sometimes, kids are mean, you know and we were no exception."

"Well, Gem and I laughed at you too, you know."

"You did? Why?"

He grinned lopsidedly, "you always pretended to be so tough but we knew you weren't. Sometimes I wanted to sort of shake you to see what was inside, I once told Gem, if we shake her hard enough maybe the real her will fall out" Gem said, "maybe more than the real her will fall out and your eyes will pop." I did wonder then if Gem thought I had a thing for you and was alluding to it in her own subtle way."

"She did. She thought you had a crush on me but later I think she knew you loved her. But I was always careful not to show any interest in you incase she got the wrong idea."

"Your friendship with Gem was important to you, why?"

"I've never analysed it, I think because she seemed so unconventional. She did whatever she felt like without thought for what people would think or whether it was right or wrong. Maybe because I always wanted to be free like she was, to live by my own code and not worry about what the world thinks. I was brought up with strict Catholic indoctrination. Do you still not believe in God, Chris?"

"I don't know any longer, when Gem was dying and I knew I was losing her. I don't know how, but I sort of felt a strength fill me as if I was being touched by something and although I have never prayed in my life, I felt a comfort from somewhere which made my pain bearable. Gem passed away so peacefully, it was as if she didn't feel any sorrow or pain. There was something there with us, a sort of presence, I could feel it and I know Gem did too…if you choose to call that God…." We sat silently. I thought of the experiences they had both suffered and Aunty Sarah with her Methodist upbringing who had been diligent in introducing them to the scriptures with little impact or perhaps it had had more impact than any of us knew. Chris slipped his arm around my shoulders and drew me to him. "It's so restful sitting here with you, I'm glad you stayed."

I was glad I had stayed too.

Twenty Three

The little old ladies at Kasgunj turned out to be more interesting than I had imagined. Carlotta and Rebecca D'souza were in their late sixties. While Carlotta was white haired, amply rounded with a double chin, Rebecca was tall and stringent with wisps of henna coloured hair which she set with rollers to give bounce and a short fringe from under which thick penciled eyebrows and faded blue eyes glared at the world in a sort of rage. Their house was a two-roomed, single storeyed, box-like structure over which a lush rose creeper had cast its thorny blooms adding colour to their drab neighbourhood with its wine coloured petals.

The neighbourhood was populated mainly by Muslims with narrow cobbled streets and rows of faded pink and green walls with peeling doors, which served as entrances to their accommodation within.

"Long ago our house was the only pucca structure in Kasgunj and we could see for miles around but with more and more Muslims settling here, we have lost our view and become boxed in." said Carlotta, "Now what can I get for you, lime juice, tea?"

"Tea please," I smiled at her while seating myself on the floral printed sofa. The room looked cheerful but a little worn. The covers of the furniture were still bright although they had seen many washings and the carpet yet retained a little of its rust colour. Little yellow and white crocheted cushions were comfortably ensconced on each chair. In a corner, near the single window stood an antique clock, mahogany coloured, its dial yellowed by age yet still ticking.

"It's an ancient cuckoo clock," said Rebecca noticing my interest in the piece. It still chimes the hour and the little door opens and the cuckoo pops out and coos; it belonged to my grandmother." Then turning to Chris, "we thought you had quite forgotten us," raising her eyebrows archly and managing to look coy, "seems you were quite occupied," she glanced at me sharply and I felt uncomfortable under her inquisitive stare preferring to look at the print on the wall of Jesus with a crown of thorns from which blood dripped. Rebecca made me uncomfortable. She couldn't quite keep her hands still but had a habit of twisting her fingers, interlacing them again and again. Her nails were long and painted bright red, which made them look like talons on her bony fingers.

"How can I forget you," Chris was saying, "I've just been busy with the farm, it's shaping up well again," then smiling at me, "she's one of my oldest friends and was really close to Gem, her family owned Manota. I thought it would make a nice change for her to meet you all".

"I'm glad you did, " said Carlotta as she entered with a tray on which reposed teapot and teacups of fine bone china obviously very old. "Rebecca, could you bring the other plates dear".

"What a lovely set!" I exclaimed.

"Yes it is that," said Carlotta, "I only take it out on special occasions, this is a special occasion, we don't get visitors too often. Sugar dear?"

"One please, Chris was telling me you provided all the goodies we often had at Christmas, do you'll still do any baking?"

"No dear, there aren't many families now who celebrate Christmas traditionally any longer."

"Then how do you all manage, I mean, do you'll have any income. I hope you don't mind me asking?"

"We have a little post-office savings, it's sufficient." She smiled gently, "Chris helped out when Rebecca was ill, he's like the nephew we never had."

"Have you'll always lived here?"

"We went away to school in Meerut, then returned here. Rebecca's marriage was arranged with a young lieutenant but he upped and married another girl he met when he was stationed at Jaipur. Mother did a lot of baking and when father died in a train accident, it became our trade. He was an engine driver. The pension stopped when mother died but we managed together to make a good business out of our baking." She sighed deeply, "times have changed dear, people moved away, died, we just make a little for our own consumption now."

Why hadn't she married I wondered, but didn't ask. Chris was seated comfortably next to me. Rebecca and him were having a whispered conversation, which stopped when Carlotta stopped speaking. Discussing me I surmised. For some reason Rebecca seemed antagonistic towards me and kept scrutinizing me disdainfully. I wondered, if she thought I might be after Chris, the thought made me want to chuckle and feeling devilish I thought I might actually give her something to worry about. Moving a little closer to Chris, I sort of snuggled upto his arm and he glanced at me in surprise which quickly changed to pleasure as I leaned comfortably against him and smiled into his eyes. I glanced at Rebecca to see what effect this silent play was having on her and found her scowling ferociously. I smiled at her sweetly, then turned to Carlotta who was watching us indulgently.

"Did you never think of leaving Kasgunj?" I asked her, "I mean after school, didn't you ever want to do any training or anything?"

She shook her head, "my father would not hear of it, he thought a woman should get married and stay at home, he wouldn't think of us going out to train."

"Why didn't you marry....I hope I'm not being too inquisitive?"

"Oh I fell in love, with a visiting Reverend, but our romance was short lived as he contacted measles, which is normally a childhood disease, but never having had it in childhood he succumbed to it when it was being passed around some of the local children. It was very sudden, his fever rose very high during the night and by morning he had passed away. I was heart-broken. So there you have it, Rebecca crossed in love and myself having lost the only man decent enough to want me." She laughed uproariously and her laughter being contagious I found myself laughing with her. Carlotta had that effect on people. She was jolly and I felt jolly just talking to her.

"How long you planning on staying?" Rebecca said into the silence, which had fallen.

"I guess a while," I said thoughtfully, "it's really peaceful at Manota".

"A long while," Chris said softly.

"Do you work girl?" Carlotta asked interestedly.

"Yes, with a hydro-electric company but I've taken a leave of absence to do some travelling. I'll continue to other places when I decide to leave Manota."

"So which places you planning on visiting?"

"Kulu Manali for one, Simla, a few places in Rajasthan, Kovalam, Cochin, Pondicherry.."

Chris sighed, "wish I could go with you, I love travelling too but I can't leave the farm just yet it's beginning to shape up the way I want, that reminds me, I've got some fruit and vegetables for you in the jeep Carlotta." He stood up and hurried out.

"You be good to him now," Rebecca hissed as she grabbed my arm and I winced as her nails dug into the fleshy part of my arm, "that Gem she was a tart, he doesn't need another like her."

"She loved him," I said brusquely, "he was happy with her."

"Rebecca!" Carlotta said sharply, "you leave her alone now, you hear, let them be, I don't think Chris will thank you for interfering, "then turning to me kindly, "don't take no notice of her love, she's possessive over Chris, just don't mind her.."

"Who's possessive over me?" Chris asked entering the room with a basket, which he placed in a corner of the room.

"Oh nothing dear," said Carlotta quickly, "this is too much, lad. You shouldn't have taken the trouble."

Chris smiled, "I think we should get moving, looks like rain and the roads become a mess. Thanks for the tea.."

"Come back soon dear.." Carlotta hugged Chris, then turned to me "you too dear."

"Bye Rebecca," I said quietly turning to her and she nodded her head. I could see she was determined to dislike me. Her face became animated as she turned to Chris.

"You take care now and come back soon."

He grinned cheerfully giving her a warm hug and her features thawed into a bright smile just for him. I was surprised the difference a smile made to her face, for a moment she actually looked pretty.

Twenty Four

Sitting in the jeep speeding along the road by Chris's side I noticed the landscape looked gray, the sun had disappeared behind the dark clouds.

"So enjoyed the visit?"

"For sisters they are so diverse, not only in looks. Carlotta is so warm and motherly and Rebecca is like vinegar."

Chris laughed, glancing at me, "she's really nice once you get to know her, she seems to think I'm the catch of the year or something, she didn't like Gem much either."

"She made me feel cattish."

"So I noticed...what was all that about in there?"

"What, the cuddling thing? More like snuggling," he grinned.

"That was Rebecca's fault, she made me want to slither all over you just to annoy her."

"I wouldn't mind your slithering in the least bit."

"I bet you wouldn't, but relax pal, I'm not about to introduce you to my slithering, it's an art ...and rationed very carefully."

A clap of thunder reverberated through the air, the sound deafening, as lightning split the sky with awesome intensity and then the rain, a gray torrent that poured from the sky obscuring visibility. Chris pulled the jeep to a halt and we sat cocooned in its interior listening to the deafening roar of water as it pelted the jeep fiercely. Conversation was out of the question. Just as swiftly as it had begun it stopped and the silence hit us abruptly. Chris started the jeep again and we bumped down the road, which had become slush filled and muddy as rivulets of water gushed in search of non-existent drains. Another sound filled the silence, a high-pitched keening and wailing which seemed to be rushing in tandem with the jeep.

"What is that?" I yelled above the noise, noticing Chris was having difficulty keeping the jeep steady.

"It's the wind, I think we're in for a mother of a storm, damn! I wonder if it will be safer to veer off into the gardens."

"The trees might lose branches, I don't think that's a good idea Chris."

"We're too exposed here, hold on..I'm going to cut across, there's the ruins of something further ahead, the walls might afford us some protection if they're still standing."

There was no roof to the building and most of the walls had crumbled, so Chris abandoned the idea of taking protection there. By now there was no natural light, a thick blackness had covered the land and he was obliged to use the head lights whose wavering beams seemed insufficient to cut through the terrible darkness which split into zigzags of dazzling light as lightning struck the sky and thunder rolled across like drums heralding a mighty onslaught. The atmosphere was tense and humid. I wished it would rain, I felt stifled by the closeness. Chris was concentrating fiercely on the road hurrying to get us to shelter before another downpour. I clung like a limpet, jolted and rattled until I felt every tooth in my jaw would come loose from its socket. I was thankful the wind was not against us but rushed along hurtling our jeep forward. Chris fought to keep us on the road with each fresh gust, which lifted the jeep almost overturning us. A moment of startling quiet, when the wind died suddenly and the air became unnaturally calm, only the roar of the jeep engine loud in the silence, then it began. A thick, heavy drumming thumping the canvas of the jeep and the rain came out of the sky in a steady wall of water. In no time the road became a river but Chris continued doggedly forcing the jeep to respond to each challenge, cutting through the curtain of water, willing it onwards until we came to Manota and could clamber out drenched to the skin.

"That was amazing driving Chris."

"Weren't you terrified?"

"Oh yes I was, I've never been in a storm with such ferocity before, that was really something..."

"Well I hope I'm not on the road ever again in something like that, I felt so puny, almost helpless...better go and change..." he looked shaken, unnerved and I supposed it must have been horrible battling the elements, trying his best to keep the jeep from overturning.

We didn't hear them come; the drumming rain drowned the sound of everything else. They were there, seated comfortably on the verandah, four of them, their heads swathed in turbans, the lower part of their faces well muffled. They ignored their dripping clothes, squatting, silently facing the entrance to the living room. I began backing slowly again towards the door but a sharp word stopped me. Chris stepped out from behind me.

"What do you want?" his voice was harsh as he spoke in the local dialect.

One man stood unwinding the cloth from his face, his eyes burned with some terrifying emotion.

"Recognize me?"

Chris backed and I saw him pale, he looked shaken.

"Shaitan Singh", he whispered then they were on him, steel flashed and I screamed as blood splattered everywhere. I ran inside to get Chris's rifle, which he kept beneath his bed. It was not loaded and in my nervousness, spilled the bullets all over the floor. Snatching a handful I loaded as I ran. They were gone, blood pooled on the floor the only evidence they had been.

"Chris....Chris..."

He was gone too; there was no sign of him. I knew the blood that congealed on the floor could only be his. How had Shaitan Singh returned? I resolved to find out, I had to go to

Kasgunj to report Chris's murder, I didn't think he had survived or if he had I knew it wouldn't be for much longer. A search had to be initiated.

Damn the storm! I couldn't possibly drive the jeep in this weather, I had to wait. Shivering with cold and fear, I huddled in the living room, the rifle beside me. I couldn't get Chris out of my mind. Was he alive? Would they torture him, would they return? I didn't know. At times like these when a person is distraught one has the strangest thoughts. I thought of metaphysics and what I had read of it and if perhaps I could settle my mind sufficiently to practice some of it then maybe I could keep Chris safe. But everytime I closed my eyes I could see the pool of blood, which congealed. What was Chris thinking, did he care whether he lived or died, would he be happy to join Gem? Was there an after life? I tried praying but the words were jumbled and incoherent. Would God understand me? What had he ordained for us, what preconceived destiny were we to follow? What was God really like? I imagined him like some big ogre looking down on the world playing his game of chess and we were the pawns he placed according to each move he made. Aha! I take the knight...why not the bishop? Now the queen...did we have a choice? How did the dacoits get out of jail? I went from being angry to being afraid and then grief hit me and I sobbed inconsolably for Chris, for the horror that he might be facing. All at once I thought of Bhim, Chris's servant, where had he disappeared to? Hurriedly I got up and went onto the verandah.

"Bhim!" I called, "Bhim!" I yelled, shouting his name again and again, but he did not appear. I went back in locking myself securely in the big bedroom.

The rain and the wind didn't let up all night and exhausted, my emotions in turmoil, afraid and alone, I slept.

I woke to the sound of the birds chirping happily. The day had dawned bright and the sun had already dried out most of last night's rain. A banging on the door had me scurrying for the rifle. Balancing it in the crook of my arm I carefully unbolted the doors. Bhim was standing there gaping in astonishment.

"Where were you?" I yelled and his eyes widened in fright.

"Madam, I went to visit Shiva's house, the storm came suddenly and I couldn't return."

Sighing I returned to sit on the sofa, then in as few words as possible I told Bhim of what had happened to Chris. He went to look at the bloodstains and I told him he would have to accompany me to Kasgunj to seek the help of the police. He nodded in agreement. Bhim seemed thoroughly upset by the loss of Chris and wept unashamedly. He told me how Chris had rescued him from a *dhaba* outside Delhi, a sort of wayside cafe that catered food for lorry drivers. The proprietor of the dhaba had been a seedy individual who beat the boys who worked for him, keeping them on short rations, threatening them constantly with awful consequences. Bhim had been tricked into his employ. He told me how he had travelled from Rolpa, a village in Nepal, with the driver of a lorry in search of employment as his family was large and they could barely subsist on the meagre food they grew on the tiny land they owned. Being the eldest he had left, hoping to earn enough money to send some part of it home. Unfortunately the lorry driver left him at the dhaba at the behest of the proprietor who promised to pay him a decent wage to wash utensils and clean the place. He never did see a penny of his earnings and infact was beaten when he tried to leave. His life had been grim. Chris had been a witness to one of the beatings and had paid the proprietor to release him into his care. Such was his gratitude he had refused to leave Chris or seek employment elsewhere but had become his faithful and loyal servant. He told me he had been happy with Chris and Gem and he had been able to help his family with the wages he earned. He was devastated with Chris's disappearance and was just as determined as I to bring the culprits to justice.

Inspector Chauhan had long since retired, a new spit and polish, determined looking individual had taken his place. He was dark with a beaky nose and black eyes, which looked at us suspiciously. When I finished relating the story he sat silently, his eyes focused on the wall, seemingly deep in thought. Inspector Rohit Gupta.

"So you don't know that he is dead," he said finally and I nodded my head, "I see...mmm...why were you there, may I ask, why exactly did you return, you knew the house had been sold?" his eyes bored into me.

"I just felt like seeing the place again, it holds a lot of memories for me."

"I see..." the way he said it made me wonder if he really saw and what exactly was he thinking. I had a feeling he was suspicious of my reason for being at Manota, I wondered if the Inspector suspected I had tried to get rid of Chris, I felt anger building at this thought.

"Look Inspector, don't you think something should be done to try and find Chris... there just may be a chance he is alive, we can't just sit doing nothing?"

"Please," he held up his hand, "I am thinking, this area is full of hiding places for dacoits, we cannot just rush around, we have to plan. If what you said is true I have to discover how it is that Shaitan Singh was released from the central jail."

"But by the time you plan and make inquiries about Shaitan Singh what little chance there is of getting to Chris might disappear, if he is alive that is.."

"You have given your report," his voice was abrupt, "it is now my duty to discover what is the truth and what is not. You will be required to sign a statement, kindly write, the sooner we dispense with formalities, the sooner I can discover the whereabouts of your friend, that is ofcourse if you don't really know.."

"Look, what is it you are saying, are you thinking I've got something to do with this?" I yelled furiously, "I'll write your bloody statement and I'm going looking for Chris even if you aren't."

"Madam, madam..no need to get excited.."

"Excited! My friend could be dying out there and all you can talk of is formalities. I think I wasted my time coming here, it would be much better if I began making enquiries about Shaitan Singh in the villages. I'm sure I can discover something…" I stalked out of the office seething.

"Wait, wait," he called, I'll organize a search, it might be dangerous for you to look on your own besides, have you thought, Shaitan Singh might want to do away with you as well as you were a witness."

"I know, but I still have to do something about Chris."

"Please, you must stay in Kasgunj until we find him."

"Okay, I'll be at Raja Govind's hotel.."

"You know Mr. Govind?"

"Yes, he can vouch for me, I'll ask him to provide Bhim with accommodation as well. Please you have to hurry with the search."

Govind's name seemed to have activated the Inspector and suddenly he was barking orders to his *hawaldars*, organising the jeeps. I left him in the midst of men hurrying and scurrying.

Govind was annoyed that the inspector had procrastinated. He called to voice his displeasure and inform him that he would be personally monitoring the progress of the search. He made a few other calls before calling me with the information.

"Shaitan Singh and four of his men broke jail. I do think the inspector is going to be a little nervous that he didn't take immediate action. I want you to rest now, catch up with you later okay?"

I thanked him before lying down to rest. For a while sleep eluded me, I thought of the Inspector and his suspicious nature, then I thought of Carlotta and Rebecca. I was sure

Rebecca would think like the inspector. I knew I had to inform them about Chris...perhaps after there was some more news. I was woken with the ring of the telephone. Groggily I sat up and reached for the receiver.

"My dear, I have bad news for you..." it was Govind.

"What is it? Have they found Chris?"

"Afraid not, it's something else..."

"Govind please, you can tell me over the phone."

"Okay... it's Manota, they went back there.."

"What?"

"There's nothing left...I'm sorry.."

"But..."

"I think they thought you were still inside, we don't really know the whole story, but last night apparently, the explosions took place and the whole place is just rubble."

"Were any of the villagers hurt?"

"Apparently not."

"What about Chris?"

"No news yet, I'm afraid. Are you okay?"

"Yes," I assured him. For the moment I was okay. Perhaps the full import would sink in later; right now I didn't feel a thing. Chris was still missing, with no one knowing whether he was dead or alive and Manota reduced to a handful of dust.

The words of Omar Khyyam so often quoted by my father came to mind;

'The moving finger writes; and, having writ,
Moves on; nor all your piety nor wit
Shall lure it back to cancel half a line,
Nor all your tears wash out a word of it.'

Twenty Five

Two days later there was still no word of Chris. I decided to visit Carlotta and Rebecca, I didn't feel I could put it off any longer.

"I'm sorry I took so long to inform you but I thought I would wait until there was more information. So far the police have drawn an absolute blank." I was seated opposite them on a single sofa, a cup of tea in my hand. Far from being annoyed at my tardiness, Carlotta looked troubled. Rebecca looked at me blankly for a moment, then her face crumpled and she began to sob, deep gut wrenching sounds that spilled into the room making me cringe with agony. Carlotta stretched her hand to pat her, then withdrew it as if she couldn't bear to touch her. The sight of Rebecca hunched in agony as she sobbed drove me to despair and I fought hard to contain my own tears, which threatened to spill. I could see Carlotta was having difficulty too. Then just as suddenly as she had begun, she stopped. I sighed with relief and waited expectantly for the tongue lashing to begin. Instead Rebecca blew her nose, seeming to have gained control of herself.

"I'm sorry," she said in a shaky voice, "I was afraid this would happen. I warned Chris several times he should take precautions or settle somewhere where he would not be so accessible. I knew if they ever got out they would come after him. He laughed at me, he loved taking risks and the lure of living on Manota was too enticing, he couldn't resist."

"I suppose he thought they wouldn't ever be released."

"No dear, he knew they would come for him someday, especially since he had taken the loot. He knew they would come for him but he just didn't think it would be so soon."

"Perhaps they haven't killed him yet then," said Carlotta.

"What do you mean?"

"Chris is not stupid, he'll realise people would be looking for him, he'll play for time and they won't kill him until they get the information where he hid their loot."

"But they'll torture him..."

We looked at each other in consternation. The thought of Chris being tortured didn't bear thinking about. I stood up hurriedly, "I think I have to inform Govind about this. He will make sure the police step up the search."

"I'll come with you," said Rebecca.

"I'll make a novena for him," said Carlotta, hugging me. "Thanks for coming..."

"This definitely puts a different light on things," said Govind, "If Chris is smart enough to stall them. There's also the fact that he was wounded, we don't know how badly and he may not be able to take their torture... I'll talk to Gupta."

"I'm going back to Manota with Bhim."

"I don't think that's a good idea," said Govind, "they're bound to return there to search for the loot. It could be dangerous for you. Let Bhim return with a police escort first. When it's safe you can return. Where will you stay, the house is only rubble. I insist you remain here." I had to agree with him.

Late in the evening Inspector Gupta came to see me. Not the arrogant Gupta I had met at the station but a chastised man bent on apologizing.

"They returned to the house," he said. "We should have posted a guard there but you do understand we are short staffed..."

"I understand perfectly," I said quietly, "and I feel guilty I didn't think of this earlier.

According to Bhim there wasn't anything for them to find, but of that we are not certain and there is no clue as to which direction they took." He was silent for a while. "I don't think your friend would be alive..."

"I hope you're going to continue searching..."

He was quick to reassure me.

"I hope it's alright for me to go now, Inspector? I'd like to return to Manota, has Bhim stayed there at the village?"

"Perhaps it would not be safe." He spoke carefully.

"I'll chance it," I said "and I will return here before nightfall."

"Would you like an escort?"

"No. I'd like to be on my own."

Govind was furious, "you're being foolish, they will return and this time it will be you who is the target."

"I'm still going Govind, if Chris ever manages to escape them, he will come there. I'm sure of it, I just want to see what's left and talk to the villagers."

"Then take an escort..."

I shook my head and he sighed, "you are stubborn."

That night I slept fitfully and early morning I left for Manota. The sun was not yet up and the landscape had an eerie stillness to it. Morning squatters searched for a place to defecate, the banks of the river were already dotted with them. I concentrated on the road. The breeze felt fresh on my face and I inhaled deeply.

Perhaps I was being foolish in returning but it felt right. I tried to think of what Chris would want me to do and I knew he would want me to stay. I knew so little of Chris's life. Maybe the answers lay at Manota, if only we could get a clue as to which place to search for him. I suspected the Inspector was right. Chris was doomed...but I didn't want to think about that now.

Bhim received me at the village with a woebegone face and I suspected he mourned Chris already.

"There's still a chance we may get him back," I told him, "we cannot give up hope so easily. Is there really nothing left of the house?"

He nodded his head then asked me to follow him and as I accompanied him to Shiva's house he told me there was someone waiting there to meet me.

Lunch was a simple meal of *dal*, vegetables and wheat *rotis*. To please Bhim I ate with pretended enjoyment, which seemed to revive his spirits somewhat. He seemed happiest serving food and doing his normal household duties. Neetu, Mira's daughter had been waiting patiently to get my attention. She was almost the exact image of her mother. With her was a young girl of sixteen whom she introduced as her daughter Gita. They squatted on the floor opposite the *charpoy* on which I sat.

"He said you would come," said Neetu.

"Who said I would come?"

"Krist Baba"

"When was this?"

"During the new moon."

"Is there talk in the village, Neetu, does anyone know where he went?"

She scrutinized me for a while, her eyes giving nothing away.

"Has he gone somewhere?"

"Don't pretend," I said tersely, "you know he has been taken by Shaitan Singh and his men." A look of fear crossed her face, then she stood pulling her daughter to her feet.

"We must go..."

"Wait, please...if you know anything you must tell me, his life could depend on it..." But they were gone as quickly and silently as they had come.

"They won't talk," said Bhim. "Shaitan Singh has made a deal with the police. He has taken his family with him but the villagers won't talk, they still fear him..." he hesitated a moment, "Neetu's daughter...she used to come to Chris baba..."

I looked at him puzzled then suddenly the meaning of what he was telling me hit me and I looked at him sharply. He looked away in embarrassment.

"Do you think she knows something?"

"I think she just came to have a look...it is said in the village you would marry..."

My burst of laughter made him smile too. I supposed that's what the villagers would think and I couldn't resent their simple deduction. "What happened to Mira, Neetu's mother?"

"She died, it is said she was poisoned by the *buniya*'s wife. He left her to live with Mira."

"What happened to the buniya's wife, did the police take her in?"

"There was no evidence, Mira's body disappeared."

"Poor thing, what an unhappy life she had. Who did Neetu marry?"

"Neetu is not married..."

"But she has a daughter?"

"They live on the outskirts of the village...it is the same profession."

I understood what he was implying. And Chris had used Neetu's daughter...

"Bhim, I want you to mingle in the village, see what you can pick up. We just might get lucky. Don't ask any outright questions...you understand what I want?" He nodded his head.

Chris had made the *pucca dillan* into his room. I wondered if there was a reason. It was the only room which stood although front and side walls had crumbled. The room smelled of something indefinable. I couldn't place it but I gazed around the room which had a few trunks stored in a corner and two wooden almirahs and a chest of drawers which had been torn apart. The ceiling still had the old wooden rafters which looked as strong as before. The beds were no use to anyone having been thoroughly smashed and Bhim had taken them to the kitchen to be used as fuel. One cupboard leaned drunkenly, its drawers upended and a leg missing. I opened the top trunk and saw that Bhim had dumped papers and clothes back into it as best he could. The envelope lying on top caught my eye and I recognized Gem's handwriting. Feeling curious, I lifted it out to take a closer look and noticed a letter was still inside. It was dated two days before I had returned to Manota. How could that be, hadn't Chris said Gem had died in child birth? I read the letter.

My darling Chris,

Please return to Delhi. You put yourself at risk by staying at Manota. Even if you have the death wish, think of me and the love I have for you. I know you cannot believe me but I took a conscious decision to become Anil's mistress not because I had fallen out of love for you but because I couldn't bear the change in you nor cope with it. Anil is old and tired, I am his only consolation and he provides well for our child. I do not understand this desire you have to belong to that place. We never really belonged. I could understand the sadness you felt after your mother died but what I cannot understand is your revulsion and hatred for Annette. It is not her fault that she was born deformed but what hurts me more is your

attitude. This pretence of yours that she doesn't exist kills us both. If Anil hadn't agreed to accept my services, we would now be destitute. I cannot believe you chose to abandon us. I look at it as temporary insanity. Please return Chris, you know where to find me.
Yours as always,
Gem

I took a deep breath. Gem was alive. Why had Chris lied? Was he so ashamed at having a deformed child that he had abandoned them and pretended they had died? I thought back to the day I had arrived. His tears had seemed so genuine. My thoughts were in turmoil. It seems as if you know a person then suddenly something like this makes you realize you don't know them at all. What of Chris had I really known. I focused on the fact that Gem was alive. I needed to get in touch with her. Frantically I went through the other papers searching for an address but I couldn't find one nor were there any more letters. When I turned round Bhim was standing in the doorway looking anxious.

"I'm looking for Missy Gem's address," I explained.

He shook his head. "She died," he said sadly.

"This letter is dated two days before I came here, she is alive," I said sharply.

"She died," he said stubbornly.

"He told you that?" He shook his head.

"I was in the hospital, she died and missy baba with her."

"Bhim this is Gem's handwriting and the letter is dated..."

"Chris baba, he told me they died."

"But you didn't actually know that they died?"

He was quiet a while, "he came home in the morning, I was preparing breakfast to take to the hospital and he said they had died in the night. He was tired, he went to his room and slept. When he woke he went out saying he had to make arrangements for the bodies. I never saw them again. They died."

I could see Bhim didn't want to believe anything else. To him Chris's word was gospel, if he said they had died then he intended to believe him and that's all there was to it. Then a thought occurred to me.

"Bhim, did you ever meet Dr. Sharma? Did he ever come to the house?" but he was already shaking his head.

So that was that, there was no address on Gem's letter and until Chris returned and I could confront him...would I ever know the truth?

I wrote to Ivan, it was a month before I received a reply.

"It does not surprise me in the least that Chris is unhinged. Perhaps to him Gem did die in childbirth. The years of abuse have finally taken its toll; Chris is a victim of circumstance. Not all humans are able to cope and do the right thing. In rejecting Annette and Gem, he's only doing what a lot of people would do when they can't cope. Don't judge him and don't give up, he may yet return..."

Another month passed before I was certain that the nausea afflicting me was not due to the spicy food. I took the test to be certain and when it came up positive felt myself thrown into emotional turmoil. We had weathered the storm but not our emotions. I had succumbed to Chris's overtures once out of the storm, enjoyed them. In fact our passionate natures had sought and found release in so many different ways and at that time it had seemed so natural to express our relief at being alive by loving each other. Our spirits had been so exuberant and then had come Shaitan Singh and his men and with one fell swoop had changed our joy to sorrow. But I couldn't regret the life growing within me. Ivan was right he may yet return...but what of Gem? She still hankered after Chris...I would wait...

Bhim, Neetu and Gita had put up a new *chappard* and rebuilt the kitchen. I didn't object to Neetu and her daughter having taken up residence with us. They had appeared one day just as suddenly as they had gone and without explanation. Gita drooped with sadness and exhaustion and I presumed they had searched for him until hunger and thirst had brought them to me. It seemed to console them to be near me and I rather enjoyed being pampered for a while though the thought nagged as I wondered what explanation I would give when they discovered I carried a child. I hadn't yet decided what to do with myself, going to any of the family exposed me to ridicule and condemnation while staying here though a temporary solution was not the ideal environment to have a child let alone bring her up in it. Neetu had inherited Mira's skill as a masseuse and while Bhim took on the chores of the water carrier ferrying water from the well, Gita took over the cooking and I rather enjoyed the preparations she concocted.

"There are murmurings in the village," Bhim said one evening as I sat on a charpoy under the star filled sky and sipped a cool lemonade, "the women object to their presence…" he indicated Neetu and Gita with a tilt of his head.

"What has their being here got to do with anyone?" I asked annoyed at his words.

"It is a question of *izzat*," he said, "their profession…" he hesitated while I interrupted him.

"They don't do that now and who are these women who complain."

"They only wish to protect your reputation, you being a woman after all…"

"So what your saying is it was alright for Chris baba to keep them but not me." He bowed his head sheepishly.

I shook my head at the narrow minded way in which the village women confined themselves, but how could I condemn them either, this was their world. To them Neetu and Gita's profession put them beyond the pale and I suppose in normal circumstances I might have ostracized them just as easily. I felt like a hippocrite at my attitude. Would I in normal social circles have cohabited with women who were social outcasts? I didn't think so, but here hidden away in a remote village I had felt free to do as I pleased, imagining I was not being observed. What would they think when they came to know I carried Chris's child, would I be beyond the pale too? It bothered me that although I tolerated Neetu my attitude towards Gita was not all it should be, was there a little resentment because of her involvement with Chris? Why did I keep her here then? I knew the answer immediately I wanted control of him, I was sure he would allow it. In my twisted thinking I felt by keeping them with me I was sort of paying a debt, because I couldn't take away their livelihood without compensating them in some fashion. I knew I wouldn't let him keep them now should he show.

The next morning brought news of Ivan and a surprise in the shape of Gem and Annette. Stylish with her hair set in a blunt cut, well manicured nails in peach and pedicured toes crimson, she presented a picture of wealth and grooming a far cry from the simple girl who had worn a made over dress and scruffy sandals on her first date. Annette threw me altogether, her body was grotesque, short, stumpy and twisted but her face with flamboyant curls down her shoulders captivated, with wide-spaced green eyes the colour of moss agate and her perky little nose perched above luscious pink lips. She was angelic! I collapsed in turmoil. How could Chris reject someone so beautiful. One look into those gorgeous eyes and her body paled into insignificance.

"He hasn't seen her since," lamented Gem, "she wasn't so beautiful as a baby."

"That's still no excuse," I said quietly. We were seated in the cool of the chappard while Annette dosed on a charpoy and an attentive Gita fanned her diligently to keep the flies away.

"I still can't believe Chris is gone!"

"Why did you suddenly decide to come, Gem?" She looked away avoiding my eyes but I prodded her, "Gem?"

"I will be getting married, I wanted to leave Annette with Chris." She looked at me defiantly. "Satti doesn't want Annette, I thought it was time Chris took some responsibility."

"Satti, I thought you were with Anil?"

"At first, then I met Satwinder Singh, I have my own beauty parlour now..." she preened a bit patting her hair, "Oh dear, he's not going to be pleased...I suppose you couldn't..."

"No Gem, Annette is your responsibility and besides I will have my own..."

"You're married," she looked excited, while I shook my head and then she laughed as realization dawned, "Oh God, not you too! Whose the father?"

"I'm not going to discuss it..."

"I tell you all my secrets but you never do..."

"I won't discuss it," I repeated. Wild horses weren't going to drag the confession from me, I decided. To distract her I told her about Rebecca and Carlotta but what caught her interest more was the news that Ivan had decided to visit.

Ivan came on a Tuesday; I remember it well because Bhim had suddenly decided he was going to be a Hanuman devotee and so took himself off to find a Hanuman temple in which to pay his respects. He had informed Gita loftily that he was on fast for the day and would require an early meal at night. Nobody came to visit in the afternoons and since Bhim had taken himself off Gita had decided to bathe in the compound after fetching water from the well. She was the first to greet Ivan on arrival and what followed would perhaps not have been noticed had Gem not remarked on the change in Gita's demeanour. She no longer slouched but walked confidently, almost strutting and her look was bold, somewhat challenging. Her confidence restored at having captured Ivan's attentions.

Ivan had changed from a gangly young man to a well-built person of good proportions. The added weight and the gray above his ears suited him immensely; he had aged well. I felt relieved I no longer craved his attention, the time spent with Chris seemed to have restored my confidence. A successful lawyer with a thriving practice, two sons almost adults and a wife who still doted on him but he confessed, there were problems. Patrick had died from poisoning and Alaida resided in his mansion now, Ivan took care of her affairs but it sort of put a strain on his marriage. Linda suspected Alaida had a hand in Patrick's death but nothing had been proved and she hadn't been at the house at that time either.

"So you think Alaida is sane now?"

"Definitely," said Ivan with conviction.

"The police still haven't discovered who poisoned poor Patrick...well I tend to side with Linda."

"I thought you might," said Ivan absently but his eyes were following Gita as she teased Annette and played with her.

"You always think the worst of people," said Gem and I looked at her in surprise wondering what had brought that on. Was Gem piqued because Ivan seemed more interested in talking with me than paying her attention?

"I do think you should come stay with me a while," said Ivan, "the old woman can look after the place and Gita can come to look after Annette."

"Oh lets!" said Gem excitedly, "its so hot here, I think we'll enjoy Chhaoni for a bit and it is nearer the town.."

"I thought you were thinking of going back to Delhi?" I interrupted.

"Not right now," she said smiling into Ivan's eyes and I saw where the land lay on Gem's side.

Bhim finally came back late in the evening and we left him to look after the place though only the kitchen had been rebuilt and the damaged part of the pucca dillan. Neetu insisted on accompanying Gita (I explained to Ivan she wasn't really old, just looked it after the hard life she had lived) and we didn't have a heart to dissuade her from coming too especially since she felt in some way she protected Gita though I for one felt Gita required no protecting more able to get what she wanted with her artful wiles than we did with straight talking. I told Ivan about the gossip from the village and how we seemed to have tarnished our reputation by having had them stay.

"Well, you could leave them with me," he said casually, "Gem will be returning and you won't really need them here..." I hadn't yet told him I would be leaving and he just assumed I would stay.

"I'll probably be leaving soon too," I said, "I don't think Chris will return now...how long will you be staying?" I still couldn't refer to him in the past tense.

"Awhile...I've been toying with the idea of building a school at Chhaoni."

Ivan did stay awhile amidst the dust, heat and flies. He seemed not able to help himself. Gem had left in disgust when she had discovered a half nude Ivan with a sultry Gita wrapped around his thighs in a somewhat compromising position. Her disappointment had been so acute she had forgotten to take Annette with her and since she had not bothered to leave a forwarding address we couldn't send her to her either.

Annette was the perfect excuse for Ivan to extend his stay despite Linda's entreaties and Gita who doted on the child, took on the task of her well being as a matter of course. He made provision for the three of them to continue to stay on at Chhaoni after he left and that too only because Linda threatened to take the next flight out.

This I learned later from Ivan who wrote frequently to the tiny seaside resort in the south of India where I had closeted myself to have my baby. Rebecca wrote too but just to inform me that Shaitan Singh had died without revealing what had happened to Chris.

I couldn't sleep that night and feeling hot and restless decided to take a swim in the sea. I swam further out than I had intended being lulled by the calmness of the water, which stretched endlessly like a sheet of glass. When the wave hit I was suddenly plunged into a torrent of foaming water, which somersaulted me almost half the distance I had come. As I floundered to get my breath and probably swallowed a bucketful of water I could feel the strong undertow pulling me out to sea when suddenly my legs were grabbed and I was rapidly hauled into safe water. I don't remember the rest of it apart from waking in the sanitized room of the St. Mary's nursing home.

"You were lucky that fisherman was on the beach," scolded Sister Paula, "if it hadn't been for him you wouldn't even be alive, foolishness in your condition..."

A condition I no longer had, I thought dully. The pounding in my brain worsened as I closed my eyes and tried to shut out her voice. I felt remorse at having lost the child but a part of me felt relieved too and that was a feeling I didn't want to acknowledge. Now no one need know what one night of passion had cost me, I thought guiltily, and immediately the thought made me cringe. I had just lost a child and yet my first thought was for myself, it only made me feel worse. In a sad guilty sort of way I was also glad Chris had not come back. How happy we had been all those years ago, what dreams and aspirations we had had. I had always thought I would live a life others would envy a life impeccable and principled. Gem had been right, I had thought myself better than them and discovering I wasn't any different had chastised me. Perhaps of them all, I had changed the most or perhaps I had only become more human. Suddenly it felt good to no longer be looking down but to stand at par with them all. I had made mistakes the same way they had and like them had found myself wanting. It felt comfortable to come to terms with my lowered standards to think of Gem with compassion and Ivan with amusement but what felt right were the tears which finally fell not only for my daughter but for Chris. It had taken a while but he had managed a feat I had thought impossible, he had penetrated a heart long held in isolation and breeched the fortress leaving me exposed but I could only think of him fondly.

That night I walked on the beach for the last time letting the sand sink between my toes and the warm breeze caress my cheek as I said a last farewell to a child whose life had ended in such a cruel manner. Too late to wish it had been different now! A single star popped into the night sky as I gazed upwards and a deep peace entered my heart as I stared enthralled. It felt like a sign from above; a sign telling me she was alright...or perhaps, that again was only my imagination!

Epilogue

"The Indian sun vanquished the clinging mists which had obscured the stately splendour of the hills, hoarding their secrets in cold dignity. Dark and mysterious, their silence mocked the valley where everything was exposed to the relentless onslaught of harsh sunlight sweeping away the shadows which night had enclosed. "His voice was low pitched, his eyes distant. "In the valley where they had been born, the pack of wolves had dwindled rapidly. Humans with their greed and their capacity for reproduction had overpopulated the land and the wolves had no option but to move out of their natural habitats to strange pastures. If in retaliation due to the scarcity of food they began to forage in the human habitats occasionally feeding on humans, who could blame them? It is a natural inclination of humans to grab what others have and when they had finished possessing the wolves domains, they thought to drive them to extinction by starving them. The wolves in desperation began to feed on any humans foolish enough to venture out of the villages alone. Taking umbrage at their own kind being devoured and fearing their own extinction they began to hunt the animals banding together from all the villages in the valley, flushing out the creatures and with each success drawing more and more hunters to the area. Some escaped into the hills and were lost but three, having been cut from the pack ran deeper into the plains to survive the merciless hunt and escaped from the valley in the hope of finding something to eat. Male, female and the last of their litter ran tiredly despite the scarcity of food sniffing hopefully. The heat of the sun had diminished by the time they left the valley behind. In the distance, the fiery orb now faded to pale fingers of gold began its descent behind the hills, bright sky turning an indeterminate gray, heralding the onset of night. Their foraging had taken them further afield and they found themselves near a river from which they drank thirstily but yet unable to appease the painful pangs of hunger, which wrenched at their guts driving them almost insane. The female was weaker than the other two and sank into the soft sand to rest tired after the long trek. They had found no succour. A rat scuttled in the sand and the younger male took off after it diving into the long sword grass, which grew in clumps near the banks of the river. Pawing at the clumps, it tried to dislodge the rodent which remained hidden when suddenly its sharp ears caught the sound of voices and it raised its head, pricking its ears." He took a deep breath noting the enthralled faces before him, they were engrossed in the story and waited with bated breath for him to continue.

"Instinctively it feared humans, hadn't they been hunted by them before? But hunger is such a driving force, it drove the wolf into being bold. Sniffing at the air, it's ears tuned, it followed the sound of voices until through the bushes it could see them. A plump woman and two children, the younger child lagged, trailing in the wake of his mother as he dragged a thin stick behind him in the sand the only source of amusement as he made strange wiggly lines. The saliva drooled as it contemplated the well-rounded shanks, which were bare of clothing due to the heat and the fact that it was easier for him to urinate whenever the urge took him. Slinking along, hidden from view by the tall grass the wolf followed waiting for its opportunity. Marking it's prey... stealthily it crept nearer.

As the first fingers of the dawn crept into the sky lightening it, Shyamlall Singh yawned as he left his house and wandered down to the river, an aluminium *lota* in his hand. He shivered as an icy wind penetrated the cotton shawl he had carelessly wrapped around him. As he squatted beside the water to fill his lota he smelled something. Probably a dead dog he thought as he looked around and saw a bundle lying a few feet away. Curiosity getting the better of him he stood and cautiously went near, then reared back in horror as he looked into the staring eyes of what had once been a face. Something had obviously frightened the animal, which had been feeding and it had abandoned the pitiful remains. He wondered why it had not returned then looked around in fear.

Perhaps the creature was near. Hastily he departed for the village shuddering as he ran muttering to himself, calling the name of God. "Ram, Ram, Ram, Ram." . There was a dread within his soul. Demons were haunting his village, the boy Kishan had been the first victim; who would it take next?

He was right in his assessment that the creature had been disturbed. A lone figure stood near the river still and watchful. He was being pursued; he felt the hair on the nape of his neck rise. He could feel the malevolent eyes of the wolf bore into him from the bushes nearby. His face split into a huge grin and for a moment the idiot look was gone replaced by one of mirth as he sensed the wolf. He knew the creature feared him and a tiny flicker of compassion almost made him hesitate then remembrance of what he had seen; the pathetic remains of what had once been a laughing, gesticulating child hardened his resolve. He didn't understand this power he had over animals, he just knew he could command them and now he compelled the wolf to come nearer, to show itself.

The wolf cowered, it feared the man but it also knew something was forcing it to move nearer, it bared its fangs in a horrible grimace, then in a rush charged from out the bushes and launched itself at the man who stood willing it onwards, his broad frame standing easily, legs apart, the sickle gripped tightly as he waited. The impact of the sickle hitting bone with a sickening thud shook the man as it sunk deep into the wolf and snarling and snapping, crazed with pain drove it to make a desperate attempt. Twisting its body it flung the man to the ground and lodged its teeth deep into his throat. Taken by surprise Ramu reacted slowly, letting go of the sickle, he tried with his bare hands to wrench the wolf from him but already in the last throes of death the jaws had locked tight and he could feel his life's blood gushing, weakening him. His mind clouded and as he sank into cool, dark oblivion remembered nothing.

Fishermen returning with their morning catch came upon the tableau, the heroic battle of man and beast clearly depicting their struggle as they lay dead in the sand."

The wizened old man finished his story as he lifted the last leaf of the canvas book and slipped it over the back of the wooden board. His eyes were faded with age yet retained some of their original colour, the colour of moss agate. Squatting on the sand he waited expectantly as the men and women stood and stretched their limbs. No one spoke and in silence dropped their contributions into his cloth bag, which gaped invitingly. Soon he was alone and the silence continued unabated as he contemplated the *beedi* (the local rolled tobacco leaf he had always smoked) his thoughts turned inwards. Master storyteller he moved from village to village telling his tales with the aid of his story-book, a set of pictures painted onto canvasses. The colours were bright and mesmerizing and held the gaze of the crowd while he told his tale. Squinting into the harsh blaze of the sun he looked southwards and could just make out the outline of the ruins. He felt drawn towards it as nostalgia rose up engulfing him. Why not? he thought, no one would ever recognize him now. Those who knew him were probably all dead these many years. He had weathered many things even the attack by the dacoits and had survived, eking out a miserable existence, wandering from place to place but now he would go home. There was nothing there he knew, just his memories but it was the perfect place to lay his tired bones, his final resting place, but first he would take the time to remember...he was asleep before his thought could take shape and his dreams took him home as they had on many an occasion, when he woke he would remember nothing and would journey onwards in search of that elusive something; a shadowy place called Manota.